Esther's Wars

Also by Maureen Mitson and published by Ginninderra Press

Paper Chase
Jumping the Cracks
Take Time… (Pocket Poets)
Insulae (Pocket Places)
Beatrice's Commonsensical Approach
Rupe (Pocket People)

Maureen Mitson

Esther's Wars

This a work of historical fiction based on fact. With the exception of public figures and events recognisable from global and domestic Australian history and mentioned in the context of the story, all names, characters and incidents depicted are the work of the author's imagination. Any resemblance therefore to actual persons, living or dead, is entirely coincidental.

Esther's Wars
ISBN 978 1 76041 241 8
Copyright © text Maureen Mitson 2016
Cover photo: Wild red poppy © ZoomTeam

First published 2016 by
GINNINDERRA PRESS
PO Box 3461 Port Adelaide 5015
www.ginninderrapress.com.au

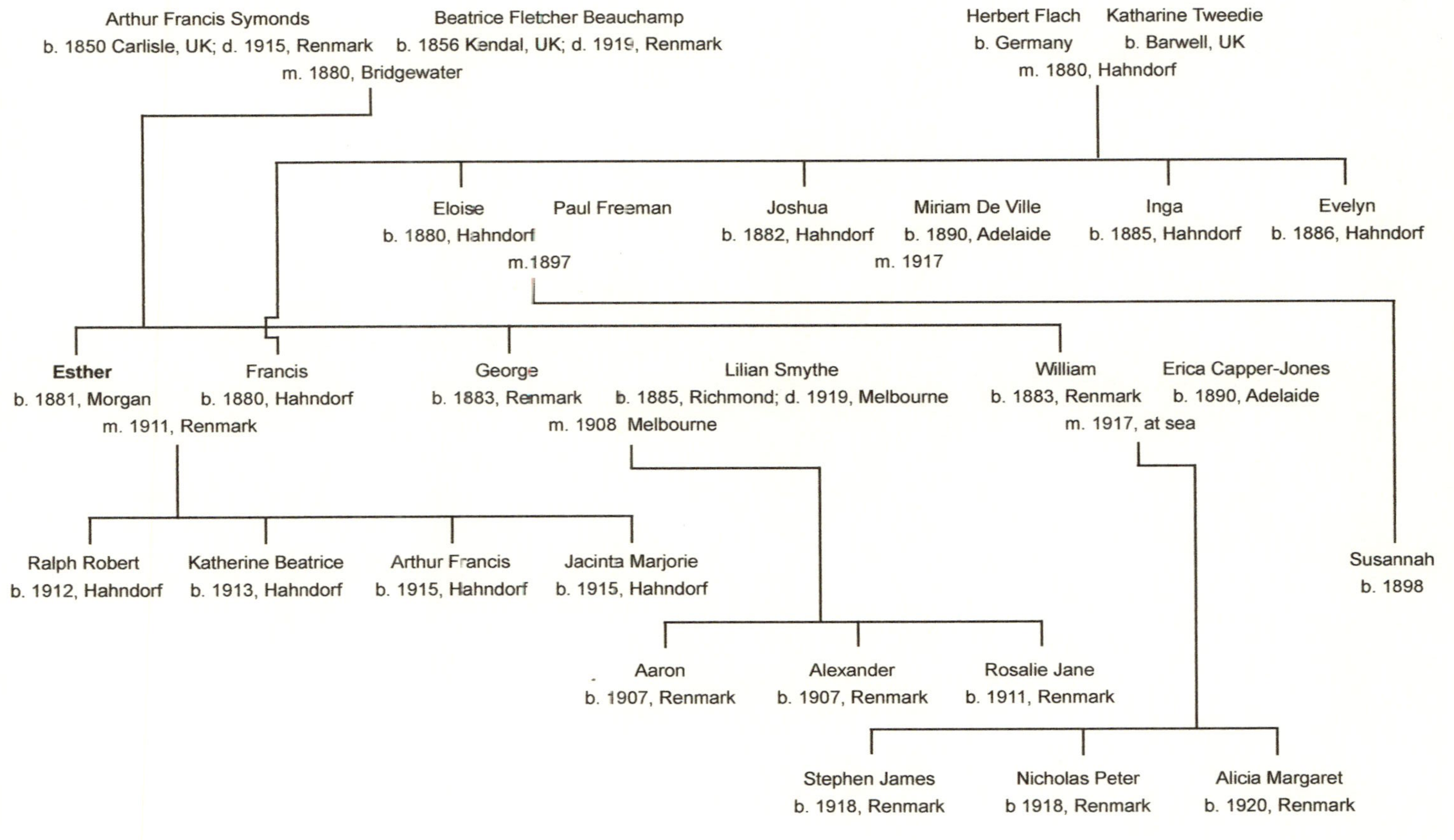

Arthur Francis Symonds
b. 1850 Carlisle, UK; d. 1915, Renmark
Beatrice Fletcher Beauchamp
b. 1856 Kendal, UK; d. 1919, Renmark
m. 1880, Bridgewater
Herbert Flach
b. Germany
Katharine Tweedie
b. Barwell, UK
m. 1880, Hahndorf
Eloise
b. 1880, Hahndorf
Paul Freeman
m.1897
Joshua
b. 1882, Hahndorf
Miriam De Ville
b. 1890, Adelaide
m. 1917
Inga
b. 1885, Hahndorf
Evelyn
b. 1886, Hahndorf
Esther
b. 1881, Morgan
m. 1911, Renmark
Francis
b. 1880, Hahndorf
George
b. 1883, Renmark
Lilian Smythe
b. 1885, Richmond; d. 1919, Melbourne
m. 1908 Melbourne
William
b. 1883, Renmark
Erica Capper-Jones
b. 1890, Adelaide
m. 1917, at sea
Ralph Robert
b. 1912, Hahndorf
Katherine Beatrice
b. 1913, Hahndorf
Arthur Francis
b. 1915, Hahndorf
Jacinta Marjorie
b. 1915, Hahndorf
Susannah
b. 1898
Aaron
b. 1907, Renmark
Alexander
b. 1907, Renmark
Rosalie Jane
b. 1911, Renmark
Stephen James
b. 1918, Renmark
Nicholas Peter
b 1918, Renmark
Alicia Margaret
b. 1920, Renmark

1

It was Christmas Day 1910 and Esther knew it was turning into one of those tedious festive dinners. Noisy, too, with the clatter of cutlery and clink of glassware adding to the chatter of Lilian to her toddlers and the arguing of the grown brothers William and George. In Esther's opinion, her mother should rule the table and restore some order. Esther preferred order.

As if on cue, her mother came to her feet at her end of the dining table, her chin raised in determination and her finger uplifted in waiting. Beatrice was a tall woman in her mid-fifties and a striking, imposing figure. Her sudden authoritative stance had subdued the two toddlers. They were staring at her, spoons poised. Her husband Arthur just smiled at the silent admonition of that finger.

The very room was expectant. The rattle of the holly streamers drying against the wall in the warm breeze seemed overloud.

Beatrice looked slowly around the gathering, smiling at each attentive face. She played with the cameo brooch at the high neck of her blouse. 'Thank you, my dears. It's not too hard, is it! A little hush is welcome. I want you to know how delighted I am that all my family is around this Christmas table, here at Cumquats. William is back after years studying law in England, Esther has relinquished her teaching duties to take her place within the family and George and Lilian are due to present us with yet another young Symonds – after already giving us these two lovely little fellows in Alexander and Aaron.' She waved that finger in turn to the two curious toddlers sitting on their high seats, each with his messy spoon still poised expectantly. 'I am so very content, as I know is my dear Arthur, your papa and grandpapa.' With a little nod, Beatrice sat down again.

Taking advantage of the silence, Arthur came to his feet and, with an elaborate music hall bow, saluted his wife with his glass, only to fall back into his seat with perhaps less dignity than he had intended.

George guffawed and a second chortle caused Esther to lift her gaze. Their father was waving a peremptory finger at his elder son.

He then spoke from his chair, even achieving a straight back throughout. 'My lovely Beatrice, I hear you. And I speak to the other ladies, my dear daughter Esther and my dear daughter-in-law Lilian. I speak in *vino veritas*, if I may be so bold, my own happiness having been a little over-indulgent.'

He gave a little cough for attention and cutlery ceased clattering on the plates. 'I do feel it has been a tumultuous year – in many respects. Certainly it has been a good one for Cumquats, and most of our part of the world, the South Australian Riverland. Indeed, there have been happenings all around and yesterday I read on the noticeboard at the post office that the British general election yielded a dead heat, two hundred and seventy-two seats each for the Liberals and the Tories. Asquith stays on as their prime minister…'

A groan from George as Esther winced. *Oh, Papa. What is still so exciting about English politics? Come, Mama, intervene and cut him short. We'll be here all day!*

Coincidentally, Beatrice obliged. 'Come, come, Arthur. After all, we are here and though we do – occasionally – have to realise all that is happening on the other side of the world today is Christmas. May I suggest we now devote ourselves to our plates before too many wretched flies flock in through that window and perhaps enlarge on our seasonal debates later?' She smiled and resumed her seat.

Cutlery clattered once again as they all fell to with a heartiness that defied the summer heat outside – after all, it was Christmas!

Lilian had one of the spoon-waving toddler twins to her right. Esther had one oppositely placed to her left who was equally fond of brandishing his own implement. An indulgent merriment ruled as mother and grandmother focused the toddlers' attention on their messy eating. Even so, a blob of gravy still landed too near to Esther's starched lace cuff for her comfort. She dabbed it with her serviette.

So being Christmas means having these messy children seated at the table amongst adults. When I was small, with Will and George also, we ate in the kitchen. We knew our place! And now, well, I don't even have a place. It's all Lilian this and Lilian that…

Esther had returned to the family property a few weeks earlier, having relinquished a senior teaching position at a prestigious Melbourne girls' school. Coming home to the chaotic domesticity of the family vines and orchards had been unsettling. Not only was it a very quiet part of the world with no theatres or civilised shopping, but within the household there seemed to be no logical sequence to daily events. As a senior staff member at school, she had been in control, with her programme well-organised. Not so at Cumquats Farm.

Esther considered her mother a contradiction in human dress, quixotic in the extreme within the household yet, when out among her vines and citrus trees, totally organised and predictable. Her father had even assured Esther that her mother's impulsiveness was her 'perfect antidote to boredom'. Esther had to continually remind herself of her reasons for returning. She knew her father hoped to encourage his daughter to stay at home and manage the areas where his wife lacked interest. Her mother just wanted someone else to run the household. Sorry, parents, leave me out of your comfortable equation. I'm not staying…

Arthur pulled up again onto his feet, leaned somewhat uncertainly to replace an errant holly sprig onto its hook above the light fitting, then called down the table to his wife. 'Beatrice! Are we to enjoy some spicy pudding this special day?'

A three-year-old voice piped up to Esther's left. 'Gan'papa! Is not Beetroot! Is Gan'mama!'

The adults erupted in laughter and Grandmama Beatrice, doting wife to Arthur, laughed until she had to dab her eyes. Even Esther was prompted to smile, although to serve up such a thing as a traditional English Christmas fruit pudding in a hot Australian summer, she considered digestive madness.

2

With the menfolk absorbed in their sticky fruity Christmas pudding, Beatrice was holding court at her end of the table and enjoying it greatly. 'That Asquith in England treats women with little or no respect. He's making them wait so long to be acknowledged as worthy of the smallest recognition. I do despair that those British suffragists will ever win the vote. To him, women simply do not signify! The death of that wonderful woman, Florence Nightingale, received sparse attention from him. After everything she had achieved! A life of loyal, dedicated nursing and service to her country, and she was ninety.'

Esther smiled. 'Yes, Mama, but he's a politician. Here today, gone tomorrow. What of their majesties? Edward is dead and we have a new George on the throne. Does that not promise surprising new beginnings? Hm?'

William had overheard and could not resist interrupting with a chuckle. 'You said it, Esther! That reminds me…saw Comedy King win the cup at Flemington a couple of days after I landed at Port Melbourne. Aptly named.' He raised his voice. 'Pa, what do you think? Huge crowds at the race. I didn't realise it was the cup's fiftieth year, though.'

His brother George snorted another laugh and renewed his father's glass.

Lilian, his very pregnant wife, saw her chance. 'Oh, you men. Politics and sports. Well, horses for courses, brother-in-law. Comedy King or not, it's another George on the throne now. That means we females need no longer endure the tightness of so-called Edwardian dress styles! Such tightly laced figures, like hourglasses as I believe one admiring fashion writer called them, were not welcomed by me, certainly not when I was developing this baby. The early Georgian styles with their high waists and bubble skirts seem to better accommodate the natural figures of healthy women. After this baby – which is growing so huge – I'm sure I'll need a relaxed fitting for a few weeks at least.'

George and even Arthur laughed at Lilian's personal interpretation of historical events. William raised his glass with a knowing smile towards Esther.

George, mouth now full of cheesy biscuit, nodded to his wife. 'You have been a fruitful wife, my love, and you shall certainly have at least one new gown for visiting after your coming event. Yes, it's been a fruitful year for Cumquats all round. Or so I feel.'

There was laughter around the group as they saluted the pregnant couple.

William rose to his feet, glass in hand. 'Everyone! Feel I should say, glad to be back here. Whatever I do from now on, wherever I practise the law of my training, I shall remember this jolly dinner. Mama, my thanks. Now, I know you all recognise changes in me – you've all dutifully told me. Big brother George despairs of my lack of aptitude for ploughing and mocks my inability to distinguish cumquats from mandarins – so he has told me many times. In my defence, perhaps, it is surely understandable after so long living away with Grandfather Fletcher in England. They don't grow oranges over there! However, because I laughed at the Comedy King's win, I don't want you thinking I lack respect for the monarchy. When the last king died in May, such a panoply of grief shaded all of London and to a degree, a small degree mayhap, I was infected by it.'

Arthur interrupted. 'Oh my boy! You made us proud, being at Oxford. But even here, we had daily bulletins about the king's illness and its consequences. Of course, he was our king, but even I feel he was a little removed from our Australian reality. He was ill, we were sorry for that, but we had endless newspaper reports of the funeral, the ceremonials and everything that followed. Ad infinitum. Must say, William, I did think enough was enough.'

'Papa, envision all that tenfold in England. A bright note, however: it was around the time of his illness that I was staying in the City, so I took some friends to see the Australian artists' and sculptors' display at the Royal Academy. Now that was a massive surprise to me. Papa, I had never heard of Bertram Mackennal – with an "L". He's a gifted sculptor and he's been commissioned to do a bust of Gainsborough to stand in Gainsborough's birthplace in Suffolk.'

'I seem to know the name. Is he an Australian, Will?'

'Yes, George. He did a fabulously lifelike bust of Dame Nellie Melba, you know. Some of his work is in Melbourne. I must visit to see them, one day. Mama, you, I know, would admire them. Fantastic figures… But at the RA, that's the English academy, I also saw some wonderful oils by Tom Roberts and Arthur Streeton, and others whose names escape me. You know, I could almost smell the Australian dust – they were so realistic. In truth, I felt quite homesick.'

William was in good voice. 'And Papa, Mama – you mention the interminable mourning for the king, well, that was quite a turning point for me. There I was, of English parents, had lived with my English grandfather, but I realised then that I wasn't one of them. I didn't have that sense of loss, nor could I grieve to their extent. I realised it was time to come home. Even so, when one newspaper described Edward as a bit of a rake, I thought those harsh words for describing a king, if arguably true. There is one notable development out of it all: the new king George V is to head the House of Windsor. That's to be its new name – they're to forget the Saxe-Coburg-Gotha lineage, or so that same newspaper opined. It will be a sensible move, no doubt, to mark a difference when the cousins in Europe are so busy sabre-rattling.'

Esther realised she was nodding in agreement. *William speaks like the lawyer he hopes to become. He certainly has something to say. Go on, Will…*

'You had Lord Kitchener here in Melbourne. I read that his success over the Boers was highly praised here and he responded, according to the papers I read, by praising young Australian men for "showing such natural military qualifications" and urging us to set up a sound military education system ensuring that we, Australia, could field a force of a standard on a par with "that of any European power". Frankly, I found the reporting of his comments rather gratuitous. Importantly, I sensed he was aiming to butter up our politicians to ensure we would send such young men in support of Britain should the need arise. I feel he was doing some sabre-rattling of his own.' Looking suitably solemn, William sat down.

Arthur had crossed his arms and was frowning in thought.

Beatrice raised an eyebrow at Esther but she returned the gaze with a wary shake of her head. There was enough of a mix of ideas and opinions for digestion already around this table. However, she put up her hand as a signal and called to William, 'So, Will, you're again an Australian and you've left your Englishness behind?'

He opened his mouth to reply just as Lilian leaned across to Esther and tapped her sleeve quite sharply with her fan. Esther turned to Lilian who, with eyes closed in that superior fashion she favoured, thereby not noticing her sister-in-law's irritated expression, made her appeal.

'It's so good to have you here, sister. You'll be such a great help to your mama and, of course, to me when this child arrives, if you would be so kindly…erm…available? That is if you're staying until when he or she does arrive. It will be about the end of January, I think.'

Beatrice intervened. 'I must agree with Lilian, dear. It is lovely to have you here. It's more than a year since your last visit, and William, well, he seems to have been away for ever and a day. It constantly seemed wrong to me, having the twins half a world apart for so long. Yet they're quite opposites, do you not think? We said years ago, did we not, how they were like chalk and cheese.' She gave a little chuckle. 'As for William, English or not, he does speak like one, don't you think?'

It was her turn to be tapped by Lilian and she turned politely to her daughter-in-law. Esther felt an almost childish resentment; felt even more she was sitting on the outside, looking in and not a part of it. Her mother had just announced her pleasure at Esther's taking her place in the family, her father referred to her as the daughter of the house, yet Esther didn't feel any of it was true. Lilian seemed to have taken over that role. *Oh my…now WHAT!*

The door banged open and little Anna Dodd came in carrying a tray loaded with more biscuits. Esther stood to steady its weight for the little girl. Anna's even smaller sister Jeanie came too; she had been promised payment if she helped.

'Anna, dear, have you and Jeanie had some roast dinner and some fruity pudding?'

'Yes, Mrs Beatrice. Thank you. An' Mrs Slope gave us our own plates full up!'

Jeanie piped up. 'An' the best meat. An' if we ate the cabbage all up to the last scrape, we could have custard wiv our fruit cake, she said, an' we did. An' we can go play in the garden with the others.'

Beatrice smiled and sat back, content to watch the process. She looked over at her daughter and tapped her sleeve gently. 'Esther, do you not wish to say a word or two?'

Esther leaned to her mother. 'Later perhaps, Mama, to you, not to everyone.'

Beatrice edged closer. 'We will talk, Esther. I'm not finding it easy, because there's so much I don't understand. Where is that sparkle in your lovely hazel eyes, and that twitch of your nose as you sense a challenge? They so loved you at that Melbourne school and your decision to leave was precipitate, so unexpected, so very out of character.'

Then Lilian intervened – again. 'You know, Mil, you look as if you're worrying for the world! Can I help? Or is it something George has said, or done…again?'

Beatrice smiled. 'Thank you, dear, but no. I was only remembering Christmases past and just indulging in the pleasure of having all the family together for Christmas this year. And you, dear, how are you feeling after enjoying a substantial meal? You seem to have hardly any room left for eating, that baby of yours seems to be so big. Surely it's not to be twins again?'

Lilian smiled. 'No, Dr Roberts is confident it will be just the one, and I am so hoping for a little girl this time.'

Arthur spoke sleepily from the depths of his chair. 'Beatrice, my love, it's the season for music, festive music. So will you play for us? "Deck the Halls" perhaps?'

Esther watched her mother nod in acknowledgement and make her way to their old, but well loved, piano in the far corner of the dining room.

3

Beatrice settled onto the old stool, thinking. She needed only an occasional look at the music sheet, knowing the lovely carols by heart. This one took her back to that Christmas 1879 at Bridgewater. Then, she had played this song for Anderson, the Welsh-born landlord of the inn. It was there she renewed her acquaintance with Arthur, the oh-so-handsome Lieutenant Symonds and, with him, had later discovered Cumquats Farm. Without the encouragement of Anderson and his housekeeper sister, Sissy, she knew she would not have found the happiness she had today. The two of them had given her, so new to the colony, a start to being independent.

She trilled the final chords as a voice called out. 'How about "The Holly and the Ivy", Mama? Please. My favourite.'

That was George. Farmer George, as she called him with affection. Beatrice remembered how it was her father's favourite too, in their farm days in England. He had always asked her mother to play it for him at Yuletide. Dear Papa. He had so enjoyed his visit here. It was just after her friend Mrs Mary Lee was credited with campaigning and persuading Parliament to give women the vote, back in 1894. Beatrice leaned back and smiled, almost missing a note, as she recalled his wife, the second Mrs Fletcher, expressing astonishment that women here, 'in a mere colony', had gained the vote before women in England! That had been a priceless moment.

She rattled off another verse, needing no music for the traditional favourites. Then almost at the end, Lilian, with her lovely contralto, broke into a final chorus. As she played a chord or two at the end, Esther tapped her shoulder.

'That's enough, Mama. I'll take over for a minute or two. Papa's almost dozing and yet, would you believe it, singing tunelessly in his chair. Some fresh air might be called for! Off you go. Take him away from his cushions and into the garden. See if you can steer the conversation your way for a while.'

Beatrice smiled as a shuffling of feet indicated the others making a move.

As she took her place on the piano stool, Esther whispered, 'What's this Millie or whatever it is that Lilian calls you?'

Beatrice grinned and whispered conspiratorially in her daughter's ear. 'It's M.I.L – short for mother-in-law. I think she read it in a magazine. She's always reading fashion magazines. Her mother sends them to her. I rather like the term. Now, as you suggest, I think we'll all end up in the garden but first, dear girl, can you play "Silent Night"? Then, if you feel inclined, little Anna loves to play "Chopsticks".'

At Esther's grimace, Beatrice gave an apologetic smile and fled.

*

Left on her own, Esther felt calmed by the quiet. She trilled a variant of the lovely carol 'Silent Night' as Mama had requested.

'Dear old piano. Your keys are looking worn, going a bit yellow, yet you're in tune. One thing Mama would not let slip! You do bring back the memories and I'm sure you've been in this corner almost for ever – well, since the parents bought this place. I was a mere infant then. Mama was my very first teacher and I remember her rapping my knuckles at times – oh yes, I do. William used to play a bit. Wonder if he still does? George never wanted to, as I remember. Twins, yet so different. William is happy for George to be Papa's right hand on the property and I'm glad there's so little rivalry between them. All William wants to do is set up his shingle as a lawyer, or solicitor, or barrister – I'm not sure which legal eagle is which. Do you know, Piano?' She laughed out loud.

'I feel good playing you, dear old piano. I've missed you over the years. I've spent so long away and grown apart as a result but you, you are the constant factor in my ever-changing lifestyle; always ready and waiting here for me. Papa had to learn all about growing grapes and getting water onto the land. Mama taught me the notes but I hated practising the scales. Then Mama embraced the grape-growing and I did quite a bit of solo playing as she was out creating a vineyard. I belonged here, then, I had a place. Then I went away teaching and only came back for short breaks in between. Is that why I don't feel this is home any more? Wonder why they kept the name Cumquats? Seems to me the grapes have taken over and the cumquats, tangerines and the other citrus don't get the attention they used to… Oh, this pedal's a bit slack.' She pumped it a couple of times and wriggled to the right level on the seat.

'Well, Esther Symonds, come now, show some backbone. Let's play a bit of Chopin. So you and Mr Piano have exchanged memories – that's a rhetorical statement.' She sighed. 'This is my life so far, Mr Piano. We are such friends you and I, growing older together. I'm twenty-nine, nearly into the next decade. You're much older than me and still play a pure note. Oops, that's A flat – huh? But I still played you when I could. I really missed you while I was at Adelaide University. I went into teaching and of course there was an instrument there, but not as friendly as you, no scratches smiling at me. That was at Lauriston first, then to the Methodist Ladies' College. I chopped and changed – as Papa says – gained lots of experience in different subjects but always preferred English and Classics…'

'Pardon, Miss Esther? What's classics?'

She looked down in surprise. *Oh goodness, I've been prattling on, and out loud.* 'Sorry, Anna. I was reminiscing. Erm, just talking to Mr Piano. He doesn't talk back, though. How would you like to come on the stool with me and we'll play "Chopsticks"?'

Anna needed no coaxing and clambered up alongside. 'Can a piano talk back, Miss Esther? Do they understand?'

'Well, they make music, don't they? That's their voice… Now, shall we play? Let's see your fingers.' *And with luck that'll banish at least another hour from this interminable Christmas Day.*

The young lass was no stranger to the instrument and Esther enjoyed teaching her new melodies on the keys. It actually seemed too soon that little Jeanie came rushing in, quite excited.

''Scuse me, but Mrs Slope's going home an' says she'll take us home now, Anna, 'cos she wants to pop in an' see Mum but Mrs Beatrice wants to see us first an' she says she has a Christmas present for us, so c'mon!' She paused for breath.

Anna slipped down and, to Esther's delight, bobbed politely to her before racing off. Esther stayed on the stool. She randomly scaled her fingers up and down the keys. Some energetic pushes on the pedals and hammers on the base notes came later as her thoughts intensified.

The door swung open. Beatrice entered ahead of an ear-bursting cacophony of toddler cries and masculine laughter. Esther turned as her mother hastily closed the door to seal off the noise and make her way over to the piano.

She slid onto the other end of the stool, wriggled into position and wrapped her arms around her first-born. She whispered into Esther's ear, 'Those last few notes of yours were angry ones, dear girl. I've seen the little Dodd girls off with their presents and now, while we're alone, please tell me what's wrong. Something is, I know. Do confide in me while it's so quiet and we're alone. You're not in trouble?'

Esther rolled her eyes. 'Mama, why is it the first thing a mother thinks of when a daughter isn't wed? For goodness sake, Mama. No, I'm not pregnant with anyone's child but…well, in its way, that *is* the problem.'

Beatrice chose to prevaricate. 'Esther, my dear, you're young, you're at the peak of your career, the career you chose – quite deliberately. I'm confused. Look, let's sit down together you and me, in peace and quiet.'

She cocked an ear to the other door. 'I think they've all gone down to the bottom of the garden to see George's tortoise. Hopefully we won't be disturbed. Do tell me, my Esther, and know that Papa and I will support you in whatever it is you need, or want.' She smiled. 'If we can, that is.'

Esther stood, closed the piano, and set off across the carpet. 'Come on, Mama, back to the armchairs.'

They flopped among the cushions.

'Mama, I'm twenty-nine. You talk of only twenty-nine whereas I think of it as almost into my third decade. *Tempus fugit*, Mama – *et numquam revertitur.*'

'Esther dear, I know – time flies and never returns. But…'

'No buts, Mama. Thirty is to me the start of my growing old, too old for some purposes anyway. I know my physiology, Mama. I have now spent years teaching young misses and young ladies – and believe me, society marks the difference – and I've been complimented on my techniques, on my inspiration. Would you believe it?'

Quite uncertain which way the conversation was leading, Beatrice chose to nod ingenuously. 'Yes, I do. You were always extremely good in explaining points of view. You have a clarity of thought and a way of infecting others with it whenever questions pop up. But now?'

Even as she was trying to ask questions, others were plaguing her. *Is it money? No, she received a good salary and her living was supplied by the school. Is it a man? If so, who? Ahah – does she want to teach a mixed class of boys and girls – she has always been for equality.*

Esther noticed puzzled expressions fleeting across her mother's face. 'Mama, I was teaching young girls, some with promise and others without, yet when they left my care I could credit them with potential. Every single one! I'm a good teacher. Then one Thursday I sat back in my room, marking papers and…well, it just came to me.'

Beatrice was quite mystified, but maintained an expectant expression. 'Esther, please. You talk of inspiration. Are you now talking about an inspiration for yourself?'

Esther got up from her armchair so that she could stand and be the dominant speaker, another common-room technique for dominating the argument. 'Mama, I want a child, children of my own so that my talents, my learning, can be put to their advantage and, thus, my own.'

Beatrice was quite nonplussed. She raised her eyebrows. 'For children, my lovely girl, one needs a partner. Erm, you haven't mentioned one but…do you have one in mind?'

'Mama, do you remember Francis Flach? Frank?'

Beatrice's eyebrows shot to the ceiling but before she could even squeak in surprise, there was a thunderous banging on the door and it flew open.

In rushed George, carrying a struggling Aaron. 'Mama! He fell over and his nose is bleeding. Lilian is lying down, can you…?'

Beatrice at once turned to the little boy. 'George, take him into the scullery. I don't want a mess on this rug.' She turned, 'Esther, do wait. I'll just…'

But a frustrated Esther was already leaving. *Oh ye gods, what an interminable day. I have to get away, go out…* She ran up to her room and closed the door. She would go for a ride. Fresh air and wind through her hair, blowing away the uncertainties, the frustrations. Her mother's crotchety old horse would have to do. *Where are my jodhpurs, my trews?*

At the thought, she dropped her skirts around her ankles, kicked the fabric across the room and pulled out her hairpins to shake her long brown hair around her shoulders. She stood by the cheval glass, turned around, assessing her all-over shape, and then posed sideways-on to her reflection, hands on her waist.

Eyes? Mama calls them hazel-coloured. Bright enough, long lashes. Frown lines above my nose, better start smiling a bit more. Good complexion, if a bit pale. Not a bad figure, must admit; still have a narrow waist, straight back. I don't look as tired and worn as some women of my age but of course, I haven't had a child each year…

She pulled on her trews and boots, headed down the rear hallway and out to the stables. *Yes, fresh air, find that breeze…*

4

Beatrice looked for Esther later that afternoon but the girl had apparently saddled up and gone off for a ride. When she did return, she escaped, or so it seemed to Beatrice, down the hall for a bath. And in the evening when they all collected for a sherry and some of Mrs Dodd's smoked almonds, there hadn't been an opportunity for the two of them to renew the conversation.

Only later in bed could Beatrice try to relive her surprise at Esther's remarks. Of course she remembered Francis. His mother Kate – Katherine –Tweedie had been Beatrice's first real friend in the colony, in Bridgewater, until she married Herbert Flach from the nearby Lutheran settlement. Kate had twins, Francis and Eloise; she and Arthur had stood godparents. Since then, there had been the occasional letter exchanged.

Beatrice had said nothing to Arthur about Esther's apparent quandary. He had been over-full of Christmas heartiness till bedtime and fell asleep as soon as his head rested on the pillow. Yet to her it seemed as if their dear girl – woman – had looked for and found an answer to it, whatever 'it' was, although it all seemed too chilling in its matter-of-factness. But then, a logical practicality had always been evident in Esther.

A woman doesn't marry just anyone because she wants a child, or that was Beatrice's thinking. If Esther's plan was to do just that, even though she had always been a most practical daughter, in plotting her career, her life choices, she was stretching her common sense to extremes. She tossed and turned as her subdued muttering disturbed Arthur. He grunted in protest. She was still formulating a plan to buttonhole her daughter when she drifted into sleep.

The moment came next morning in the dairy. Esther had been helping the eldest Dodd girl, Maisie, separate milk from cream. Maisie was a gem according to Beatrice, who could never, herself, manage to make a decent cheese. Maisie could.

Beatrice beckoned her daughter and they walked, arm in arm, up to the vines and along the lush green avenues in between. Residual raindrops were glinting on the clusters of leaves, the soil beneath smelled newly mudded and a few ducks flapped around their ankles teasing up the snails from underneath.

Esther raised her eyebrows in enquiry.

Beatrice smiled. 'Cheeky things, aren't they? And that lovely, lovely smell, the sense of reawakening earth after rain. Breathe it in, Esther. It has a name, petrichor, or so one of my winemaker friends – he's taught me a lot – tells me. He's been to France for the vines and also tells me how to rate the terroir of a wine – he says that's the place where the vines breathe and grow. Worlds ahead of me, dear. Now where was I? Ahah, the ducks. They keep down the weeds and feast off slugs and other pests. The cumquats were heavily laden this past winter and we sold some of the dried fruit in the township. The Dodds' church group has a stall regularly. And the grapes look healthy too – promise of some good bunches there. We usually pick in April, so there's time yet. We only have a small area, and most of the vines I developed from plantings made before Renmark even became known as a township.'

Beatrice reached into her apron pocket and began to scatter a bag of chopped bacon rinds for the ducks. 'Now, my Esther, we're alone with only the birds. Finish your tale of last evening, please. This talk of partners or marriage…'

Esther stopped, pulled away from her mother and leaned on a post to look her in the eye. She had rehearsed her argument many times, reciting the main points over and over in the peace of her room or in the small hours of some mornings. 'Mama, women teachers are considered the lesser breed. No matter our responsibilities, the preparation and extra hours we contribute, we're paid much less than the men and, importantly, thought of much less. We're considered to be on a level with governesses, and you know how governesses are neither family nor servant in our society. Personally and professionally, to study all those years and not be recognised, no matter one's achievements, is an injustice.

'I've worked hard, I've achieved, I have talents and I have skills. Some of us from a number of teaching establishments paraded through Melbourne to the Education headquarters and left a petition there. The Lady Teachers Association reformed and joined the Public Service Union in 1907 – I think it was then. We asked that our salary reflect our training, skills and achievements. We were assured of a hearing. No one was notified of a hearing, the matter was brushed aside and, what was worse, the newspapers called us "latter-day suffragists".

'I was hurt, angry, frustrated – all of that, Mama. I had reached my peak of usefulness. Then I sought consolation in the thought that I could have my own children, to teach and develop and know life, life as I've been able to know it thanks to you and Papa. With Duncan…'

'Duncan?'

'He was teaching at a nearby partnership boys' school. For more than a year, Mama, we went to the theatre, shows, especially musical concerts, and I was beginning to think I had met my match – literally. Then, out of the blue, he told me he was betrothed, engaged, to a woman from near his family country home and was leaving Melbourne to marry her. It had been arranged for years. He had never mentioned her to me at all. I was outclassed, Mama. Duncan's newly affianced partner had millions in real estate and her father was influential in country stock breeding. Mama, your eyebrows are meeting your hairline! Please understand: it all became so unrewarding. In my opinion, I had reached the pinnacle of my career. I could go no further.'

Beatrice looked ready to cry and moved over to hug her daughter. 'Oh, my dear girl. You never wrote of this. And that was quite a speech. My dear, why didn't you telephone us and we could talk…' She stroked Esther's rich brown hair back from her brow, smoothed a frown from between Esther's eyes, then stood back. More was to come.

'Mama, you know how you and Papa dislike the telephone and you go on and on about listeners on the party line knowing all your business.

Why on earth should I add my private business to the mix? Then last October I had another letter from Frank.'

'Another? And was that why you came home?'

'He had written before, Mama. Oh yes. It started when I was at Lauriston actually, so a few years ago. Our correspondence was only spasmodic at first. I was writing to Eloise and he added a bit to her responses. Then he started writing. Mama, he has asked me to consider marrying him. His letter seemed fortuitous…'

'*Marry?*'

'He was prolific in his letter writing, Mama. He has a wonderfully free style of writing, you know, as if he's in the room talking. In our letters I feel we've learned even more of each other by not being face to face. I'm confident we have done so. And then, at times, he would use his business telephone, organise a trunk call to my school and, well, we could actually talk.'

'Learn, Esther? His ways are not your ways, if I remember correctly.'

'You're quite right, Mama. As a boy, Frank was quite obnoxiously chauvinistic. That was how he had been brought up by Herbert, his father.' She grinned. 'He describes his father as being typically Teutonic! However, please try to understand, I do want to utilise what skills and talents I've worked hard to attain, to see results and perhaps to have that expertise recognised – even acknowledged.'

Esther straightened her stance and looked squarely at her mother. 'I've thought long about all this. I've weighed the odds, analysed my feelings, projected probabilities of happiness and achievement – all that. That's my way of doing things, Mama. I don't think I'm overly maternal. In fact, I'm not sure just what that means. However, I do think I'm still – for another short while – a suitable candidate. I do enjoy children, speculating on what they can achieve with guidance, work and ambition. I've questioned my motives, dismissed my doubts, then…it's been quite a see-saw, Mama, an emotional battle, but I have decided.'

'Esther, surely the emotions involved in such decisions include those of the heart? Love, nearness, not wanting to be without that person, more of that would convince me. Does Francis – erm, Frank – does he, for instance, stir your feelings, make you feel, well, reckless?'

Esther had to laugh at that. 'Oh, Mama, do listen. Eloise is close to Frank – after all, they are twins. Eloise was always interested in news of school and lately she's admitted to me that she and her husband want Susannah, their daughter, to be a doctor. I admit I was becoming muddled in my thinking, Mama, then Frank's letter told me of their hopes and his faith in me as a mentor for the young girl. That was the catalyst.'

'Goodness me, Esther, I know there are women doctors now. In fact, years ago, I heard of a girl being accepted into medical studies at Adelaide University. There was something of a local outcry, the general feeling being that doctors had to be men to give the profession some respectability. There was an article in the newspaper about some men declaring they would never allow a woman doctor to examine them. I must admit I don't know of any women doctors practising around here.' Beatrice moved on through the avenues of vines, found another post and leaned against it.

Esther faced her from one opposite, watching her mother's face, ready to listen.

'You know, Esther, I stayed awake last night for hours, just thinking. There's some background to all this that you might find helpful to know. Kate wrote me when Susannah was born. Eloise took as a husband Paul… let me think…Freeman? He wasn't a member of the settlement, his father calls himself a currency lad, I believe, born in Australia. His father came out in the very early days – to Hobart, I think. He was made a freedman by however means they did it then, took that name as his own, married a convict who'd been deported for stealing lace, a former governess, I think. She apparently taught him to read and write and then, with his natural business acumen and her accounting, they progressed. They had only the one son, Paul's father, and settled in Sydney. Paul was later raised there. You know, we really should approve the endeavour in that settler's tale. True of so many. I gathered from Kate that Herbert Flach, Frank's father, disliked the young man on sight. Had Paul been of German extraction, or of the Lutheran faith, it might have been more acceptable. Eloise and

Paul moved elsewhere to live – they had to. Must admit, I really didn't realise their little girl was old enough to, well, talk of careers. I just haven't counted the years. She must be twelve or even thirteen by now.'

Esther stood quietly, digesting this new information. She hadn't known of that animosity and it would be helpful to know of this Flach family situation; certainly her mother was digging deep into her memory bank.

Beatrice frowned in concentration and moved to another line post, and leaned against it, facing her daughter. A curious magpie flew onto the rail nearby, its head cocked as if listening.

Beatrice held up a finger and scuffled her feet around in the loose soil as she pondered. She fidgeted in her apron pocket and held out a stray smidgin of bacon to the opportunistic magpie, which actually took it from her hand – a cheeky move that prompted her daughter to smile. Esther knew her mother had a fondness for the black and white birds; perhaps the feeling was reciprocated. She waited, enjoying the caress of her unbound hair blowing across her face.

Beatrice felt she had to ask. 'Esther, this Susannah – isn't she able to go to that girls' high school in Grote Street? And her father, Paul, isn't he making a success of some city business? But you, you have just left your position. How do Eloise, her husband and Francis – or whosoever – think that you can be of help? And this talk of a catalyst intrigues me.'

'You look stunned, Mama. I'm sorry. Well, though I will be glad to help little Susannah, and I'm sure I can, I want my own daughters and, God willing, sons too. Frank wants me to marry him and educate our children with my ideas and what he calls my style. He wants a family of his own. He started looking around some time ago – believe it or not, this was in his letters to me. He says he searched for so long and then, in telling me the story, realised he was actually using as a sounding board the one woman against whom he measured all the others. Mama, I am she. Isn't that a lovely story?

'As Frank grew up, with his mother a former teacher, he recognised – he says – how an educated woman can open children to ideas and opportunities. Those are his words. When he decided he didn't want to take over the cooperage business, his mother understood but his father was quite unpleasant to him. He called it breaking a tradition but Frank argued that this is a country where the old traditions are broken regularly. Happily, they're now reconciled, I believe, because Joshua took Frank's place. Josh always did want to work with his father. So, Mama, Frank now has his own business, doing what he likes best.'

Beatrice nodded, exhaled with a little whistling noise, and then beckoned Esther to walk on further with her. 'While I'm here, I'd like to check on the dam. Coming?'

The curious magpie hopped along behind them in its comical fashion, making Esther smile. Birds and animals…

'Mama, do you remember how Frank once carved me a little fox, stalking its prey?'

Beatrice nodded.

Esther continued. 'You know, that little carving is so lifelike, so very artistic. I have always loved it. It's a symbol to me of the past that Frank and I share, Mama. We haven't seen much of each other over the years but somehow we share a lot. His wood carving is becoming known. It's the key to his new industry, a specialised carpentry. He earns money by carving doors, railings and fences, stairways and things he calls corbels – and much of that kind of thing is for public buildings as well as mansions and churches.'

She smiled, gazing upwards at a flock of pink and grey galahs shrieking against the bright blue sky. Somewhere along their route, the magpie had been joined by another, a grey-back. She smiled at its comical, hurried gait.

'Yes, it has been a battle, Mama, deciding, but Frank not only has prospects, he's realising them. He's renting a house in Grunthal outside Hahndorf at the moment but he's negotiating for one just up the main street in Hahndorf itself. It's for freehold sale, it has three bedrooms and, Mama, he has bought a bathroom water closet from a newly arrived English immigrant who needed the money and he wants to have it plumbed in…'

'Esther, do stop there. Goodness me, I do keep my nose to the ground, you know. I've heard of water closets – the old queen had one. But metal piping isn't a timber worker's area of skill, surely… Nor is it my own preferred conversation, so please let us continue about such things when Papa can join us.'

She stopped to give her daughter an affectionate hug. Then, standing back, looked into her eyes, a serious expression on her face. 'I'm not against this plan, totally. I think it's just a little…businesslike. Marriage requires commitment, affection and love, many other qualities. I do respect your common sense, Esther. However…'

'Mama, I told you Frank respects me, admires me. Deep feelings, Mama. This is not only a business arrangement. I really like him, trust him and respect him. Mama, I cannot say I love him because I don't know how love, as an entity between a man and a woman, can be measured. Duncan was the only other man who appealed to my senses. So, Mama, do think back. You told me once how you were not of a mind to marry when Papa came wooing you, that you had the best advice that in this new place you needed a man behind you, or alongside, for support, that perhaps you should take a commonsensical approach to a liaison without fearing you would lose your independence. Was that not so?'

Beatrice broke into a tentative smile, it widened and then – to her daughter's surprise – she broke into a chuckle. 'Dear Esther. You are certainly my daughter! I cannot deny your sensible approach, can I? And I do know that love grows when nurtured by two people who want it to. Just allow me a minute or two or three to think of what it all may mean, to straighten out some confusion.'

At the banks of the dam, where they both noted quietly how low the water level was despite the recent rain, Beatrice turned to her daughter. 'You're a woman grown, a woman of experience, Esther. I do respect your logical decision-making. I do want, above all else, for you to be as happy as I have been. Your mention of internal battles implies a measure of doubt in your decision, however. Just please give me time to think well over this.'

They linked arms.

'Esther, one more thing: can you explain the word "chauvinistic" to your dear old mama? It's new to me.'

Esther chuckled. 'Oh, Mama! You know in the Napoleonic Wars…?'

The voices faded into the distance and the magpies seized the moment to scatter the ducks and snatch the remaining pieces of bacon.

5

He took some convincing but Arthur Symonds eventually accepted the idea of his daughter's unexpected marriage. She wanted it to be on the Saturday of Easter weekend, 15 April 1911, a date to etch on his heart. To Arthur's mind, time seemed to be flying by, and that allowed him only a limited time to, as he put it, see how the land truly lay for her. He had enjoyed a quiet discussion with her in the stables, undisturbed, and that seemed to settle much of his doubt.

Arthur recounted to Beatrice that Esther might be well past the age of needing his agreement, but she had always been close to him and wanted his blessing. As he saw it, there was no agony of indecision, so her battles, as she called them, were not a full-blown war; all was still open to reconciliation then. He wanted to be sure in his own mind – or so he told Beatrice – and this well before the preparations started. He said he would travel to Hahndorf to see for himself but the rest of the family could be told he had business in Adelaide. April was a busy time for the vines, but that could be organised, George had assured him, so he needed to go as soon as possible.

'Arthur! This won't fool Esther. She will know what you're up to. And Lillian's baby is due imminently, so I'm needed here… Oh, Arthur.'

'Come on, Beatrice, Dr Roberts tells me he foresees no problems with the infant, that after the twins, this should be an easier delivery for Lillian. Mrs Dodd was a midwife for years and Dr Roberts will be on call and attend Lillian just as soon as George rides to tell him or of course, he can telephone. Hrrmph. I still can't get used to that intrusive and minimally useful item being here in this house, my dear. Also, this infant is not Lilian's first, Beatrice. Come, come, surely you want an assurance of Esther's future welfare?'

'Oh, you know I do. I do know that she knows her own mind and she's resolved but I cannot see her settling easily into a tradesman's, even a craftsman's, way of life, despite her assurances to me. And a small town like that after Melbourne? Yes, I admit to misgivings, but I do want her to be happy.'

Arthur grinned. 'Oh, how I remember your doubts, my Beatrice. Our Esther is very much your daughter, in many ways, my dear. However, and seriously, I wish also to know more of this special tutoring to young Susannah that seems to have cropped up, to ensure, if you will, that this Frank is not casting a sprat to catch a mackerel.'

He drained his glass. 'You know, dear Beattie, when we met, your determination to remain independent and go it alone as your friend Mrs Lee thankfully dissuaded you from doing – that worried me dreadfully. Not least when I contacted you after our first meeting and realised your newly-found presence of mind.'

He grinned and ducked his head as she made a mock striking motion with her newspaper.

*

He left on 18 January – a Wednesday – planning to take the mail coach to Morgan and the train from there to the city. He thought longingly of the spur planned for the train from Paringa – so much closer. But for now, the train from Morgan must suffice; from Adelaide he would take the train to Bridgewater. Beatrice wanted him to check whether her dear old Anderson friend had remained in the inn there, or moved to Adelaide to live with Lucille. From the inn he planned to telephone Herbert's business in Hahndorf and hopefully gain a ride to where Frank was living. He wanted to learn for himself of the young man's prospects. It would be interesting to know of the young man's parents' thinking regarding the planned linking of the two families in this way.

Another, recent, concern was a sense of growing anti-German feeling among ordinary people. He'd read of it in the *Advertiser* and spoken quite a bit on the topic to William – who had a London point of view on the Kaiser's activities, as had most who lived in London. Opinions were formed apparently since they saw the Kaiser ride at the old king's funeral. Also, in his own estimation, the occasional newspaper reports about the Boer War situation were coloured by English thinking and therefore best kept for readers over there, not here. Germany's support of the Boers was a fact but unfortunate in that it prompted a predictable antipathy. It was a pity that the advances in telegraph services meant that such propaganda was too easily transported to the colonies. Yet Arthur hadn't heard of anything unpleasant in Renmark. He would like to ascertain if any such prejudice existed in Hahndorf. If ever there was a place that it might, Hahndorf was surely high on the list.

He knew William was travelling to Adelaide shortly to contact Ralph Schulze, a prosperous lawyer, about work opportunities. The man had been recommended to William as a useful contact while he was in London. Surprisingly, this Ralph was none other than the Rauf who had married Lucille Woof of the Bridgewater Inn at the settlement, years ago and Beatrice knew them well. From that meeting, some truth of this anti-German feeling might eventuate and hopefully be mitigated by one who would know, or so Arthur hoped; he knew William would keep him informed, anyway. Nevertheless, when in casual conversation with a fellow traveller on the train from Morgan he mentioned that his daughter was to marry into a Hahndorf family, he was surprised to be asked if he was going to allow it.

'May I ask why you think I should not? The young man has a thriving business and is well able to support a family. Also, he's my godson so, you see, I know the family well.'

'Well, sir, I hope your wishes are realised. But those people supported the Boers in the war, you know. They were on the wrong side and their settlements in the colony are very much for the Germans. I don't wish to speak out of turn, sir, but I do know their alliance is very much to their own race. They speak their language in the shops, in their churches – and don't like it when you only speak English.'

The fellow traveller, who had introduced himself as Armstrong, shook out his newspaper, a copy of the Adelaide *Advertiser*, as if to read. 'If you only visit the capital infrequently, sir, you may not be aware of the increasing strength of feeling against Germany, not least because of this Agadir business. You know, of course, that the Germans are kicking up a storm about protecting their Moroccan interests, sir – apparently against what they call France's interference. It's not for them to impede world trade, sir, and Britain may be called upon by France. This is German mischief, sir, if it comes to pass within the next few months. Mark my words! I recommend that you take care. Nonetheless, I wish you well.'

William's past mention of sabre-rattling by the German royals added weight to this exchange and gave Arthur plenty to think about.

When he arrived in Hahndorf on his borrowed mount, he recognised an obvious increase in German patriotism. The shop signs and windows were predominantly in German script as were many street signs. Nevertheless, they were all well painted, clean, and had a prosperous air – and a pleasant one in his eyes. He wasn't entirely surprised, because Anderson, still of the Bridgewater Inn, looking well and quite Pickwickian in scarlet braces had regaled him with the local news during a drink or two the previous evening. Anderson had no prejudice and was an admirer of what he considered German efficiency in business.

It was only a short ride from Bridgewater and Arthur left the inn promptly after breakfast next morning. In his well-used, broad-brimmed hat, shirt and moleskins, he rode in leisurely fashion up the Hahndorf main street. Anderson had suggested he mark the solid building of the mill – steam-driven apparently – information Anderson knew would interest Arthur, a steam engineer. He didn't stop, however. The street was lined with a variety of European trees – he recognised the leaves of the chestnut, and the elms and even a plane tree. They were an attractive and well aligned planting of attractive shade trees, quite mature, possibly twenty or thirty years old.

The Hahndorf Academy was a little further up the street, though on the same side, and presented as an impressive building with a mown green surround. Surely that was an oak tree, *quercus quercus*? Must have been brought from the old country – or somewhere in Europe and planted at what was, according to its sign, the academy. Anderson had recounted rumours of its forthcoming closure and Arthur thought that a pity. There was a little timbered school further up the street after a row of neat and tidy cottages and as he passed, a bell clanged and a file of children, boys and girls, walked sedately towards some outside benches, apparently to eat some bread and drink their water.

Must be midday lunchtime recess. Hrrmph – I'm later arriving than I thought. But how well behaved they are, most unlike the noisy mob that pour from the Renmark school at the end of their day. The thought raised a smile.

As he rode along, the growth and development of what had been the Lutheran settlement – or German Town – surprised him. It was now becoming widely known as Hahndorf and he knew it was named after Captain Dirk Hahn of the *Zebra*, the sailing ship that brought most of the town's founding families to South Australia in 1838.

Arthur noted that the houses were linked in lines, next to one another and fronting a street. They seemed to have garden spaces behind, but not the long lines for cultivation as in the old. What had that pastor called it when he and Beatrice married – *hufendorf?* Certainly its German origins and loyalties were well displayed, judging by the names over the shop frontages. Arthur saw nothing wrong in that. It was a busy town and a friendly one if the smiles that greeted him as he rode along the street were a true indication. English-sounding names like 'street' and 'lane' were frequent also. He knew from Esther that one of Frank's friends, who he described as an arty type, lived in a delightfully named Billygoat Lane. How much more English could one get!

The Flachs' house looked less raw in its setting than when he had seen it last, too many years ago. A high hedge either side of the gate, some perfumed white blossoms among shiny green leaves giving it a comfortable, settled appearance, and he recognised the creeper to be the same as one on the dairy wall at home, planted to keep the wall cool against the sun.

Herbert was watching for him at the gateway and took the horse's reins as he dismounted. They shook hands heartily and then a rueful Arthur rubbed his behind.

'No seat for a saddle nowadays, must admit, Herbert.'

'I'm sorry I couldn't collect you from the inn, Arthur. Whatever cart was available has ferried some produce to the market. Been such a good season.'

A stocky young man came running from behind. 'I'll take your mount to the stable, Mr Symonds.'

Herbert grinned and gave a nod in acknowledgement as the horse was led away. 'That's my Joshua, Arthur. Oh, man! It is so good to see you!' Herbert smacked his thighs in happy emphasis then held out his arm for Arthur to pass up the path. 'Come, I'll take you in. Kate and the girls have been baking in readiness. I think we'll have a tasty bite this day and I shall enjoy it!'

Kate was little changed from how Arthur remembered. Still quick to move, though less supple in the waist, as he thought, her welcome was as warm as ever and her eyes as blue as Beatrice had described. A tall young woman with long blonde braids in her hair smiled from behind Kate, her likeness to Kate unmistakeable.

'Our youngest daughter, Evelyn, called for her godmother, Evelyn Lee.'

The young woman gave a delightfully old-fashioned bob in greeting then walked away towards a dresser bulging with breads and cheeses. Kate explained that Eloise and her husband did visit occasionally, now they were supposedly all reconciled, but they lived in Adelaide nearer to her husband's business. They hoped to come to visit tomorrow if Arthur would be staying.

Arthur determined he would be – he wanted to meet that daughter, and her daughter, the child prodigy apparently destined for high medical office under his daughter's guidance.

Joshua – still unwed – came back in to shake hands but asked to be excused as he was to meet with some friends, then attend some celebration at his football club. Kate explained that Inga, who was a year older than Evie, was married to a teacher and living up north somewhere near a place Arthur remembered well, Cobdogla, and with three-year-old twins!

He thought it fascinating that twins seemed to be an inherited trait bridging the generations. *Lillian is certain she is carrying the one baby this time but she certainly is a monstrous size. Any day now, I suppose…*

It certainly was an enjoyable meal, though as it was almost four o'clock when they finished, Arthur was uncertain if it was intended as lunch or dinner. A tasty soup, vegetables, cold meats and cheeses and bread, and when Arthur thought he couldn't eat anything more, in came a cold apple pie with cream. Well…

Joshua excused himself and went off to his club. Arthur found it difficult to reconcile the grown-up Evelyn Mary with the baby he remembered. Attractive and friendly yet with a firm set to her mouth, he calculated she must be about twenty-four or so, the age Beatrice was when they met, all that time ago. *Surely I have visited since then?*

Kate noticed his interest and invited Evelyn to speak of her work. She explained that she enjoyed helping her mother in the home, was in no hurry to leave it, and was able to give herself the time to study art with a family who lived locally and who did wonderful works in oil paints.

'My goodness, Kate and Herbert, you have a talented family. Evelyn and Francis both seem to have a creative talent.'

Kate seemed ready to agree, but Herbert raised his eyebrows with a pejorative sniff. Kate bit her lip, looking sideways at her husband as he replied to his friend.

'It has not been easy for me, Arthur, losing one son from the cooperage.' He sighed. 'But Joshua is a clever woodworker and also meticulous in the iron banding of the barrels. So I am content, I think. He is also happy to work with me and – what is that modern phrase – ah yes, we get along fine together. Frank is my elder son but we have argued because he wants always to diversify into other ventures with different timbers. However, I am proud of what he fashions – drafts the drawings also – with fancy trims for houses, and for the churches. Yes, other churches too. He is better doing what he does and happier for it. So all in all, it works well.'

Arthur noticed that Kate seemed to relax at his comments, allowing a smile in relief.

They talked of the township's growth and how the original settlement had been subsumed into what Herbert called Hahndorf busyness.

'I would like you to come and see our cooperage, Arthur.' Herbert gave a self-satisfied and friendly smirk. 'We now have a double landholding at the end of the lane and Josh's customers for the wheels have room to turn. It is really quite convenient.' He stood, still with that happy smirk on his face. 'The British surveyors of this town have imposed a grid style of village layout here which incorp– erm, incorporates the *hufendorf* we had before. It seems to work better than some feared.' He clapped his hands. 'Now we will enjoy a beer, I think.'

He brought a stone jug from the cool dresser, swept the lace tablecloth to one side and smacked the jug onto the boards. '*Hier ist mein Krug*, my friend and in it is my own brewed ale as my father used to make. You will share with me, I think?'

'Oh, I will, Herbert. Yet my Beatrice tells me I have to stop drinking so much. I'm getting rotund – her words, not mine!'

Kate laughed and signalled to Evelyn. 'Come on, Evie, let us clear away and we shall busy ourselves elsewhere!'

Evie whispered, 'Mutti, he is a most handsome man, this Arthur. So tall, and his hair has hardly a greying whisker!'

Kate grinned at her daughter. 'You know, I have always thought so, and he really hasn't aged much in the years in between.'

Evie winked at her mother and they both laughed out loud.

The men were indulging their thirsts. Herbert poured the two large steins of the frothing, milky brew. Its yeasty smell appealed and Arthur grinned. He readied himself – or so he hoped – for some discussion on the prevailing and as yet unmentioned matter of his Esther's marriage. He would bring up the matter, if Frank did not. Later.

'Herbert, my friend. What is this talk of Josh and…wheels, you said?'

'It came about because of his aptitude with the iron hoops on the barrels, Arthur. One day a carter came along asking if we knew of a smith, as he had a buckled wheel. Josh went to have a look and tempered the metal next day, fitted a new rim and the man was delighted. I fixed a price with him and – well, another little business plan came to light. The boy is good, Arthur, and keen. It pleases a father, does it not?'

Kate brought a plate of cheese and a board of bread. 'Here you are.

Food for thought, no doubt. Evie and I are escaping from your man-talk. We are sewing in my sitting room. Arthur, please do stay the night after the beers. There is a trundle in Frank's old room. Herbert will show you. Know you are welcome.' She smiled as she exited the room.

Herbert's grin was nearly as wide as the door. 'Evie is good company for my Kate and, it seems, is in no hurry to marry. I confess I hope not, Arthur. Let us go and settle your horse for the night, then we can talk this man-talk my dear wife allows. Over some beer and then maybe some schnapps, hey?'

Arthur was not at all unwilling and raised his beer mug in salute.

6

Next morning as the cock crowed, Herbert and Arthur shared the icy water from the standpipe in the yard, pouring it over their heads from an enamel drinking mug and gasping with the shock of its chill.

'By George, Herbert, man. That schnapps of yours is lethally alcoholic.'

Herbert grinned. 'You have not the head for it, my friend? Fear not, Kate will be having a good meal ready for us, Arthur. Let us make our way inside and see if we have the means for recovery on the table.'

Arthur threw back his head and roared a loud laugh, quickly brought to an end by a wince. His host was already throwing his towel over his shoulder and making for the kitchen door.

'Goodness, Kate! You must have been up hours before that cock-crow to have bread from the oven so early.'

Joshua walked in the door. 'No, Mr Symonds, sir. I ran over to the bakehouse and it is they who suffer from lack of sleep. For my mother, no more. She bakes her lovely cakes and things, but the bread and the kneading and rising I can organise for her now.' He cut thick slices from the long loaf and took a bite of the crisp crust. 'To the hunter the spoils, eh, Papa?'

Kate brought mugs of coffee to the table. 'Please help yourself to honey and cream, Arthur. Herbert always drinks his black, says it starts his heart for the day. Evie is frying bacon for us all and it will be here soon.'

They laughed as Arthur exclaimed at the taste of his chosen chunk of bread heavily layered in white butter. 'Oh, man! This is as good as the butter Maisie Dodd conjures in our dairy.'

A platter of piping hot bacon was presented and Arthur forked up a few rashers onto his bread. 'This is a feast, my friends. We eat well at home, I must be honest, but I suspect this bread has rye flour in it and the bacon – oh, it must be a special smoking you do, Herbert. It is excellent!'

Kate excused herself and left them eagerly exchanging the comparative values of certain types of timber for smoking. She whispered to Evie, who was at the sink, 'They seem happy enough. Soon, Arthur will want to talk with Frank. He said he would come around this morning particularly. I will have the coffee ready.'

Even as she thought, there was a loud 'Halloo!' from the rear gate and Frank leapt over it, calling to his watching mother. 'Some of your coffee, please, Mother!'

Mother indeed! 'Hello, my boy. Arthur is here, Esther's father…'

'I know. Vati's expecting me. Ah, thanks…' as she held out a steaming mug of coffee. 'I'll share some bread with them, if I may. Wish me luck, Mama.' He strode into the hallway.

Evie looked at her mother and signalled 'shhh' as they listened. Frank spoke first, and boisterous greetings were exchanged between the men and then the door closed, tightly.

Kate pursed her lips. 'Hmm. C'mon, Evelyn my girl. Let's leave them to it. I'd like your thoughts on the market stall. Seems to me…'

*

Arthur stood to shake Frank's hand, glad to register a firm but not aggressive grip. He then smiled easily at the younger man. Frank's smile was a little more cautious.

'Good day, sir. It's good to see you again.'

'I'm pleased to see you, Francis. Or is it Frank?'

'Day to day, sir, and with family and friends, it's Frank. If my parents call me Francis, I know I'm in trouble.'

The three of them laughed easily, and that set the scene for the ensuing conversation. It was not, as Herbert had feared, an inquisition. For him, almost as much as Arthur, it was an education. Of course he knew of Frank's cleverness with timbers, but when Frank pulled out a packet of photographs – the better to demonstrate some recent applications for local houses – he felt a father's thrill of pride.

The plates showed the shapes of his carvings arranged in an artistic fashion on some plain dark cloth, the better to show their dimensions. Arthur found them absorbing. There were curves and angles, much as he had expected, but also a springing cat, some owls with feathers beautifully and cleverly separated and eyes that seemed to see. There was a parrot, its head to one side…

'My word, my boy. That parrot has a decided curiosity in its look – it's a marvel! Are they all in different timbers or…'

'I carve them in whatever woods I can find that is spared from other – what Mutti calls serious – work. Mostly softwoods. One day I shall hope to be able to import timbers from the tropics up north of here. One day. But please, sir, come perhaps tomorrow to my workshop. I have many there, some waiting to despatch, others waiting for a home! I find that lately I have been asked for decorative angled pieces to fit above veranda posts. Doorknobs, and finials and spindles are my bread and butter for turning, when other work isn't waiting. Also, I would like to show you where we – that is, Esther and me, sir, with your blessing – will be living. I would like you to see the house.'

'That, Frank, would please me very much. Herbert, would you show me the way?'

'Arthur, my friend, it will be my pleasure. I, too, want to see how far the building is developing. Is that all right by you, my son?'

'Yes, Vati. Perhaps we can go over there together now. I'll see if Mutti is happy.' He scrambled off his stool and strode eagerly to find his mother.

Herbert looked enquiringly at Arthur, his honest face requiring no words.

Arthur put out his hand. 'My godson seems to me a fine young man, Herbert. Steady, ambitious, talented and responsible. Let us see his home and then perhaps we can all speak this evening and share our plans – and hopes.'

7

The men decided first to see the house on the main street that Frank was buying. His purchase had only been settled three days ago and although it had been lived in and was now vacant, it was obviously going to need quite a lot of work to make it as habitable as he was planning.

The house had a wide frontage and there was a large outbuilding to one side that Frank envisaged as a workshop. Arthur was concerned that the house seemed somewhat isolated, though no doubt that was an advantage for the business side of things. It was quite separate from the main group of shops, heading slightly westward from the High Street towards Adelaide. However, it would only be a walk of maybe ten minutes if Esther needed the shops.

The three men entered the little iron gate and walked up a neglected brick pathway. Arthur liked the outward look of the house, not only the woods, stones and timbers, but the care and planning that Francis had already put into it for the woman he had chosen. On entry, the ceiling was high enough for missing the beams, even for Arthur, who was taller than many men.

'You are dividing this big room to make two smaller ones? Bedrooms perhaps?'

'Exactly. The short pieces of rough timbers you see here are the noggins, sir.' Frank picked one off the pile. 'These are for noggins, for the partition walls. This wall is separate from anything structural so the noggins help keep the wall from moving around too much as the house shifts and the construction material expands and contracts due to temperature changes and humidity. It keeps the studs from moving around too much. The little work spent putting in noggins will save us from having to re-lime the walls too often because these walls won't shift!' He grinned.

Arthur was impressed. The work was being carefully planned and executed by this young man, floors, ceilings and now dividing walls. Even modern plumbing. It boded well for a comfortable living for his special daughter. This young man seemed, like Esther, to know his own mind; such a shared practicality could only be a positive sign. He listened to more plans for improvements and renovation and was content, recognising that Esther would be in good hands with this young man.

'It is a sturdy staircase, Frank. Now please, do show me more of this house my daughter is to be making into a home.'

He watched as a wide, joyous grin spread across Frank's face. 'Yes sir, Mr Symonds! Does this mean I may marry Esther, with your blessing?' He grabbed Arthur's hand and pumped it vigorously. 'You will not regret this, sir. I will treasure her for always.'

'I know you will, Frank. She knows it too, I think. She is a grown woman, I respect her decision and I'm content it is a good one.'

After spending another hour on the property, even discovering some fruit trees, seemingly one of everything but all needing some pruning, they decided to head back to the Flachs'.

Arthur turned to Frank. 'The land is a generous size, my boy. Good for business, no doubt, to have the sounds of your industry not too close to neighbours. Was that one of its attractions?'

'Indeed, sir. I agree with Vati – my father – that good relations with neighbours must be respected. The cooperage is down at the other end of town, in an area where to be a wheelwright is a disadvantage and a nuisance to those living nearby. His business with coopering and wheel rims is predominantly noisy metal ding-dong-bangs.'

He laughed and gave his father a gentle knuckle blow on his upper arm. 'Is that not right, Vati? Each strike of the metal over the stone sounds like the bells of the town hall clock!'

Herbert smiled. 'We do have a bit of a noise problem at times but as yet there is space around us, too. I am working at ways of muffling some of the noise. Now, you my son, will need a sawmill for some of the work you do. Any thoughts on that?'

Frank nodded to his father. 'I do plan to have a saw pit of some new design, active in the back garden. We have an acre, so there is the space. I do need to plan a proper workshop, though, and one where I can exhibit items to sell. That area there is perhaps the most suitable. We're near enough to the main road from town to be noticed for what we do. I thought to look for designs for new saw pits, one to cope with furniture, table tops and such. For long timbers, floors and such, there's the mill not far away… My work is mainly small pieces in comparison, Vati.'

Arthur had listened carefully to this exchange between father and son. 'If I may intervene, Frank? And Herbert? As you know, I know steam. It was my work and is still a devouring interest – so Beatrice tells me.' He grinned in a conspiratorial way. 'Agreed you wouldn't need a mill here but even a saw pit can be much easier to operate with the aid of a steam-driven rotary saw. There is such a thing being developed, by a friend of mine – lives just over the border from us. Until recently it required two men above the log and another in the pit below, working hard. I visited him recently on an irrigation matter and he has put his knowledge of steam-driven irrigation pumps to another use. We spent hours, he and I, designing and adapting our various experiences to a much smaller enterprise and his ingenuity is most admirable! For that saw pit, he employed strong men to work it in rotation to saw the timbers he's cleared off his land. However, three of those men are giving notice to leave his employ to make more money in a factory. My friend will have a problem with production…'

Frank was watching his future father-in law in great interest.

Herbert laughed out loud. 'Oh, mine goodness, Arthur! You have now caught the attention of this boy. Anything new…'

'Not so new, Herbert. I was quite surprised at some of the innovations I've witnessed using steam. It's so simple, and so effective. Now, take my friend, for instance. The straight, long timbers he ships elsewhere for milling but he's building a new barn. He claims that additions to his property will need smaller pieces up to say nine feet long – for instance, for wall planks. These he wants to trim on his land and save transport costs. So he and I contrived a design – still on paper – using a small steam engine with an eighteen-inch-diameter cylinder that he owns already. It was made in Glasgow, which I like, thinking of my own beginnings in the steam industry. I'm not sure how he acquired it but I could ask. It's generously sized for the jobs in hand. Fences, shingles and such everyday splitting jobs he can cope with.'

He stopped. 'Oh, I'm sorry to be talking so much, Frank. I'll keep you informed, my young friend, should anything come of our steam thinking.' He laughed. 'That's if you would like me to?'

They arrived back at the cooperage to find an attractive young lady waiting for them with Evie. Kate had gone to visit a neighbour who was unwell.

'May I introduce my lovely niece, Susannah, Mr Symonds?'

'Oh. No need to be so formal, Evelyn my dear. How lovely to meet you, Susannah. I've heard a great deal about you from your uncle Francis too.'

Evelyn suggested they all sit down for a biscuit and a drink, bringing apple juice for Susannah and making piping hot coffee for herself and the others.

Arthur liked what he saw of the young lass his Esther was to help with homework. She was polite and asked lots of intelligent questions of her uncle and grandfather; not so many of himself. *But then, I'm new to her and she to me. Nice broad brow and eyes not too close together. She'll be a beauty one day.* He asked her if she knew much of England, where he came from, and that led to lots of questions about geography and if she enjoyed learning French. From that, the conversation switched to music and her joining a school choir. The hated school uniform led to comments on fashion. He watched, amused, as she argued with Evelyn on the fashionable styling of hair.

He answered her questions about Esther and how she had liked school; whether she had brown or blonde hair; and it seemed all too soon that Evie apologised and said she had to take the lass up to the church for a choir practice and they must not be late.

'Lovely young lady, Herbert. If she wants to be a doctor, I think she will go far.'

8

Meanwhile, chaos was reigning at Cumquats, or so Esther was convinced. Lilian seemed to be having a prolonged labour. It was now two in the afternoon and it had been before six that morning that Mama had called for Mrs Dodd to take her place at the workers' breakfasts. She would be needed elsewhere, Esther knew. George had been pounding the bedroom floor in his heavy boots until his mother banished him.

'George, for Heaven's sake, and mine, get the horse and do some ploughing in the second paddock. Papa wants that done, as you know, and here is your opportunity. It's perhaps unfortunate that William's in the city. All right, I know you don't consider him much of a hand on the property but he is willing. I'm sure Esther will look after the boys and I will look after Lilian. As it happens, Dr Roberts is coming on a routine check visit this morning, so he should be here soon. Lilian's doing well, so believe me, son, just go and let us all get on with it!'

Esther made her way to check on the little boys. Alexander was crying and Mrs Dodd was trying to soothe him.

'He heard his mumma crying out, Miss Esther. Perhaps you stay with him. Worried about her, he is. Hard to explain to a littl'un that all is really well.'

Esther smiled and ruffled the little boy's hair. He put up his sticky-biscuit hand to grip hers and abruptly stopped his sobbing.

Aaron had cleared his plate. 'Mumma gotta headache, Aunty Esther.' He nodded assurance. '"Take a powder an' get well." Mumma says it all time. Baby kicking, wants to get out. P'raps she should give him a powder, you fink?'

Esther smiled at the three-year-old's summary justice. 'Mrs Dodd, let me take the little boys outside for a while. A distraction would be good for them, and for us, I feel!' She held out her other hand to Aaron. 'Come on, young lawyer. Let's all go out and play ball.'

Beatrice looked harassed. 'Oh, my dear, I'm so pleased. If you can keep them out perhaps for a half hour or so, it should all be over by then. The baby is almost crowning, I do believe, although Mrs Dodd has it all under control.' She wiped her forehead with the back of a hand. 'Well, at least let's hope so!'

As they left the house, the doctor's trap turned up at the front to be met by George. *Thank goodness, now Mama may relax.*

Esther led the little boys into the small paddock, noting how rapidly the boys forgot about their mother's distress when distracted by the thought of some fun. She threw the ball to each in turn, encouraging them to catch. Unused to such young children, she had to restrain herself from grumbling at them for not being able to trap the ball in their hands.

'Hey, you two, shall we go among the vines and see if we can catch a rabbit or two?'

'Yeah! I win you, Aunty!'

'No, I win you!'

The pair took off towards the boundary gate, their mumma and ball games forgotten. Rabbits they knew and understood.

*

Esther enjoyed calculating the boys' progress and development as they played.

'Boys, you are exhausting! You play that kickball football game you like and I'll watch for a while. Aunty Esther's running out of puff.' She leaned against a vine support.

You little fellows who aren't listening to me. I've enjoyed running over the grass but you know, instead of just playing a game with you, here I am measuring your reaction times – and progress – for your age. Is this what it is being a mother? More to the point, is that how I'm going to be as a mother – clinical – rather than motherly? How will I know before I am? She clasped her hands, twirling her fingers. *Oh dear, am I doing the right thing?*

The boys were by now over at the edge of the field so she called loudly. 'Time to go home, boys! Time to go.'

Mrs Slope was in the kitchen. 'Made a pot of tea, Miss Esther. Would you like to take it along to them? Lovely news it is, and they'll want to tell you.'

'Tell…? Oh! How…but first, perhaps, Mrs Slope, could you please just pull off the boys' boots and wash their very dirty faces and hands for me?'

Beatrice came down to the kitchen followed by a smiling Mrs Dodd.

'Mama – please! Boy or girl?'

Beatrice was almost crying. 'Oh, it's a little Rosalie, Esther dear. Rosalie Jane.'

Esther jumped up and down on the spot. 'Oh, how delicious, how wonderful!'

She reached for her mother's hand and Mrs Dodd's and the three women, laughing and smiling in relief and joy at the safe arrival of the infant, skipped around the kitchen in a circle. Then they barely managed a sip or two of tea before George came cluttering down the hall, calling for the doctor to join him in a brandy.

Beatrice shook her head. 'Typical man! No mention of the lady student he brought along. Here's his two boys with milk all over their faces. That's good. Thank you, Mrs Slope. I'll just take them to see their mumma and little sister. Lilian was asking for the boys and it will be good for them to see all is now well. Esther…'

'Mama – lady student? Or a lady doctor? I'll go and talk with her. You do the right thing, Mother. Off you go for a cuddle!'

The lady student, as Beatrice had called her, came over to Esther and held out her hand. 'Hello. I gather you're the daughter of the house. I'm Erica Capper-Jones.'

'Lovely to meet you. I'm Esther. Come and sit outside with me and I'll organise a coffee. Or perhaps you'd prefer a sherry?'

'No thank you, though I dare say the sun is well over the yardarm, as my father would have said! Hot tea would be delightful.'

'Here's Mrs Dodd – as usual, she has anticipated our preference!

Thank you, Mrs D. Now, Erica – oh, may I call you Erica? Good. Tell me, are you joining Dr Roberts's practice?'

Erica stirred her cup of tea. 'Oh, this is delicious. Yes, I hope to. I'm on probation but I am qualified. Adelaide University. I finished the year before last. Spent 1910 gaining experience under a group of doctors. They called me an apprentice! I was the only female. My speciality is prenatal and paediatrics.'

'Is that now a dedicated arm of the profession? I'm so pleased if it is.'

'Yes, and having given it a name means that we women doctors are being more highly regarded, accredited by prospective patients. It's only recently that people stopped thinking of women doctors only as assistants or students – like your mother just said.'

'An oversight on my mother's part, I assure you. There is none more passionate about recognising a woman's profession than my mother! She will be pleased I know, to have a female doctor – but do you also do daily doctoring?'

Erica laughed. 'You mean what they're now calling general practice. Yes, I do. Dr Roberts isn't yet ready to retire but he is looking to the future, so he told me when he engaged me. He believes women bring gentleness and an understanding to the profession that females of all ages appreciate. Those are his words, by the way. However, I believe it's more a matter of acceptance. Strangely perhaps, many women don't trust a woman doctor. Or they see us as very good nurses. They think that any illness requires the gravitas of a rather lordly gentleman!' She laughed. 'Even Dr Roberts assumes a rather alien pomposity to some older women patients because that's what they expect.'

'I really can understand what you are saying. As a senior teacher, and some even called me inspirational, I had to fight for respect from many of the male teachers and, sadly, some of the parents – despite the improvements their daughters made under my tuition. Not only that but women teachers, no matter what level they reach in their career, are paid considerably less than a male teacher. Purely a male versus female thing. We marched, were called copycat suffragists. I found it very frustrating.

I knew myself as qualified, both academically and in experience for headmistress of my school but, quite precipitately, I decided to leave the profession when the post became free. The governors would have denied me – I'm female. I was advised – delivered rather condescendingly – that I could apply for the deputy position and I was expected to be grateful. And this was a girls' school! I'm just so tired of fighting the rigidity of the establishment.'

'Oh, I see. Dr Roberts did say you'd returned home.'

'Nearly two months ago now, but I'm not staying, Erica, though my mama finds it hard to accept. I plan to marry and I'll move over to the Adelaide Hills region, Hahndorf actually. I hope for children of my own to teach and also to indulge in a consultancy practice.'

'So Esther, I'm sorry to make your acquaintance only to have you leave. However, I admire your commitment to an ideal. But Hahndorf, isn't that a German town?'

As Esther nodded, Erica assumed a solemn face. 'I've read that there's strong feeling in Adelaide against some German-born settlers, and even their Australian children. I haven't witnessed it myself, but would that not be a concern?'

Esther smiled. 'I haven't noticed it myself, though perhaps there aren't many German families around here to form an impression'. She laughed. 'We must believe in ourselves, Erica. You and I both have experienced a form of discrimination and feel confident we can rise above it. We will overcome such prejudices by our strengths, I'm convinced. Now, come and be more acquainted with my mother.'

9

Next day, Esther rode into town. Her papa was due back in a day or two and Frank would probably send a letter back with him. Nevertheless, she hoped that one perhaps was waiting in the post office from a week or two earlier. Frank knew that Cumquats was on a telephone line but she had not encouraged him to call her at home despite being so very keen to know how they had got on. They were on a party line and she was sure she had heard others listening in at times. She had been angry when her mother confessed that Papa's main business was to meet and talk to Francis and the family; that he wanted to see what Frank was providing for her and also to know that the Flachs approved of the liaison. Then reason took hold – it was a good feeling to know that parents cared, even when one was almost thirty years old!

She also had a couple of notes to put into the post for Mama; one to Evelyn Lee, her Adelaide friend from early days in the colony and one to Kate Flach, her future mother-in-law, telling of the baby's arrival. *Lovely name, Rosalie. Wonder where it came from? Jane was Lillian's mother's name, I know, so nice to pass that on too. Rosalie Jane Symonds – has a nice ring to it.*

Aunt Evelyn Lee, daughter of Mrs Mary Lee, still lived in Adelaide but didn't write many letters, Esther knew. Mama and Papa had been talking about her only recently and whether she would stay with the Telegraph Department. Mama thought she worked on the telephones, connecting conversations. Apparently, the South Australian government had relinquished control of the Northern Territory to the Commonwealth government, only at the start of this year, and Papa thought that might affect Aunt Evelyn's position. Mama had written to Evelyn some months earlier and she had replied promptly, hopeful that she would be granted a position in the new public telephone offices that had been set up in Stuart, the town near Alice Springs Telegraph Station. They knew Evelyn had travelled with various parties of telegraph linesmen and officers to the station, she was highly valued and, according to Beatrice, it would mean much to her to be judged on her own abilities instead of living in her heroic suffragist mother's shadow. Mama had asked Papa to see if Aunt Kate knew of Evelyn Lee's movements. Miss Lee was godmother to her Flach namesake and they possibly communicated more often.

The coach had arrived and the sign was up saying things were being sorted. She ran in and the sorting was almost complete but the clerk recognised her and shook his head. No post at all for Cumquats that day. Nothing from Frank; she was terribly disappointed. Now she would need to wait for her father to return.

Oops! She had letters to post; in her hurry, she had almost forgotten. Her mount was just outside, secured to the rail near the water trough. As she looked up the street, standing by the halted coach and in the shade of a pepper tree – surely that hat, that big carpet bag, was Papa! Yes!

She ran down to meet him, presuming he'd come on the mail coach. She gave him a hug; grown woman she might be but this was Papa. 'Good news, Papa. You have a granddaughter, Rosalie Jane. Isn't that sweet? All is baby chaos at Cumquats. I must admit I was pleased to come for a ride to drop these in for the mail. I'll tell you more soon but first I must arrange the despatch of these letters.'

'A girl! Oh, Esther dear, that will please everyone, I think. Such very good news. You know, daughter, I was just deciding whether to ride or to hire a trap. Now you're here, let's sit in the shade a while and enjoy a cool drink while all the mail is being sorted. Then I'll hire a mount and ride home with you. I do have a packet for you from your fiancé, Esther. Yes,' as her eyes opened wide, 'it is all good news, I think. But let's talk properly at home or I shall have to repeat it all for the benefit of your mother and my throat is cracking already with dust!'

Esther almost ran into the post office, relief sweeping over her. Her father seemed quite accepting of Frank as a son-in-law. Wonderful! She could marry without his approval but she wanted his blessing. He is Papa, after all.

*

Esther chatted on the way home, trying to draw her father, out to entice news from him about what he'd seen in Hahndorf, and of course whom! She realised he was determined to tease her by making her wait for news of Frank. He enlarged upon the old man Anderson from the inn, the man who'd been such a friend to her mother when she arrived in the colony all those years ago; Mama was concerned to know how he was faring. Arthur had been surprised at his own feelings on staying at the inn again, reliving his courtship of Beatrice and their wedding, for which the inn had hosted a happy wedding breakfast. Papa had learned how Anderson had been so badly affected by his sister dying a number of years ago, he had little enthusiasm for running the inn any longer without her by his side. However, it seemed he was reluctant to sell. His niece Lucille had offered him a home with them in Adelaide but he didn't think he could settle in their way of life.

'Anderson feels Lucy, as I will always call her, is now too grand with a well-thought-of lawyer for a husband. Her Ralph is making his way in chambers and aims to be head there eventually. Yes, he changed his name to Ralph from Rauf. I didn't realise he's the one William was advised to contact, so I really look forward to hearing of that. But old Anderson feels he would have to be on his best behaviour all day and every day if he lived with them. He said, "I'd have to watch me Ps and Qs and I'm too old now to change." I can see he'd miss the friendly camaraderie of the inn – his bar and regular callers. It's been his life for so long. So I really can't say what will happen with him, although he has many friends careful of his feelings. As for Hahndorf, there are changes there too. Not all for the better, I feel, or perhaps I'm being too pessimistic.'

'Papa! How do you mean? It's not Frank…?'

'No, dear. Hold your horses. I'll enlarge on things when we're home and your mama can hear everything. The family are all well, it's just that there are…well, undercurrents in the township. You'll be pleased to know Herbert's quite accepting now of Joshua taking Frank's place – no hard feelings hanging on, just that Herbert had assumed Frank to be the natural inheritor. Josh has grown into a friendly and capable young man and he's extended their business into wheels. It seems his expertise in coopering – all those metal bands around the barrels that he has made his own task – has all become useful, as wheels need metal rims. Thereby, a useful sideline for the business.'

Thunder started to rumble and they both realised the sky was blackening. Esther didn't have a hat…

'Come on Papa, let's gently boot these beasts into a faster pace.'

As they clattered into the yard, Max Dodd offered to take their horses. 'I'll put Gemina into her paddock, Miss Esther, and that other old bloke could maybe enjoy a roll on the grass too. All right, Mr Arthur? We be in for some rain too. Ain't that good news?'

'Thank you, Max. The ostler's kindly agreed to collect him tomorrow as a service to me. It's all been agreed.'

10

Easter Saturday, 15 April 1911, and Beatrice gathered her new ankle-length skirt up from around her dainty shoes. 'I fail to understand why she had to have her wedding aboard that little boat, Arthur. When Esther promised she'd marry in Renmark, I didn't realise she'd be offshore! In the river, bouncing about in a little boat. A boat, a little peebee – a paddle boat – I ask you…!'

'Come on, Beatrice. Let me help you up the bank. It's a bit slippery. I thought it a lovely wedding, if a bit crowded. Certainly unusual. The *Etona* is actually a mission boat and reaches out to all settlements along the river which don't yet have a church. And you know, that young man Montgomery who pounded the little organ, Bernard Montgomery to give him his full name, he's actually the son of the Bishop of Tasmania over here on a short break. Been to India too. He told me he comes over for a ride up the river whenever he can, though he's shortly to return to England. So it's solidly a Church of England initiative. I agree it was unusual but it doesn't matter for me, as long as our girl is happy. Happiness is what matters, Beatrice, the only thing.'

He bent to whisper in her ear. 'He actually told me, that young man, that he blames the Kaiser for cutting short his leave! Remember William telling us how Britain is growing angry and frustrated with the Kaiser – and he a cousin of our own royals? This Montgomery's with the Royal Warwickshires – I think that's right – and he's been told to report back to his regiment as soon as possible. Says they've lined up an adjutant's post for him and he's not too pleased about that. Must admit, impressive attitude. No doubt he'll go far. Can't be more than twenty-three now. His father, maybe because of his position in the church, is involved with the *Etona* in some way. No doubt that's how the son could wangle leave from the army.'

'Goodness me, Arthur, how you talk. Of course I know about the little chapel boat. It's sponsored by that English school, Eton. No doubt that Tasmanian bishop sees its service along the river as a mission. Yet I do wonder why Esther gravitated to that church. I did think she would have adopted the Lutheran. I really thought Frank would have insisted. I wonder if her choice is influenced by the school in Melbourne?' She sighed. 'Why she chose it doesn't really matter. She's the bride, her prerogative. The deed is now done. No more mental battles for her.'

She turned to look at him. 'What does surprise me, Arthur, is your indulging in below-stairs gossip.'

'Beatrice, it was no idle tittle-tattle. That young Montgomery fellow told me the Etona is to be sold soon. A Captain Connor, I believe wants it for trading – again. There's your shame. However, with more churches popping up along the river now, its days are over. You know, my dear Beattie, treasure the fact if you will, weddings like our daughter's are rare on board, though they have performed many baptisms over the years. Have to admit, I like the thought that their marriage will appear in the records that are eventually taken back to England, as will copies of their registration papers. And on the other tack, you know that Frank and Esther will have a blessing service when they're back in the Hahndorf community. Beatrice, do smile, please. It's Esther's day, you know. A mother feeling sorry for herself is not the best memory for her! Our Renmark friends are happy for us and also about celebrating in this hall, and it is a lovely setting. Frank's parents were in the boat with us and most of our closer family. Must admit, Lilian stood aside with unexpected grace, knowing it would have been impractical to have her little boys – and the baby – on board.'

He looked up ahead. 'Seems they've all arrived now, though – family and the Renmark crowd. I suppose most are waiting in the little riverside institute for the celebration and even Lilian with her noisy brood. So, my dear, you'll have plenty of people to speak with and share your maternal delight in our daughter's special day. It will be good for Kate and Herbert to meet them all, too. Come, let us lead the procession over there. You are the bride's mother after all. So no more of the sad face, my Beattie.'

Katherine, called Kate, Beatrice's closest female friend, came over from the crowd and gave Beatrice a huge hug. Arthur beckoned Herbert and the four fell into line.

Kate was relishing the occasion. 'Esther's a lovely young woman and Frank is smiling like that Mr Dodson's Cheshire cat! They look so very much in love, do you not agree? I've been reminded by Herbert that I'm not losing a son but gaining a daughter. To know that our families are to be united in this way delights me. Frank is quite in love with Esther, or so I feel. It all bodes well, does it not?'

Beatrice had to smile at the analogy. 'Oh that Cheshire cat! Lewis Carroll, isn't it – his Alice stories? Esther brought one of his books home with her from the school. I love the idea of Frank smiling as widely! Seriously, Kate, your Frank has turned into a most personable young man and I can see why my very independent daughter is content. Arthur came back with some wonderful tales of what Frank has achieved and how Hahndorf's grown as a town. I'm truly delighted with everything. If I look a little bit pensive, it's only that – oh dear, I was so glad when she came home, and now…'

'What! Oh, Beattie, come now, there's the pastor, or whatever he's called. Reverend Severn, is it not? Now the fun, the celebrations and the speeches can begin! Frank tells me a photographer is taking a big photograph of us all. Is that not magnificent?'

Arthur and Hebert were joining with the reverend in conversation.

Beatrice smiled. 'The photographer's from J.C. Reiners in the town. And I'm really looking forward to having a lovely picture to remind me of Esther's big day and all of us being together, not least because she'll be leaving so soon after the celebrations…' She blew into her lace handkerchief. 'When Esther was teaching away, I grew used to her not being around, but the last few months have been so companionable. She has organised so many of the chores, scheduled tasks between Lilian and me, and of course the Dodds and Slopes. She has such a very workmanlike head on her shoulders, you see – so practical. As for her wedding suit, as she calls it – but in a pale blue? It's not as if she's blue-eyed. With her brown hair and yellow-brown eyes, why not cream? Or ivory? Lilian and George's wedding – well, Lilian was glorious as a bride. Oh dear – I don't know if it's fashion or if my daughter is just determined to be different!'

Kate bent over in laughter. 'Oh, my dear Beattie. She is your daughter, very much so. You've commented on her being so commonsensical, yet now you're asking if she really knows what she wants! No more confusion, Beattie. Let's strike a pose for that wonderful photograph. And this is altogether a lovely Easter time. I'm so looking forward to staying with you for a few more days.' She tucked her arm through Beatrice's. 'Seems we're to stand in the middle, we two mothers, yet the fathers are to sit on chairs. Oh, my goodness, how formal! Now, do whisper to me, what time will the young marrieds set off back down the river and in which of the peebees – for I've forgotten its name – are they to travel?'

'Ah, that I do know! It's a Goolwa vessel, so Arthur tells me. You remember he used to work on the peebees? This one is the *Oscar W* and it will take them all the way to Morgan, then they'll take the train to Adelaide. This *Oscar W* is, I think, the second one of the name – oh, Arthur would know. He knows them all from his days working on the river.'

Beatrice did relax as the afternoon became jolly and the speeches pleasantly correct, especially Herbert's, the poor man perspiring from nerves. Arthur spoke of his love and pride in his daughter; his words prompting tender tears from Esther, who was comforted by Francis. His brother Josh raised a laugh or two with his occasional ribaldry concerning his older brother but it was all received with good-natured humour. The ladies of the institute had put on a lovely casual meal – lots of food on the tables in the hall, and cool drinks and massive enamel teapots outside on the wooden tables under the trees.

For Beatrice, it was much too soon to hear the *Oscar W* sound its hooter on approach. A cloud of pink and white galahs swept upward from the taller eucalypts on the bank, to form a sweeping formation over the water and then into the distance. There were cheers and happy welcoming calls from the younger folk in response to the steam whistle's sonorous note echoing among the tall trees. Some of the younger Renmark folk had to be shooed away by the captain as he tied up at the narrow wharf. The peebee's only load from here was to be the young couple and their belongings.

There were tearful and somewhat riotous farewells all over the green but the captain refused to allow any farewells on board. 'Bad luck, so it is!'

Esther came over to her parents and gave them both energetic hugs. 'Mama, Papa, thank you so very, very much for all your understanding, and I will write. Also, now we can telephone each other as long as we don't mind others listening in. I may write, Mama, for preference!'

There were handshakes and pats on backs all round and Arthur stayed dry-eyed although Beatrice noticed a suspicious wobble to his chin. Too quickly, the steam whistle signalled its readiness to leave and the young couple were urged to climb on board and join their baggage as it was stowed. With its farewell resonance again scattering the bird life, the yellow-white wake curling after, the *Oscar W* chugged its way midstream and much too quickly round the bend and out of sight.

Lilian's two toddlers came over holding their father's hands. 'Gan'ma, we wanta go on boat!'

Beatrice bent to hug the twins and hide her tears. George winked at his father, who smiled at his co-conspirator.

'Well timed, my boy. Not the first wedding for the Symondses, was it? And it won't be the last. Let's greet some more of the friends who came today then perhaps you and I can organise the carriages home. Been a lovely day. It'll keep your mother crying happily around her vineyards for a good few days, no?'

11

Esther sought her warm lambswool slippers from under the bed. The wedding suit was hanging in her robe with some other clothes that had once been a slimmer indulgence to fashion. Her bulk, as she termed it, was to blame on the coming baby girl. So much had happened since that day, what – fifteen months ago. This was her second wintry July in Hahndorf and she disliked the strength of the wind. Their little household was cosy enough, though. Their house renovations were almost complete; the house was now quite capable of thwarting the worst of the winter.

She let the ginger cat in from the scullery; it too had comfy quarters and looked very satisfied with life. Ahah – let's hope its smirk means it caught that mouse near my bread bin.

Then, with a rush of cold wind, the rear door from the backyard was pushed open. Frank edged in, laden with logs for the fire, kicking the door closed behind him. 'I'll bring more later, and smaller ones for your mother's bedroom, Ess.' He stood upright and sniffed. 'Oh, I do like the smell of cake and bread baking. It's better than a coffee smell!'

She smiled as he dumped the logs. 'It'll be so good to have Mama here again, Frank, oh yes!'

Beatrice had visited last September for Esther's thirtieth birthday and the whole Flach family had collaborated on a busy few days of eating, feasting and talking. Beatrice had been a great help in making curtains and some lovely big cushions for their well-worn but very comfortable sofa, called a settle – a gift from Mama Kate. She had also painted some of the box room walls, a little room now to be employed as a lying-in room and then nursery. A baby was then only a declaration of intent, and she had escorted her mother all over the township and nearby countryside in the little trap. They had even spent a day in Adelaide. This visit would be less frantic, not only because it was a rather wet winter, not conducive to picnics in the garden, but also because of Esther and Frank's baby, due in only a couple of weeks' time. Esther was impatient for the baby girl, for so she predicted – she felt so huge, so clumsy.

Frank tidied the bundle of logs into the half-barrel by the open hearth. They'd chosen not to close it in but instead Frank with Joshua's help had repacked the brick surround and limewashed it, then fitted two small seats, one at each end. A massive mantel beam formed the arched support facing the room. There were indecipherable carvings upon it, letters of a name perhaps; also something that looked like a mermaid or a sea horse which Frank had discovered when stripping it of old paint. Rumour had it that it actually came from an old ship. Frank liked that idea. To Esther, it was just a sturdy support to one of her favourite places in the house.

The stove was central to the wide inglenook, and was already installed and in that position when Frank bought the house. He had spent hours with a metal brush ridding it of rust marks, then rubbing it over with black lead paste to intensify its colouring and making it as good as new – so he proudly told her! It was made in Sydney by Metters and stood on legs, which gave it extra height; had a side grate which allowed easier access from the wood stocks, and six hot plates on top. Frank's mother, Kate, admired it and liked its two-shelf oven. Its hinged oven door was embossed with the inscription 'Beacon Light' with shafts of light radiating from a light house. It warmed the house and the water cistern, and it baked cakes. *Each one is better than the last. I'm growing used to its temperament!*

In Esther's opinion, the arched inglenook with the stove was the central point of her home. She could sit there on the coldest days and stay warm. Because its separate flue went up through the ceiling and thence the roof, there was little smell, and no smoke indoors. The flue ran between the dividing walls of two of the bedrooms upstairs, keeping them comfortably dry and warm. Frank had done most of the carpentry and even built the brickwork flue.

Mama liked it when she came last year; before when it was just working but not at its best. *Now it looks good and works wonderfully. The seats are in the inglenook and the bedrooms are kept warm. Oh Mama, having you here for the baby's birth, that is so comforting.*

The ginger cat rubbed against her legs.

'Come on, Mog. You're here to kill mice. If you've checked out the scullery, I'll put you in the washhouse. Mama hates mice. So go earn your keep!'

*

Beatrice had found the time to write often to Esther since her daughter had left Cumquats. She didn't care much for the telephone party line – she felt a telephone call was always being listened to by the local exchange – but she and Esther had enjoyed a lovely chat that way over the previous Christmas.

'I prefer letters for privacy, Arthur, but responses can take too long. When Esther has her baby of course, she'll have less free time, but for now we can talk – and talk more, generally, than we ever did when she was away at school.'

'I can't share your enthusiasm for that instrument, Beattie. It's so intrusive. Calls for me tend to interrupt my drafting, my thoughts or even our conversations. Woman talk is different. Your daughter is so like you in outlook – oh yes – in so many ways and now that she's married and to be a mother, you have much more in common than before.'

'Well, for whatever reason, Arthur, I'm so enjoying our exchange of views and opinions, whatever the risk of gossip.'

Despite Esther's years away teaching, Beatrice had always wished her daughter to be nearer. She had another female companion in Lilian of course, or so Arthur consoled himself, but Lilian's range of interests seemed limited to women's fashion and the children. Besides which, in Arthur's opinion, Lilian should do more to support George in his work on the property.

'As we're exchanging confidences, Beatrice, I'll swap one with you. I asked George how the new cuttings were coming along for the transplanting and he said he'd check with Lilian and then when I asked again, he was setting them himself because she'd forgotten! So we missed transplanting them in the sun-warmed soils. Even with young children – and she does have help – the setting of new plants is not too laborious a task for a young woman. Look what you used to do from morn till night! She cried off taking over the dairy supervision too when Esther left and now Mrs Slope helps Maisie. I'm not impressed by Lilian's apparent lack of interest in the property and yet she'll be the mistress of Cumquats when George takes over.'

'Oh, my dear, that's not for a while yet and I do believe she's already expecting again. And you do love little Rosalie, and she adores her ganpapa. As for another, well, she hasn't told me so but I do have my ways of knowing these things. I stress, that bit of news is confined to the letters. So let that console you: we are establishing a dynasty! Perhaps another grandson this time…'

'God forbid another pair of twins! They're mischievous little tinkers, that Aaron and Alex. You know, I find each one harder to distinguish than George and Will ever were!'

'That's because our two were different in character from the start, my dear Arthur. I too find it hard to differentiate one from the other and they even like the same things. At least they're now learning to write the alphabet and seem keen. Unlike their father. Remember how George hated lessons and even when the school began he wanted to play football all the time? His lesson results just worsened as he grew older. Yet you yourself acknowledge his instincts as concerns the maintenance of the property and its reputation for healthy produce – although it's not as expansive as others. Also, we really must appreciate Lilian's accounting abilities – they're a necessary part of her role and she does that side of things very well. It's so necessary for the future of the property, my dear, so on that account – pardon my pun – you can relax.'

He gave her a rare hug. 'You're correct, as always. I just wish I could take the time to come with you to see our girl. Oh, and if we start early tomorrow, I'll drive you to the train at Morgan in the car. You must write me every detail.'

12

Beatrice was forced – if reluctantly – to admit that their new vehicle, the Ford from the Duncan and Fraser garage in Adelaide, covered the miles to Morgan in record time.

'I cannot call this the most comfortable way to travel, Arthur, though it is quick. It's exciting to know I can reach Morgan so quickly to catch the train to Adelaide, then catch the other train to Bridgewater and arrive there in time for a good night's sleep! Truly expedient, my love. Also, I'll have a chance to talk with dear old Anderson.'

'Well, Beatrice, you can thank David Shearer for the motorcar. A man ahead of his time, he was. He made his own motorcar years ago, you know, and do you remember I visited him back in '97 or '98 at his invitation to see its steam engine transmission? I doubted it at first. After all, he and his brother John had developed a plough industry. I was curious, though, about the transmission of the power being enabled from an engine to wheels. I was quite enthralled, I admit, and of course, you read in the paper of his drive around Adelaide in 1900. It could reach fifteen miles an hour – what a speed! That was the start of it all for me. Even the wonders and simplicity of steam were forgotten when I thought of being able to drive quickly from A to B over these country distances. Oh yes!'

'All right, Arthur, I admit it's a huge benefit but let's hope it's a lasting one. This new motorcar of ours cost an enormous amount of money. I want to justify it.'

She arrived at Hahndorf two days later, on Thursday 11 July 1912, as she later noted in her journal, and promptly settled into the domestic routine of Flack's Master Joinery as if born to it. Esther had every aspect of domesticity so streamlined that everything happened or fell into place exactly on cue. Such a gift for organisation, she freely admitted, had never been hers! At first the changed spelling of the name on the new sign board surprised her, but knowing from the newspapers of what she called William's sabre-rattling nonsense, considered the change common sense. Only one letter had been changed, anyway; it was still pronounced much the same. She believed she understood the reason and regretted it, hoping it was not a portent.

She approved the house renovations. 'You and Frank have worked so hard on the refitting and in finishing the paintwork. My goodness me. It has distinct possibilities for extension, Esther, should your family grow. And the new plumbing in that bathroom is very modern.'

Esther liked to have her house admired, and with her gift for organisation she deserved the compliment. One aspect of Esther's attitude to the house disturbed Beatrice yet she couldn't find the right words to convey her concerns to Arthur, nor did she feel it would serve any purpose; he too was the practical one. It was that she had noticed how Esther always spoke of it as the *house*, our house, and no mention of *home*. She rationalised the thought; perhaps she needs time to grow into the idea of being married, of sharing and all that goes with it. She was sure things would change after the baby was born.

On the factual side, Esther's routine, she knew, would please Arthur, so she was happy to be able to reassure him that, although heavy with her pregnancy, their daughter had already managed a small stock of bottled fruits, including tomatoes from a healthy crop last summer. She had no dairy, but a can of milk was delivered to the gate of the house each morning by a local farmer who made it his business. She didn't make her own bread, though her oven would have dealt with it, in Beatrice's opinion; the stove in the house seemed new and looked more efficient than the one at Cumquats. However, there was a wood-oven bakery only ten minutes' walk away and the little lad called Al who helped round the place brought a loaf to the house whenever Esther wanted one. Cheeses and other dairy products were available in a little delicatessen (a German word new to Beatrice) and it was quite near, too.

She was quick to explore the delicatessen because she wanted to extend their own Cumquats range of cheeses for the new weekly markets in Renmark. She doubted ever being able to turn out the boiled or fermented sausage meats, wrapped in skins and tied with string, that were obviously a German heritage touch; she was also unsure if they would be to Arthur's taste. She admitted to having sampled some at Esther's urging and had admired the clever herbal mixes but was unsure about the strength of the garlic in some. Esther called these sausages 'wursts' and had them on the table regularly for Frank.

Cabbages and other green-leafed vegetables were under Frank's supervision in the garden, as were the fruit trees and a green-fingered young lad with the unlikely name of Alphonso, Al for short. Frank was finding he had little time to dig around in the garden and, apart from its planning, was happy to delegate its operation to their part-time gardener, Bertie, and his little off-sider.

To Beatrice's surprise, Kate Flach made a vinegary sauerkraut with cabbages from their garden, even the tougher leaves. Beatrice didn't like *sowerkrowt* at all but admired the economy of it. She wrote to Arthur that it was grated cabbage and onion or something else in a vinegary mix and was used with roast meats but was also a way of preserving the cabbages out of season. However, she didn't think Arthur would care for it either.

Another concern for her was the apparent lack of displays of affection between the young married couple. They cared for each other – literally – but there were no open displays of affection such as hugs, certainly no kisses and no secret smiles bestowed when 'Mama's here' or 'your mother's looking'. It seemed to Beatrice they were just as Esther had many months ago described – two very good friends fulfilling a purpose.

As to that catalyst of Esther's initial proposal to her mother, Susannah came over from her *Oma* Kate's house most Saturdays. Apparently she stayed most weekends at her grandparents' so that Esther could review her past week's school work and help if any problems had occurred. With Esther now expecting, it was her habit to come to Esther rather than, as previously, Esther walking to the cooperage. Beatrice thought Susannah delightful; she and Esther would have their heads over the table solving whatever topic required revision most of Saturday afternoons. Both young women obviously gained a lot from the exercise and it pleased Beatrice to see Esther's teaching skills in action.

Susannah always visited Bertie in the garden hut too; he quite openly adored her and she would go back to Kate's loaded with cabbages or whatever was in season. Bertie was considered a rough diamond by Beatrice who, after tasting the produce from the garden, carefully nurtured by him, considered him as valuable to the little household as the gem of that name. He was friendly and obliging and had a commonsensical approach to practical matters. His little hut was tucked away in the far corner of the garden as he preferred and, though somewhat weathered in appearance, was sound enough with an interior refurbished for comfort by Frank.

To young Alphonso, Beatrice was a curiosity. Though she was the missus's mother, she was neither fat nor white-haired. He knew she was English but lots of other people in his town came from England too and this woman smiled a lot and didn't speak loudly to him at all. After Beatrice had been almost a week at the house, he confided as much to old Bertie.

Bertie leaned on his spade. 'See, lad, yer come from a Latin fambly and all of yers shouts when talking. I 'eard it. Just the way of things, that is. The other English you speak of, them's the toffy kind who think Germans can't unnerstand if they don' yell. Them is called Britishers. An' yer not a German but yer have a different way o' talking English 'cos yer allus talking yer Spanish. Just know that some folks is ignorant, remember that word, Al, i-g-n-o-r-a-n-t. Not many of them as shout at yer can talk two languages like you. Remember that an' all. Mind, if an Australian yells at yer, well that's when yer done summat daft an' deserve it. Now get on wi' that dibber-dobbing fer me cabbages.'

*

On her first Sunday, Beatrice surprised her daughter by deciding to attend the morning service at St Paul's Church of England on the crest of a hill up Billygoat Lane. Not of a religious turn of mind, she was nevertheless the first to admire the sense of community, the friendships, that could foster within membership of a church group. Also, she had an unexplained desire to reconnect, if vicariously, with her own upbringing that day, brought about by remembering it was her papa's birthday, 14 July.

She wasn't sure why she suddenly remembered the date, being the first to admit she seldom celebrated such occasions outside of her own close family. And her father was half a world away in the English Lake District, living with his second wife in their new house up Beastbanks, in Kendal. He'd sold the farm, not having any sons to carry on with it, or so he had last written. She tried to work out his age – being now 1912, she thought eighty-one.

A magpie flew down onto the dirt road and cocked its head curiously. She held out her hand, which it ignored.

'Hello, Mr Magpie. Do you share with my wishes that the second Mrs Fletcher is giving him a celebration as warm as Marjorie, my mama, used to do?'

Esther had preferred to stay home that morning and enjoy a lie-in, so she said. Kate had already invited Beatrice to join her and Herbert at St Michael's Lutheran Church on the Balhannah Road but she had declined on being told that all the service was conducted in the German language. She said she would not understand a word. Frank occasionally worshipped at St Paul's Lutheran, attending only because his father pulled his strings and at least it was nearer to their home. Esther didn't mind an occasional visit with him; the German language was used occasionally at that St Paul's but seldom in a sermon. Strange having two St Paul's in a township of this size, though.

Esther and Frank had discussed religion at length. Frank's family members were all devoutly Lutheran. Frank was less so, explaining that his beliefs were his own, an assertion that upset his father but not his mother, whose childhood had been kindly influenced by both Methodists and Catholics. Herbert was upset enough at his elder son's determination to anglicise their name on the signboard by finishing it with a 'k' and not an 'h'. It had taken Kate a number of evenings persuading him that Frank was in no way rejecting his heritage, that Flack and Flach sounded the same; that whether they liked it or not it seemed to her a prudent act. Beatrice knew of this contention but was certain that a boy born in this state, married to a girl of English extraction also born in the state, a boy from a local hard-working and prosperous family, would not be regarded as an alien and an enemy.

Beatrice quite easily found the Church of England St Paul's. It stood atop a small crest, ahead of extensive pastures and at the head of a road as yet unsealed. Sturdy pine trees were planted along its front fence; her knowledge of pines coming to the fore, she calculated them to be anything from ten to fifteen years old and tall already, showing promise of great height. A plaque on the wall named the builders and it pleased her to note how both were Lutherans, a mason by the name of M.C. Born and a master carpenter J.C.F. Faehrmann. With all the gossip of rivalries and patriotic extremes currently filling the newspapers, she found such evidence of community coexistence refreshing. It struck her as a pretty little church, without the tall spires of the two Lutheran churches in the town but blessed with a friendly porch, in the English way, around its entrance door.

As she took her place on the rear, highly polished wooden pew, a few bonnets turned, and faces curious and smiling met her gaze. She found the service much as she remembered from her visits with her mother to the local village church many years ago. After the sequence of the familiar plain-spoken, simple couplets from the prayer book came a sermon not of castigation but of faith and optimism for peace in the world.

She rose with the other members of the congregation to file from the main door, where the rector was waiting to speak to his congregation.

He greeted her warmly. 'I have very good friends living near to your daughter, Mrs Symonds. It is a pleasure to welcome you.'

As other women followed from the church, some came over to speak to her, recognising a new face and welcoming her to their town. When she explained she was only visiting because her daughter was shortly to give birth to her first child, there was increased interest. They fired friendly if curious questions about her daughter and the forthcoming event with such rapidity that she finally laughed and said she had better make her way home. The rector mentioned that he hoped to officiate at the new baby's christening. He was overheard and heads bounced and smiles were wide and then a woman stepped forward and actually stabbed her finger at the rector's surplice.

She looked beneath her nose at Beatrice. 'Reverend, surely you recall the Flacks are German!'

Beatrice was lost for words. As she hesitated, the group of women just melted away.

The rector gently took her arm. 'There is a feeling, unfortunately, dear lady. But it is not everyone. The British and the Germans have coexisted peacefully from the earliest days. The lady who was…erm…enforcing her own impressions, shall we say, has been rather hurt, suffering grief in fact, because her husband and son were on the *Titanic* intending to create business opportunities in New York. You will know of that dreadful sinking back in April? She is now alone in the world, has become quite confused and angry at the blow dealt to her by fate. Our community has been trying to build up her spirits again. Please forgive her.'

He turned to indicate the remaining groups standing under the trees. 'We do have a number of communicants here at St Paul's who were brought up Lutheran but whose husbands, or wives, are only English-speaking. They wouldn't understand the other churches' lessons. I beg of you, do not let this one incident colour your opinion of our town. If your daughter and her husband choose to have the baby christened at our St Paul's, I would be honoured. If the infant were christened as Lutheran, I would understand.'

Beatrice left the rector standing by one of the pine trees and walked home, finding it hard to understand such singular spite as that red-hatted woman exhibited. Yet she had lost her husband and son; that would have been dreadful. She resolved not to mention the incident to Esther; she could not allow Esther to be upset by a woman's attitude, whatever the cause. Ironically, it seemed Esther and Frank had discussed the child being christened in the English religion. Frank was reluctantly recognising it might be an advantage for his child to be classified as British, like its mother. Beatrice, on learning of this from Esther, had doubted the need but now, as she walked along the dusty road back towards Sunday lunch, she was starting to understand.

13

Beatrice didn't muse on the situation for long; excitement was evident at Flack's Master Joinery. The dogs were barking and the front door was left wide open, young Al rushing down the path to meet her. He stopped long enough to tell her he'd been sent to fetch her and the doctor.

A noisy party of magpies was holding an excited parliament on the patch of grass and flew up to the nearby gum tree to watch what might eventuate. Beatrice spun on her feet and watched him head for the doctor's house then, walking as fast as was proper on a Sunday, made her way into the house. She closed the door behind her, pulling off her gloves. There was no sign of Esther but there was a tangible hum of expectation and exhilaration and when she looked into the scullery for Mrs Alphonso, she was scrubbing her hands and arms in lye soap at the trough. She was in readiness to play midwife! Beatrice threw her hat onto the table and ran up to Esther's bedroom.

She wasn't there! A momentary panic assailed her until Mrs Alphonso ran up the stairs and signalled her to come into the little box room.

Of course, Esther said this is where it will all happen; all scrubbed ready and a bed stripped for action.

'Oh, Mama, I'm so glad you're back. Tell me all about it later – as you can see, events have overtaken us!'

Holding her daughter's hand, Beatrice flinched as Mrs Alphonso flung Esther's shift above her legs – goodness, no modesty – and proclaimed the head to be crowning.

'What! Esther, when did all this start? It's not yet noon. Did you…?'

'On and off all last night, Mama, but I wanted you to go to church for your papa's birthday and I was sure things would take…ohwoeoh… longer.'

Footsteps were heard up the stairs and Doctor Jacowitz came into

71

the room, nodded a greeting to Beatrice and walked straight over to her patient.

Beatrice was excited, emotional, astonished… Another woman doctor in action and not under needless supervision. Excellent.

She moved to hold Esther's hand. The girl's face was a mask of sweat and grimace. Her knuckles were white as she grasped her mother's hand, her fingernails cutting into her mother's palm. Beatrice barely registered the pain she was so tense.

Then so quickly, the babe was there; slipping onto the bed, supported by the doctor who massaged its tummy and then reached for the clamps. In no time, or so it seemed to Beatrice, she was shaking her hand to encourage its blood to flow again and Esther was looking up at her expectantly.

'Mama…?'

Dr Jacowitz nodded to Beatrice, her suggestion obvious.

'Darling girl, Esther, you have a plump, healthy, black-haired son.'

'A boy? Mama! He was supposed to be a girl! Oh my, oh my, can I see?'

The midwife was wiping the baby's face. He started to cry – spontaneously, loudly – and that was the signal for Frank to burst through the door. Esther pointed, and the midwife handed the little towelled bundle to his papa.

In silence, the women in the room watched a multitude of expressions sweep over the new father's face. Tears rolled down his cheeks onto the baby's brow. Beatrice quietly wiped away a tear of her own to think that if she had waited a week she would have missed this precious moment.

Frank looked at Esther from under his brows, walked over and squatted, babe in arms, by the bed. 'Oh, Liebchen. I am papa and I have a son.'

Esther put out her hand. 'Just look at that black hair! Wherever did that come from?'

That was the cue for more cries and, laughing, the midwife took the baby and walked over to the washstand. Doctor Jacowitz continued to attend to Esther.

Frank gripped Esther's hand and cried uncontrollably, his forehead resting on her shoulder.

The baby's cry reminded Beatrice of her baby George, who had been loud, so very loud, from day one. 'Oh my goodness, dear. He has a good pair of lungs, this boy of yours.'

'Mama, we have no names ready for a boy. I was so certain he would be a girl. In view of this being your papa's birthday, perhaps we can name him Robert.' She peeked at Frank as he wiped his eyes. 'Perhaps that's one name, Frank, and we can think of another later. Do you agree?'

The doctor then signalled she wanted some time with the new mother, as she put it, so Beatrice smiled and exited downstairs with the proud new father, where he was greeted eagerly by household workers, and even his apprentice, all agog to hear the news.

Beatrice slid away from the shouting and cheering to the friendly kitchen. Frank was explaining to his friends he was off to tell his parents. Beatrice smiled, thinking of Kate. *She will be absolutely delirious. Not her first grandchild of course, but Frank is special to her, always has been. This has been a day of emotions. I need to think and lots to think about. Let's make a nice big pot of tea.*

*

Beatrice watched Frank out of the back door and over to the stable and, in very few minutes, he was cantering down the High Street to his parents'. *He can't know but I so remember his father tearing up the road at Bridgewater on our wedding day, telling us of Francis and Eloise being born. So long ago now – that was in 1880 and now it is 1912!* She shook her head as if negating the passage of time.

A voice came from behind. 'Mrs Symonds?'

She turned to see Dr Jacobwitz. 'Doctor, are you happy with the birth? He looks a vigorous baby.'

'He is absolutely as he should be, Mrs Symonds, and so is your daughter.'

'This is a happy day. Would you like some refreshment, a drink perhaps? I brought some coffee from home. Would you like a cup, or some schnapps…?'

The delicious smell of coffee soon pervaded the room as they settled among the cushions.

Beatrice was delighted to know of another female doctor, remembering her local one, Erica, over in Renmark. 'Our doctor is about your age, I wonder if you know her. I know there are comparatively few women qualified so… She qualified in Adelaide too, Erica Capper-Jones?'

'I recognise the name, I think. I'm Elena. Is she the one who writes about obstetrics?'

'She told me she specialises in…what was it, paediatrics and prenatal or something like that, so perhaps she is that one. I'll mention you to her when I get home.'

Beatrice enjoyed sharing the young doctor's hopes about ways in which positions were opening up for capable women.

She found a fresh loaf and some cheeses in the kitchen. Mrs Alphonso said how Mrs Esther was sleeping and that she must go home to cook her man's meal.

Time flew and the coffee pot chilled.

Beatrice was surprised to find it was dark beyond the windows when she heard their old horse plodding across the cobbles. 'Here comes Frank!'

He greeted them both, a huge smile on his face. 'Can I go to see her, or is she sleeping?'

Doctor Jacobwitz laughed. 'Of course! This is a happy occasion even though Esther was so surprised not to have a daughter.'

Frank came back into the room. 'She's sleeping and so is that little man, but he's moving around in his crib. Mama Symonds, may I leave him to you as I see the doctor home?'

Despite the doctor's protestations of no need, that was agreed.

Beatrice crept along to see her daughter, now comfortable in her own bedroom. She was awake and reaching to look over at the little crib.

'Mama, that black hair! Frank says he must take after someone on his side of the family. Of course, we don't know his family line beyond Herbert – they were lost in Prussia, although Herbert thinks he does remember his mother having long dark hair that she plaited in a long twist and wound round her head under a cap.'

'Hmm. My papa had black hair when he was young but I knew it as turning grey. When he came to see us years ago, I wonder if you remember his bushy black eyebrows. I don't know about the Symonds side but I doubt they were dark-haired. Your papa was always too blond, as they call it now. Ah! Here comes the new papa. Frank, would you like a bite to eat while you have a cuddle with him and little…is it Robert?'

His smile was in his voice. 'Mama Symonds, our little boy, if my dear wife agrees, will be Ralph Robert Flack.'

Esther sat up. 'Ralph?'

'It's the translation of Rauf, Liebchen. Your mama will remember Pastor Wilhelm of the old settlement. He was a second father to my father when he first came to this country. My father remembers him with great affection and he made my Vati the lovely man I think he is. I would like my son to carry that name.'

'And you don't often speak about your father as Vati, Frank. I like to hear it now and again. So, my Francis, our son will be Ralph Robert. I like it. It has a nice ring to it. Now, tell me…'

Beatrice considered a little discretion would not be amiss and sneaked out. Downstairs, warming some chicken soup for Esther as recommended by that very pleasant woman doctor, she mused on how much longer she should stay.

*

Days flew by, or so it seemed. Beatrice stacked up the log fire and sat in the inglenook sipping a most welcome cup of China tea. All was quiet from upstairs, not even a baby's cry to interrupt the welcome silence. She felt so inwardly thrilled that she had made it in time. She looked at the day's newspaper young Al had brought. A headline cried that the Royal Navy was boosting its fleet in the North Sea to match Germany. The ships had been moved from the Mediterranean, placed on patrol in the North Sea in response to the continuing German naval build-up. *Oh dear, what's that saying about letting loose the dogs of war? I won't take this upstairs to Esther unless she asks for it.*

She had to smile. It was ironic: the world seemed to be in turmoil yet here she was, sipping tea and worrying about everything back on their little farm. To fret about what was happening at home and even talk about missing it – let alone talking about going home too soon – would upset Esther. No denying, though, it was almost time to pick the cumquats; also the mandarin oranges were ripening when she left, so George would have to hire some pickers. If Lilian was indeed expecting, she would not want to go picking, so the hired help would need to be efficient. Not that the fruit this year had showed promise. The grapes would need pruning soon, the rows cleared and the geese allowed among them again to defeat the snails.

She sipped her tea. Arthur had told her to forget about Cumquats for a while, to enjoy her time with Esther. *And so I will, but...*

Water had been a problem for the Riverland this season. The drought conditions further upriver had hit the areas around the Darling and hence the flows into the Murray had been disappointing. She smiled at the thought of Arthur's organising his new steam pumps for the irrigation of the property. It was all well and good to have developed such inspiring machinery that made the best use of every drop but now he was kept so busy by others wanting to know how. His friend in Victoria had asked to patent their joint design process and she rather thought Arthur might agree.

A hearty yell interrupted her thinking. *Oh, my goodness, this baby has lungs!* Even as the thought registered, Frank came thudding down the stairs.

Mrs Alphonso emerged from outside, unbuttoning her coat. 'Is all right, Meester Frank. I go see to her now, she all right. She wanting get up and I say tomorrow. Doctor coming first then will say. I good, my husban' has finished eating. That is good. You have a son, Meester Frank. Is wonderful so much.'

Everything was in hand here but nevertheless, Beatrice decided a choice about her leaving could wait a few more days. She'd only been away little more than a week.

14

The christening was over and even Herbert and Kate had attended the ceremony in the Church of England St Paul's. Held at the morning service that Sunday, 28 July, the first available date to allow Beatrice to attend also, it was a happy occasion – for the adults if not, apparently, for the star of the event. Baby Ralph cried and yelled most of the ceremony although, interestingly to his godparents, Paul and Eloise, he quietened while the holy water marked the cross on his brow. To Beatrice's relief, there were only smiles from under all the other Sunday bonnets. Some of the men were happy to shake Frank's hand while smiling congratulations, and a number of the women were obviously known to Esther, who called them by name.

Afterwards the family went over to the Flachs, where Evelyn and Susannah had prepared a traditional lunch. The pastor from St Michael's had been invited and, a jovial fellow, he was quite understanding of the baby being baptised in, as he put it, his mother's religion. He recited an old German blessing over the little boy, which pleased Herbert and, to everyone's delight, changed the baby's mood. He was wrapped and swaddled into the old cradle and went immediately to sleep, to Esther's profound relief. Esther had to restrain herself after yet another congratulation on gaining a son. *Why is it that to have a son is so special?* Even her mother's talk was more of little Alex or Aaron than Rosalie. Yet Frank and the other Flachs were all concerned for Susannah's future career.

For a couple of years now, Susannah had visited her grandparents frequently. Eloise's Paul had made an uneasy truce with his father-in-law; Herbert recognised that the younger man was providing a comfortable living for his family, ill-conceived or not, as Evelyn whispered to Beatrice with heavy sarcasm. She had always regretted her father's cool attitude to her older sister – older by only about six years – yet it had to be admitted Herbert had discovered an admiration for his granddaughter Susannah's ambition and perseverance since getting to know her better, welcoming her parents to his place. She was also an outrageous little flirt, so said Evelyn with a smile, and flattered her Opa accordingly. As her grandmother Kate predicted, 'That young girl will get on. No need to worry about her.'

Eloise and Esther enjoyed getting together occasionally; they were almost the same age and had a lot in common in Beatrice's opinion – personal qualities and ambitions not excluded. Susannah's schooling had brought them together initially and Esther had been able to reinforce the school's teaching in mathematics particularly, and this had raised Susannah's confidence with the subject. As Esther's pregnancy had advanced, so had Susannah's attitude towards her education; a happy coincidence, in everyone's opinion. However, what once had been a weekly tuition over a weekend had now become only occasional. At the Grote Street school, she was apparently performing very well indeed. In Esther's opinion, based on her knowledge of young females, Susannah was quite capable of reaching the highest standard academically. In Kate's and Eloise's opinion, it was Esther's example that was the impetus for Susannah's eagerness to succeed; that it was her often repeated encouragement that modern girls now had every opportunity to excel and only the silliest ones failed to take advantage. Esther quoted frequently that attitude must equal aptitude. Her own mother used to quote it to her and her brothers.

This mental strength was the personal characteristic Frank had so long ago perceived in Esther. As a boy, he had been annoyed by it; as a man getting to know her through reputation, his admiration grew. As they subsequently learned more of each other through her contact with his sister, then their letter writing, that admiration strengthened to liking and a wish that she like would like him and, well, then the inevitable happened. Now, well into their second year of marriage, he felt he was as much in love as his mother fondly believed. Not an academic himself, he found the right words hard to say, his feelings hard to describe. He only knew he would give Esther the world if he could – if she asked for it!

As for Esther, logical and organised Esther, she hadn't asked herself if it was love that she felt for Frank. She knew early on that she found him attractive; liked him and recognised in him the potential for success that she admired. But how could she define love? The strength of mutual feeling she knew her parents enjoyed was shared by her and Frank to an acceptable degree, so she believed. They were both achievers – Mama's word – prepared to work for their goals. In the quieter moments of her pregnancy, she acknowledged to herself, and latterly to her mother, his qualities of strength with gentleness, business acumen and initiative and, above all, his admiration of her and his loyalty to his family. After little Ralph was born, seeing his love for the child, listening to his resolve for the little boy's well-being now and later, a wave of tenderness had washed over her such as she had not before experienced. She had actually, while sitting on more than one evening by the inglenook, nursing the babe and watching Frank pore over drawings and plans at the table, felt so quietly content and replete in happiness that she had asked herself if those feelings constituted love. If so, were the supreme contentment and satisfaction she felt at times all part of being in love.

And being the logical and organised Esther, she knew that right now it was enough to be going along with, as Mama would say.

*

Neither mother nor daughter spared the tears and the hugs when they parted on the Tuesday after the christening. Beatrice was quick to say she would be over again before too long – having the train services made travel so much easier. Kate and Herbert drove her to the inn at Bridgewater but couldn't linger because Herbert had a contact at Grunthal on the Balhannah Road, near to where Frank used to live; it could promise an increase in business.

So, after all the sad farewells, Beatrice was pleased to enjoy a merrier lunch with Anderson at the inn. He still wore red braces – or, as he said his Sydney friends called them, suspenders. Whatever he called them, Beatrice had to smile; they were certainly supporting an admirable girth!

Later, they both caught the mid-afternoon train into the city, where Lucille's Ralph met them. His instruction from Lucille – he laughed – was to take them back home for supper and then he and Lucille hoped Beatrice would stay the night before heading home. So the time unfolded.

Anderson had decided – after many months of soul-searching, according to Lucille – to live with her and Ralph at their large house in Kensington Park. Lucille proudly showed Beatrice around and then Anderson showed her his quarters, as he called them. It was obvious that Lucille and Ralph had given his comfort a great deal of thought. Beatrice felt he would quickly settle and, with a dedicated little garden area to do with as he wished, would find plenty to occupy his time. Lucille's children already loved him and called him granpa. As he said, he had always thought of his Lucy as more daughter than niece, anyway.

15

Esther missed her mother not being around to fuss over the baby at his every cry.

'She wasn't here to be with him for long, Frank, but long enough for him to expect to be picked up at every whimper. How can I just drop everything I'm doing to run to him as she did? He must not be spoilt, Frank. He must learn his place in the household. Discipline cannot start too early.'

'Oh, Liebchen, he's but a tiny baby and it's not yet more than a couple of weeks since his birth. He has to learn, *ja*, but so must you. You must relax. Mrs Alphonso can do more to help, to let you build your strength again, so when you want to cuddle him, do so – enjoy him. You get up to him in the night and miss your sleep, I know. Sometimes two times, so please, for me, look after yourself, as you're precious to me.'

She didn't know what to say at such an endearing concern; he was not a man for flowery phrases. Before she could reply, he was gone to his workshop again. Feeling somewhat overcome, she sat down in the inglenook. And how could everyone think a baby was to be enjoyed? They were hard work, and smelly little creatures. Was it really necessary to give so many cuddles? Had Frank's Mutti rushed to his brother and sisters at every cry? Surely not; she too had been a teacher and accustomed to disciplining youngsters.

As if on cue, Mrs Alphonso came in with a cup of chocolate. 'Here you are, Missus. Mr Frank say to let you rest, so here also your knitting.' She placed both on the end of the little bench. 'Baby fast sleeping now. I look after…so you have chocolate.' Smiling widely, she made her exit.

Esther picked up a copy of the newspaper from the other stool where Frank had been reading earlier. *Don't feel like knitting…*

One item dated over a week earlier, 22 July, demanded her attention. Headed 'UK Mediterranean warships recalled to North Sea to counter the German fleet', it detailed a breakdown of Anglo-German talks aimed at slowing down the rate of expansion of the two countries' navies. It continued, 'Winston Churchill as First Lord of the Admiralty asked the Commons to expand the naval budget to build four dreadnoughts, eight cruisers, twenty destroyers and several submarines to counter what he called the German threat.'

A cold chill caused her to shiver and she dropped the paper on the floor, only to pick it up to read further. There wasn't much more on that subject, though, other than to say that recruitment in Britain would be stepped up. Most of the paper was given over to the report on the 1912 Olympics being held in Stockholm. She felt a little happier to read that Fanny Durack won the 100 metres freestyle swimming – Australia's first woman gold medallist. A brighter spot of news.

Other happier news about the opening of the ski resorts Mt Buffalo in Victoria and Mt Kosciusko in New South Wales caught her eye. Skiing was something she had tried one school holiday while teaching at Lauriston. The memory made her laugh out loud. *Oh, how I fell over so many times and how long it took my thick black woollen stockings to dry! At least my skirt was short enough – the hem just below my knee – to allow long strides. But even that didn't keep me on my feet!*

Still chuckling at the memories, she took her empty chocolate mug out to the kitchen, just as a loud cry was emitted from upstairs. 'Hear that Mog? Ah well, he has good lungs. Be thankful, Esther Flack.'

A knock on the door heralded Evelyn, Frank's younger sister. 'Good day, Esther. Is it convenient to call?'

'Oh, nice to see you, Evie! I must just go upstairs and see Ralph. As you can hear, he's in full voice today. Make yourself at home. Mrs Alphonso will make you a chocolate if you pop in the kitchen.'

They were soon sharing space at the big table. Ralph was quickly fed to perch over his mother's shoulder while he brought up his wind.

Evelyn was enthusiastic about that morning's art session at the

Heysen's studio. 'It was so funny, Esther. Their oldest little girl came into the studio garden carrying the new one, Nora. Freya's only about four and the baby's more than a year and looked too heavy for her big sister to carry! Mrs Heysen, I can call her Sallie but her name is Selma, came looking for them. Sallie used to be a student of Mr Heysen and she does some lovely drawings too. This morning we were all in the little garden capturing the sunlight on the branches but I'm not too sure I made a very good job of it. Sallie said that baby Nora loves to pick up some chalks and try to draw. So young she is too! The lesson was cut short because they're moving to their new place on Heysen Road. Sallie says it is necessary because of all the children – there are seven, I think. They also have a lot of visitors now that Mr Heysen is so well known.'

'I've never met the Heysens, Evie. I suppose if they speak German you'll be able to understand, as you sometimes speak it at home. I would not understand…'

'No, no, Esther. They always speak English at home.'

'Wasn't Mr Heysen born in Germany? I'm sure your father mentioned he comes from the same place as he did. Or near to… It's good if he does speak English.' She paused. 'Probably wise, in the current political environment.'

Evelyn looked solemn, her art forgotten. 'Talking of which, my father had an experience with that new sergeant of police the other day, not the usual constable who walks around sometimes to say hello. This one's up from Adelaide doing what he calls a census. He came to the house and asked Mutti if she was German and she said not. So he asked about my father. And do you know, I didn't know what place he came from. Germany has always been enough for me – just what town or where has never mattered, nor does it now. There are so many who came over in the early ships who'd lost families and a sense of identity. They found their identity here. Anyway, the sergeant wrote on his notepad and left after talking to old Bertie, who'd brought some timber over from Frank's workshop.

'I do worry that there's some anti-German feeling growing. You can't help but notice. You know, I went in the other baker's shop, down the other end of the main street, to buy Mutti a currant bun loaf – Josh has brought some for her and she does like them – and the lady in there, and she has no reason to know me, asked me wouldn't I prefer to go to the German bakery? Just seems almost prophetic, you know? Not pleasant, anyway. Just little things.'

'Oh, Evie, perhaps…you do your hair in those lovely plaits around your head. May I suggest, have you thought of tying it back differently? Say, for an experiment, when you visit that bakery again, change your hair style, perhaps start wearing it swept up like the new fashion in Adelaide. See if she comments again.'

'What? Oh. I see what you're saying, my plaits. I should try and look more like an Adelaide girl, you think? I will. Actually, the reason I called in today was about hair. My father said to tell you he remembers very little of his mother and father, he says the smell of new-cut hay brings back his father to him but not in shape. His mother – he's firm in one memory of her, that her hair was very black. When he smells washing soap, he's reminded and he thinks she used to have it hanging down – her hair, that is – when attending to him, and it swept over his face. When thinking of that, he said it popped into his mind that his father called her his *mittelnacht Mädchen*. That means Midnight Maiden, and maybe it was because of her black hair. It was when Mutti told him of the policeman and he was drinking his schnapps and digging in his memory.'

'Oh, Evie! What a lovely memory! That's how little Ralph has such black hair, no? Yet Papa Herbert's hair is light brown, yellowy. How strange heredity is, don't you think?'

The baby stirred from his perch over his mother's shoulder and promptly bubbled a mouthful of sour-smelling milk.

'Oh no, Ralphy! Yuk! I'm going.' Chuckling, Evelyn waved a goodbye and made her way out of the door.

<h1 style="text-align:center">16</h1>

If Esther, or her mother, had wondered about her finding enough to do in a country town, the next few months would have allayed their worries. Esther's time was well taken up. Frank had a contract to make a stairwell with carved newel posts at each storey for a new hotel on the Lyndoch road and some miles away, though strategically placed for future customers, so declared the landowner. This involved some travelling and Frank was sometimes away for one or two nights.

Frank took on an apprentice who'd been halfway through a term when his sponsor died, so the lad was already well trained in basic carpentry. His father had been a seaman on a German freighter, so his mother thought. She had gained a number of other children during a dubious past, so Willem was willing to work hard and better himself and was proving a handy young fellow to have around, in Esther's opinion. He could read, and write his name, if not much more. He thought his father's surname was Ils. His mother said she could not remember but said the ship's bosun who came for his father once called him Ils and not in a friendly way. He never did come back.

While Frank was away, the lad stayed behind at the workshop to maintain the firebox and generally do some sorting out of the timbers left lying around, matching, stacking and planing of certain lengths in readiness for the boss. He had to sweep and clean the floor, clean and oil some of the tools temporarily left idle and maintain the saw pit's firebox in a ready-to-go condition. If any problems or jobs came to the door, he was to contact Joshua by telephone. Willem felt responsible and trusted and was determined not to let Mr Frank down.

Most importantly, said his boss, he was to look out for Mrs Esther. To this end, he was given a stretcher in the workshop to stay overnight so that he was always available. He didn't mind at all. In his former apprenticeship, he had slept in a box under a bench and his meals were mainly soups. Then when his master died he had to return to the hovel he called home to share a bed with two brothers in a room shared by five. Food was meagre, and he felt he was taking from his brothers. Here, Mrs Esther kept him supplied with wurst and boiled cabbage and chunks of sourdough and hot black tea at midday dinner break and he enjoyed thick porridge with Bertie every morning. He and Bertie would sit and eat together at break times and Bertie said he could help himself to an apple if he wanted or a tomato in return for giving him a hand if he needed it. However, winter wasn't a busy time in the vegetable garden. Life had seldom been as kind to young Willem.

Esther was steadily occupied with baby Ralph, cooking and baking and maintaining a watch on the front bench of the business while Frank was away. She read some books on baby care and disagreed with a number which declared that babies should be fed whenever they were hungry and cuddled whenever they cried. She began to worry about her worth as a mother: how did one mother a baby? Of course she loved Ralphy but, young as he was, surely a balanced routine was better for him? She even rang Mama once to ask her, and Lilian answered the call instead, only too willing to tell Esther what she was doing wrong. Strangely, instead of being angry with her sister-in-law, Esther put the phone down riddled with doubt. Less than an hour later, she rang again and this time Mama answered the call and eventually, after Esther managed to blurt out her concerns, she advised Esther to stop battling with her natural instincts.

'Enjoy the little fellow, dear girl. I believe always that our natural instincts are the right ones to follow. Forget the theories, my dear, stop battling with your instincts, let them rule and just enjoy your baby.'

Esther pondered her advice. *How does one enjoy a baby who cries to feed, demands attention, to be changed and cleaned, seemingly non-stop.* It was hard work caring for this little animal, as demanding as any male of any species.

Then one day when she was holding Ralph, rocking him to soothe his tears as his crying had been so horribly persistent, he suddenly stopped crying, opened his teary-lashed eyes to look straight into her eyes and gave her a wonderful, gummy smile. She just melted. It was a wonderful moment. From then on, Ralph was Ralph and not just 'the baby'. Strangely, it all seemed a little easier. She found her confidence and even took a couple of orders for decoratively carved and turned newel posts, subject to Frank's agreement on his return, and sold four of his animal carvings. Her mother need not have worried about boredom being a problem.

When the hotel contract ended and Frank could spend more time at home, another contract was negotiated but nearer to home. Young Willem would go with Frank to help with lifting and alignment work as necessary, but sometimes Frank was promised labourers to help as needed on the job. Esther hoped so; there was a lot of heavy work involved, particularly in stairwell work. Each one of the banisters of the stair contract had to be a precise length and was solid and heavy to lift. Frank would come home whenever intervals allowed. Little Ralph was his drawcard; he idolised the boy and Esther knew the feeling was reciprocal.

So Esther relaxed and found a new delight in her little son. Christmas came and went, almost unmarked by the Flacks and Flachs; they were all so busy.

In May of 1913, Esther suspected she was once again expecting and was pleased, hoping for a girl this time. A second child: it left only another two to go. She had long thought that four was an ideal number.

Her mother was pleased for her but, 'Oh, Esther dear, is it not too soon? You must have plenty of rest.'

Esther was more conscious of time moving relentlessly onwards. *And I cannot afford to waste any!*

All this coincided with a letter from her mother saying that the Symonds intended to apply for one of the boy apprentices who had left England at the end of March on the *Irishman*. It was a farm scheme. Each of the boys apparently had to pay £10 for their passage and the state treasury would hold the balance of their pay at four per cent interest until they were twenty-one, at which time the state hoped they would have saved £70 to £100, enough to buy land and set up on their own. If the scheme was a success, it would be repeated. 'Unfortunately, we may be too late to apply, but there is next time. They say this is a growing colony and we need young men and women to build up our population. I feel this is a good move, and for me and your papa also.'

Beatrice was also eager for the promise of extra help. She wrote that Arthur was starting to feel his years, in his own words. George was very busy and his boys were too young as yet to do other than basic jobs like collecting eggs and Lilian was pregnant again. If she managed to carry this one, it would be her fourth child. Beatrice had suspected back in July when she was in Hahndorf that Lilian was expecting. However, her first letter after returning home spoke of a miscarriage. William had become absorbed in his work as a practising lawyer in Adelaide and had no interest in the farm. So, wrote Beatrice, a young man around Cumquats would be useful.

Esther was more concerned for her father. He surely wasn't tiring? At only sixty-three, he looked the epitome of good health. He had healthy air, good food and enough exercise. Perhaps it was just overwork.

Frank understood her concerns. 'Liebchen, Arthur has been an active man all his life. Maybe he's not wearing out, feeling strain, but just feels the need for someone capable of the heavy lifting. Look at me. At my relative youth, I feel I need an apprentice and your father's almost twice my age. It's good thinking on his part.'

Almost the next day came another letter. Robert Fletcher, Beatrice's father had died in England, following a fall from a horse. Back in February, St Valentine's Day. *It's now late May — why so long in the post? Oh dear, poor Papa.* Beatrice was saddened by the news but felt he had died as he would have wished. He loved to ride and she knew he regularly hired a mount to feel the freedom of riding on the fells. It seemed the incident occurred near his old farm. Beatrice's stepmother wrote that she was grief-stricken, but he had left her well provided for.

According to Beatrice, 'William was upset more than me, I think, because his gran'papa was like a second father to him all the years he was at that school before he went to Oxford. However, it appears my father left him some money and also the house in Kendal to be his after the second Mrs Fletcher passes away.'

Lucky William. Poor Mama.

*

Esther's second pregnancy was considerably easier. She felt less heavy and clumsy than with Ralph. 'I'm hoping it is a girl this time, I really am.'

'Instinct,' said her mother-in-law Kate. 'Always trust your instincts.'

Kate was with Esther the day the policeman came to the door, the mounted constable based in Hahndorf, who she recognised quite readily.

'Mrs Flack, you may be aware of certain anti-German feelings within the neighbourhood. You're of English parentage, I believe.'

'Well, yes I have heard of things and yes I am.'

'And Mr Flack is not?'

Kate came to the door. 'Good morning, constable. You know me. I'm Mr Flack's mother and I am English born. My son was born in South Australia, as I think you know. Rather than upsetting my dear daughter-in-law here who is, as you can see, expecting, does it help for me to affirm the fact?'

The constable actually gave her a salute. 'Of course, Mrs Flack. Thank you both and good day.' He turned and walked off.

Kate sighed. 'He's a decent man, Esther, that one. He's only doing his job.' She sighed. 'It is certainly an unsettling time.'

Esther hoped she was right that the constable was a decent man. This anti-German feeling seemed to be escalating; it was in the newspapers frequently. Not around home so much, but there were incidents reported in Adelaide. Apparently there were plans to open an internment camp at Torrens Island, just to house people of German heritage suspected of un-Australian activities. It was also a quarantine station, so groups interned there would be successfully cut off from society. It was somewhere near

Port Adelaide, as far as she understood. Yes, there seemed to be a war in the offing, but not here, in this quiet country town on the other side of the world from the quarrelling. Besides, there were so many people here of German heritage, the numbers were too great to pick on small groups, she reasoned.

She thought herself well known in the township. Admittedly she didn't make friends too easily but she enjoyed the company of some of the women at the church. She had few contretemps with other residents; Frank was a respected workman; a number of shops had benefited from his carved balcony rails and other trims for their businesses. Also, it was widely acknowledged she was a frequent member of the Church of England community as Frank, with a measure of cynicism, occasionally acknowledged. As the months passed and Frank finished additional work at Lobethal and spent more time around his local area, it seemed that her brother William's sabre-rattling fears had little or no relevance to their everyday existence.

The winter passed. Spring brought her more regular visits from Dr Elena, as Esther now called her – although she was very correctly Dr Jacobwitz to Frank, who found it hard to accept that such a worthy personage could also be a friend.

Esther thought the baby would arrive about the middle of December, yet it was actually on Christmas morning that she had the first pain. She had intended going to the Christmas service but, only a few hours later, at twelve-thirty in the afternoon, Katherine Beatrice – as fair-haired as her brother was dark – made a smooth entrance into the world. Dr Elena and her nurse had been called despite the special day and Elena declared herself quite nonplussed.

'Oh, Esther, apart from a little cry of protest, she has been born with a smile on her face and a laugh in her eyes! What a beautiful little girl you have.'

Hearing the shouting, Frank left a protesting little Ralph with Mrs Alphonso and ran upstairs in his boots. 'Oh, my Esther. You make me so happy. We have a daughter'

He very gently handed back the little girl to the nurse who'd come with Dr Elena then, to everyone's delight, bestowed a kiss on the doctor's cheek. 'Can I bring up the little boy now?'

Dr Elena smiled and a clumping down the wooden stairs was followed by another clumping upwards and in he came with Ralph.

'This is your little sister, my Ralphy, this is little Katherine Beatrice.' He smiled at Dr Jacobwitz. 'This time we knew the names, Dr Elena.'

17

The year turned and their first event in 1914 was Katherine's christening. Like Ralph's, it was held in St Paul's Church of England, but this one was on the second Sunday after Epiphany, which the rector thought suitable for a little child born on the Lord's birthday. There were a few whispers about Esther having an un-ladylike short lying-in but the rector in his few words made it known that it was at his suggestion, and why. Afterwards, there was the same friendly little blessing at the Flachs' cooperage.

It was strangely cool weather for January, though, and as February began, so the temperatures dropped dramatically. A wet autumn was forecast and Esther knew that her parents up in the Riverland, worried about irrigation rights, were hoping for some worthwhile rains. Her father, now a respected and well known steam pump engineer, was kept busy consulting on irrigation matters. 'Advising, he calls it,' wrote Beatrice.

With two little ones taking up a lot of her time, Esther decided to give herself a period each afternoon, between baby and toddler duties, just to be herself, in her words. This time, she felt she could balance her love of routine in a more relaxed fashion. Also, while nursing baby Katherine, she could read the daily news sheets and sent Alphonso for one every morning. It became a habit; she felt she needed to keep a grasp on what was going on in the wider world. Regrettably, whichever one she read seemed to report troubles in the world, particularly in South Africa and Ireland, and the dreadful implications of most of Europe readying for a wider war. Britain's Winston Churchill was stirring the pot again, she contended, firing up the arms race. Suffragettes were constantly in the British news. In March, a group tried to force their way into Buckingham Palace; one of them was the infamous Emmeline Pankhurst. Emmeline had been arrested in Glasgow back in March as a public nuisance and when arrested in London was quoted as 'seeming frail'. Esther was openly admiring of the woman, though despairing of some of her militarism. *I wonder if she was force-fed in prison in between the two arrests? That would account for her apparent frailty. Beastly practice.*

Then in June she read of a duke murdered in the Balkans. *Where are the Balkans?* An Austrian duke murdered by a Serbian army officer.

This item of news distressed Frank beyond her expectations. There was also a problem regarding a civil war in Ireland which she thought would have concerned him more but on reading about this duke he stood upright and woke little Katherine in her pram near the fire by yelling '*Lieber Gott*, this is it, Esther. This will be the trigger!'

'Oh, Frank! Let's not anticipate the worst.'

In following days, the papers were speculating that an Austrian ultimatum to Serbia meant war. England offered to mediate between the two countries and the Kaiser took offence at what he termed 'British insolence'. He also declared war on his cousin the Russian Tsar, which astonished and horrified Esther, who was prompted to exclaim, 'That simply cannot happen. They're all one family!'

Events moved quickly from that point. Germany declared war on France; Britain told Germany it would guarantee Belgian neutrality to help protect the coasts of France. Then Germany invaded Belgium. On 4 August, England declared war on Germany.

In ensuing days, Esther read of the London crowds cheering wildly at the declaration of war. Then almost unbelievably, in her thinking – Union Jack-bearing crowds marched through the streets of Melbourne.

'That's us, Frank. Too close for my comfort. The world has gone mad. They're all at each other's throats in Europe, but why should we be? How long will this madness last?'

At the end of the month, a report quoted the prime minister, Joseph Cook as saying, 'Our duty is quite clear – to gird up our loins and remember that we are Britons.' Esther read it in dismay. All right for some. Not all, by any measure. A few weeks previously she had read that the leader of the federal Labor opposition – a man whom Frank had admired previously – was reported as saying that Australians would defend Great Britain to their last man and shilling. That angered Frank. 'I will defend Australia with my last breath but Britain's another matter on the other side of the world.' She knew from local gossip that many, even some Australians of British extraction, shared his point of view.

He spread the newspaper out on the table and his fears worsened when he read, 'Listen, Ess, the police have told the government that in Australia, a number of German clubs and shops have been raided but no evidence of espionage was found. Where in Australia, Ess? Victoria? Our state? I agree Ess, this is madness. And sloppy reporting. They found nothing wrong but now the police want all German clubs closed. *Mein Gott*, Esther, madness it is right enough.'

Frank was worried about the implications for Australia. His fears were realised when the newspapers reported how Canada, New Zealand and Australia had offered expeditionary forces.

On 19 September, Esther read aloud that the first expeditionary force was already being trained at Broadmeadows in Victoria. 'They're the 2nd Infantry Brigade and they're practising attacks and rearguard actions despite the heat. Heat? Not in Hahndorf, that's for sure.'

Frank wasn't thinking of the weather. 'There will be anti-German feeling here, Liebchen, not just the little snipes at us but – for interest, look at this – a report saying how in Echuca, on the river, hotel drinkers have refused to drink German beer, want only the Australian product! Yes, it is madness.'

That same week he came in one coffee time waving a poster and shouting, 'Esther! Look at this – it's criminal, it's an insult! Old Jaeger gave it to me, it's off the lamp post by the market, he said. It's from the Department of Defence and it says no naturalised Germans can be accepted as recruits.'

He indicated a few lines lower in the page: '"Even Australian-born men whose fathers are German should be refused except in special cases which must be approved by the District Commandant." This is an insult, Ess, an outright insult.'

'Ssh, my Francis, calm yourself. Think on other lines: it will mean now that Joshua will cool his enthusiasm. Didn't you say he wants to enlist with those other young men, his mates, most of whom will be leaving behind a wife and young family?'

He sat down with his coffee. 'I feel hurt, Esther. I'm as Australian as any Smith or Jackson or whatever. I don't want to enlist but nor do I want to be considered a second-rate citizen in my own beloved country.' He bowed his head onto his hands on the table.

She moved over and rubbed his shoulders. She didn't know what to say, so said nothing.

Eventually, he sat up, looked her in the eye and gave her a smacking kiss. 'We're all right my Esther, are we not? Our children are well and healthy and we know who we are.' He stood and pushed his chair under the table. 'Time to get back to what I can do, and what I do well.'

Being cynical, Esther thought of a newspaper report that morning that Frank might not have seen, of a gory battle at Mons in France where the British forces suffered heavy casualties and had to pull back and,horror of horrors, where Sunday worshippers in a church were killed in crossfire. Bearing that in mind, she told herself that later in the war, if it did not end by the next Christmas as they said, the authorities would care less who they sent away as cannon fodder. No one would feel second-rate then! She shivered; she had brought two children into this world and what kind of world was it becoming! Just until the last few months, everything had been so hopeful and optimistic.

There were maps in all editions of the papers, showing the progress of various armies, one of the bloodiest reports concerning the routing of Russian troops by the Germans. The detail, the target areas, seemed to be all of Europe. Esther was distressed and angry and made even more so when she read of German clubs and shops being raided in Australian cities, even closed, yet without any evidence of espionage.

'This is madness!' she yelled, throwing the paper on the floor.

Mrs Alphonso ran in. 'Oh, Missus Esther! Look, here's Dr Elena.'

Dr Elena smiled. 'I'm here to share a coffee with you, Esther. Let us blame the world together.'

'I'll make you a nice hot cup of tea, Missus. We have no beans till I go to the shop.'

Esther's angry tears turned to laughter, Mrs Alphonso believed a hot cup of tea was the answer to everything.

*

Somehow Esther survived what she considered to be a long cold winter. It had been cold enough, she mused; it didn't even have the grace to give enough rainfall to fill the tanks and compensate for the clear skies and chill winds. The children thrived in it, though, and little Ralph loved to spend time outside kicking his ball around, all swaddled in cosy warm knitted jumpers. Oma made some for him, Mrs Alphonso made some for him, and Esther found that her knitting was more required for tough warm socks for Frank and only a little hat to pull over Ralph's ears because he didn't like to hear the wind!

Then one windy October day when Ralph was crying to go out and play ball with Willem and she knew Willem was engaged in the saw pit, Frank came in for coffee with a couple of his timber works friends. *Thank heavens. Now the little boy will stop nagging.*

Frank called into the scullery, 'Just a hot coffee for us all please, Mrs Alphonso! Working outside, that wind is so fierce it cuts through my jacket.'

Esther heard the rattle of their boots on the floor. 'Come into the living room, all of you, by the fire. This is very odd spring weather. I have a good log burning!'

Young Ralph, now 'two-years an' a quarter', as he liked to tell everyone, ran to his dadda and the men all whooped in fun at the little lad's eagerness before dragging up some stools. Ralph refused to move from his dadda's lap until Mrs Alphonso brought in mugs of hot tea and, to little Ralph's taste, a platter of gingerbread.

Frank, Erni Klinger and John Moss had been friends since schooldays. They had also played football for the Hahndorf team and the conversation turned to the game then, inevitably perhaps, to timber supplies and other business matters. Not a word about the war, for which Esther was grateful.

John Moss was talking about some friends who were living in Adelaide, both Australians of German parents. They had been arrested and taken to the army headquarters at Keswick and then sent to Torrens Island; they were to be interned. Apparently the father of one was a famous pianist who had played for the Governor General. He thought himself exempt but was still arrested.

'He caused a bit of a ruckus in the camp, saying he wasn't at war with Australia. He went mad – hit out at a guard or someone. They threatened to have his fingers bashed up if he hit out again. It seems to be very brutal there. They don't care that his wife is very ill with something incurable and she'll have to cope on her own.' He put his head in his hands. 'Why is all this happening?'

Then Esther, perched in her inglenook, knitting khaki woollen socks for soldiers in response to Queen Mary's call to women of the Empire, pricked up her ears. Erni Klinger's son had been refused as a recruit, yet Erni was himself a second-generation-born Australian. The boy had wanted to join a regiment that was setting up in Bridgewater. His friends had been accepted, he had not. As if the boy's disappointment was not enough, despaired Erni, certain of that community were now excluding him from other activities. He was suddenly not one of them – the community, the friends, he'd known all his life. He was now marked out as different. Erni was worried how the lad might react to the intensity of feeling. He, Erni, had to live through any prejudice, but it was only minimal, for the sake of his business, yet now, why the boy…?

Esther refreshed the coffee pot and produced hot cakes; somehow she felt she had to do something.

Then John Moss had an idea. A friend of his in the Victorian Mallee area – a district Esther knew well – needed riders, drovers he called them, to take his sheep on the long paddock so they got some feed. The Mallee was hit with drought; the roadside grassy verges were a desperate yet legal and effective means of keeping them fed. But sheep needed shepherding and young Henry Klinger was known as a horseman. Would it help if John contacted his farmer friend? That would take the boy away to new friends, new places and give him a sense of purpose. As John said, 'This country's economy rides on the sheep's back. It's a much needed line of work.'

Erni agreed. 'Oh, I thank you, John. It could be an answer. His ma will miss him, but I'll see what Henry says. He's a good lad and I'm sure he'd like to go away and be useful somewhere. I'll tell you as soon as I've spoken with him. Me, I'd like my son to be with me but even I now don't feel safe, and the way things are…'

John had the telephone at his business and his friend's farm had a branch line so maybe things could get moving.

Esther managed to look industrious and turned the heel of a second sock before Katherine was heard from upstairs. The church women's group had already a pile of socks ready to send. She idly wondered where they would all end up: just whose feet would be kept warm by a Hahndorf sock? 'Ironic' was the word that came to mind.

18

A long letter from Beatrice asked for another family Christmas. 'The first since 1910, dear. Now it's almost the end of 1914. Do you think you all could come? And also see in 1915, with us all hoping it will turn out better than is probably most likely?'

Esther admitted to a certain curiosity about her other family: the growing cousins for her two children. It would be pleasant to have them meet each other and connect. Yet she remembered the Christmas of 1910, and not always too kindly. Lilian was now quite a stranger to her. They had spoken once or twice on the telephone, that was all. However, her mother wanted so much to see little Katherine Beatrice.

Frank thought it an excellent idea. 'It's four years, Liebchen, since you were there. You should go, but would you mind if I don't come with you? I have another big Lobethal job to organise and quote for and perhaps I can make a start as it's a quiet time for business during January. This man is influential – he was a Forty-Eighter – and he's with one of the newspaper partnerships. Could be useful advertising. Bertie and the Alphonsos will look after me and Willem is proving a competent lad in the workshop.'

'Whatever is a Forty-Eighter?'

'Oh, they were all over Europe, Ess, as I understand from him. Some went to America. They were called that because they took part in the great revolutions that swept over most of Europe. In Germany, the Forty-Eighters there wanted all the German peoples to be as one nation, like – what did he call it? – unification and democracy in government and the rights of humans to be respected. He came out on the *Princess Louise* that a special group chartered and filled with special passengers. They weren't farmers and tradesmen like earlier immigrants. He called them middle-class professionals and I guess that's more like your mama and papa, Ess, engineers and musical people and writers and, as he said, political people disillusioned with events in Germany.'

He frowned. 'Back to you, Ess. One thing I do worry about, I admit. There's trouble in Loxton, no? It's near Renmark, is it not? And I do worry that with two children you may find it hard on the trains. I'd be happier if you travelled with some help. How about asking Evelyn?'

'My dear Francis, the trouble in Loxton was unpleasant, yes, but developed from unfortunate circumstances. They were fruit pickers. My parents meet such people from time to time but seldom need to employ them. The fruit trees are relatively few and local people have helped, as far as I know. As Papa explained to me, this was a group of young Germans over here and in the Riverland on seasonal work only. They were hot-headed young men, had drunk too much, discovered a patriotism for their Fatherland they had previously forgotten and thought it no more than a joke to march – what the paper said was "goose-stepped" – down the main street to a local hotel. Military fashion. But weren't they dispersed?'

'Yes, I know, Esther, but a couple of weeks later, not long ago at all, their leader apparently drew a loaded revolver and threatened to kill the local constable. They arrested him and he'll be interned, as will many of the others. Because some of the lads were from local families, the young constable who arrested them is now the subject of considerable resentment locally. He'll be moved, I think, to the city.'

'Oh dear, we read of it wherever we turn, don't we? I'll check with Papa about the situation closer to Cumquats if it makes you feel better. As for taking Evelyn, you forget she helps a lot around your parents' place and they'd miss her if we're away a whole month. You're right of course, a companion to help would be an advantage. I will think about it, I promise.'

She finally decided to ask if Susannah would like the trip. She was a sensible sixteen going on seventeen-year-old who always found the long school break over Christmas rather boring and wasn't looking forward to it at all. She had confided in Esther that Christmas to her meant endless games of charades – not her favourite occupation. She adored little Katherine, now a most attractive and chirpy little crawler trying to walk, and was always asking about Cumquats. Yes, she would invite Susannah.

The date for departure was set as Friday 11 December 1914. Frank would take them to Bridgewater station in the trap and she had his firm instruction to hire a porter in Adelaide to swap from one side of the station platform to the other. They should reach Morgan by three in the afternoon and Arthur would have the Talbot there to meet them. Arthur and Frank had discussed the journey on the telephone and decided it would be preferable even with the little ones to drive home that night rather than have another break overnight necessitating all the fuss unpacking and packing again, and Esther agreed. Arthur calculated it would take about two and a half hours after leaving Morgan.

On their last evening together, they were sitting at the table in the living room, sharing a chocolate. 'I hope it warms up for you, Frank, but if summer suddenly hits, do remember to drink plenty of water and wear your old hat to shield your eyes.'

He didn't answer, just sipped his hot drink.

Esther was thinking of their travel. 'It'll be a long day's travel, Frank. It'll be more restrictive for Ralph than for Katherine but then they can run around when we arrive – it won't be dark until about nine o'clock.'

He took his cup to the sink. 'It's a comfortable car, Liebchen. I saw a picture in *The Motor Magazine*. Your mother wrote of it, didn't she, said how proud of it your father is. Apparently there were then only three of them in Australia. Your papa would like that it was built in England. Didn't your mama say in Westminster?'

'Yes, Mama loves it. It was shipped out to Brisbane in April from where Papa's Paringa friend had obtained it. He fell out with it, so Mama wrote, and sold it to Arthur for a song. We shall be comfortable. It will be nice to see Papa again.'

He pulled her to her feet and looked her straight in the eye. 'Esther, my Esther, I will miss you very much. It will seem a long time without you.'

She laughed. 'Come, come, Frank. In truth, you'll miss your children, not their mother. You always tell me I argue too much. You can have peace and quiet while I'm away.'

'I don't have the gift of words, my Esther, but if you don't know you are the most important person in my life, please know now. Your comfort matters to me, as well as the children's. Beatrice said the Talbot has lots more room than the Ford. Your father told me George has that one now to get about in, but this car has two double leather bench seats that are really comfortable. It has two doors each side, a big boot to carry your luggage, and a canvassy-rubbery roof that can be put up or down. Your father describes it as a type 4-MT with a ninety-millimetre by one hundred and forty-millimetre bore and stroke. Not that I know what that means. Now. Liebchen, the fire will smoulder till the morning –' he looked sideways at her, grinning – 'as will I.'

Esther gasped in surprise at his words then smiled almost shyly as he continued, 'You and I will go to bed while those children of ours are sound asleep. Then I may show you just how much you mean to me.'

Mog considered it inconsiderate of the two tall humans to race each other up the wooden stairs and in their hurry boot him from his usual vantage point. Not seemly at all!

*

Departure day arrived and they met Susannah at the Adelaide railway station as arranged. William was also there! Esther was delighted that somehow William and Susannah had become acquainted with each other. Apparently he had joined her at the appointed spot.

'Mama told me where you'd be meeting this young lady, Esther. I hope you don't mind.'

Ralph was so fascinated by the noise, the bustle and the excitement of the station and then totally engrossed watching whatever passed by the window for most of the trip. 'Mumma, it's so fast!'

Susannah was excited too, looking out of the windows and exclaiming at whatever caught her eye. She had been on a train regularly up the hills, but not on this busy route to Morgan up the river. Nor had she been onwards to Renmark. It was all new country to her.

William had never met her before and whispered to his sister that she was a very pleasant youngster.

Esther laughed. '"You are old Father William," so sang the turtle. No, it was Alice, I believe! At least your hair is not uncommonly white...' She chuckled. 'Yes, she is intelligent, Will, and ambitious. And she'll grow into a beauty.'

'Oh, my dear sister, not a blue-stocking! She'll scare off all the suitors. Aha, here we are at last.'

Arthur was delighted to see both his younger son and his daughter. 'It has been absolutely ages, you two! And these delightful young Flacks. Hello, Ralph, may I shake your hand? And what a young blonde beauty is Katherine.' He turned to Susannah. 'I met you at your grandparents' house before my Esther's wedding. Lovely to see you again. Now let's all find a spot in the Talbot.'

'Honestly, Pa, you call it by name repeatedly. How positively pretentious of you!'

'William, I am unashamedly proud of it and make no apology. Motor cars, automobiles as the Americans call them, are the way to go. We're in a new century now and many new marvels are happening all around us, even in the wide country. Now you get in the front and so... Tell me, do you have a motor in Adelaide?'

There was plenty of seat room for Esther and the children and Susannah, though Ralph spent most of the ride spread along the back seat, his head on Susannah's lap. They didn't put up the hood; it was a balmy evening. Little Katherine soon curled up over her mother's lap with her feet alongside a length of Ralph. If it wasn't that she was scared of dropping the baby, Esther would have dozed off.

At some point, William filled the tank with petrol from a can tied alongside and its pungent smell made her queasy – not that she dared admit to it!

The sky darkened and was picked with stars. Arthur passed over a couple of rugs for the children and Esther tucked them up.

'Papa, how much further? It's just over one hundred miles, I know, to Renmark but how far to Cumquats?'

Arthur turned. 'It's about eighty-five or so going on this road but not long now. Should we have stayed overnight in Morgan, do you think?'

William lifted up his own sleepy head. 'No, Pa. This is a lovely comfortable motor. Your dial says forty-five miles per hour is your speed and at that rate it's a manageable ride. To get home and only unpack the one time is worth every minute! I think Ess agrees with me, don't you?'

'I do indeed. Really? Forty-five miles an hour? Oh my, that is fast. The children are peaceful and that sky is worth every mile – it's like an upturned bowl of stars, only interrupted now and again by tall trees. Driving through the dark, the glow of the headlight's beam showing the way. Oh yes! This is lovely country and I shall long remember this sky. Can't match it even in Hahndorf. Too many hills, you see… Oops! What's that? '

'The brake, my girl. We don't leave the gate open at night time, you see. William, could you stretch your long legs again and undo the gate for me? I'll give the horn a short burst. That'll send the birds from the trees!'

It did. Suddenly doors opened and rectangles of light shone from all openings. The dogs barked a welcome and Beatrice was there at the open door, arms extended. This was Cumquats.

19

Beatrice was quite overcome seeing Katherine. 'Oh, she looks just like you did at that age, Esther, except for the blonde hair.'

After an enjoyable cuddle she put her down on the kitchen floor and Katherine immediately shuffled along the floor to the cat, calling 'Mog! Mog!'

'Your cat's the twin of ours, Mama, but I've never heard her call its name before! That's her first real word! And it's a cat!'

All their bags were taken along to the bedrooms. Ralph wanted to know where the stairs were. Then followed the questions, one after the other. To the little boy, beds were up a flight of stairs. Beatrice offered to show him, sensing that a few interesting weeks lay ahead of them.

So it proved. From the next day, when nearly four-year-old Rosalie was introduced to her cousin, it was obvious there was a twosome in the making. Rosalie climbed up onto a table and gave Ralph a ginger snap from a jar. She dragged him out to look at her pet baby lamb – a late addition that needed bottle feeding. The friendship was sealed from that shared moment. Little Katherine was taken under the wing of Alexander, or it might be Aaron, thought Esther, resolving to find out once and for all who was which. Both boys were tall for seven years old and seemingly similar in temperament. Also, they seemed well matched as playmates, those twins. They were both to start school in the first week of February. Esther remembered their father and his twin, William, frequently arguing as they grew. George was more the outdoors type, always to be found among the animals or in the glass house planting seedlings; William was more of a book reader or preferring to play board games like Snakes and Ladders or Draughts. The Double As, as Arthur called them, liked different things but were amicable enough when together.

105

It was obvious they both enjoyed making Christmas streamers. They each cut a pile of nine-inch strips of old newspaper and glued them with flour and water paste in a circle, then linked them with another one, racing to see who could make the longer string. It proved a safe occupation for some hours at a time. The others joined in, though Ralph couldn't use the scissors. Rosalie showed Ralph how to paste and, between them, they too managed a passable string to hang in their bedrooms.

There was only one incident: the twins left the bowl of paste on the floor one day when they heard a horse arriving and toddler Katherine found it. When Esther realised her little one was missing, a search ensued. She was found, happily eating grubby flour paste between brushing it all over herself and the carpet. Mrs Slope was horrified but Esther and Beatrice caught the giggles.

Esther was quick to apologise. 'It all washes, Mrs Slope, and I'll clean her up – you have enough to do. Then I'll come in and help with the mince pies. Then if you like, I'll make some Hahndorf Christmas ginger biscuits.' She hesitated to call them *pfefferkuchen* which, like *stollen*, had become a favourite of hers to share with the Flach family at Christmas time. Nevertheless, she thought how it was a pity politics should intrude on family fun. Just go along with the traditions of Cumquats, Esther; they were once your traditions too, remember.

*

Lilian was no easier to get on with. She had grown exceedingly plump. Fat would be more accurate. *I swear she has five chins! No, but two at least. Papa says she does very little outside work, uses little energy. Planting and pruning are not her strengths apparently.* In Esther's opinion, she acted like the lady of the house, as if it were all her own, laying down the law regarding the children, where they could go and what they could do, even saying what time Ralph and little Katherine could have their baths. It annoyed Esther to see her mother so compliant. When Esther remonstrated after one incident and spoke to Beatrice, all she received in return was a shrug and a comment that 'It's easier to keep the peace.' Lilian's last pregnancy had ended abruptly and too early for the babe to survive, so Rosalie was still her youngest and Mama was eager to treat Lilian gently to compensate.

Lilian was prejudiced against the Germans; Esther could understand that, but was becoming increasingly annoyed at Lilian's all too obvious denial of Susannah. When taken to task by Esther after ignoring a friendly remark from the girl, Lilian's comment was that she was a child with a foreign upbringing and one who actually boasted of having a rough convict, even two rough convicts, as ancestors. Esther reminded her that Susannah was her niece by marriage, an intelligent and attractive girl who wished to make an ambitious career, and was likely to. Lilian asked why she then spent so much time in the dairy learning how to make cheese. 'Hardly a calling, is it?'

It had been a source of amusement to others of the family that the young city-bred girl had little idea of growing vegetables and none at all of how cheese was made before coming to the table; they certainly had no objection to her being kept interested in this way. Esther thought Lilian was quite simply mean-spirited. However, when Mrs Slope repeated a remark of Lilian's made after Ralph had taken a newly baked biscuit off a plate on the kitchen table, Esther sought out Lilian and let her know of her anger and disappointment. *She has a vicious tongue, that one!* Mrs Slope had thought the incident funny, because the little boy had handed one to Rosalie and the two had run off giggling. Then later she heard Lilian telling the post boy, 'Such behaviour, like stealing, is no more than one can expect – the boy's half-German!'

Then, when Lilian was making one of her customary explorations around the kitchen, lifting lids, smelling cooking, sampling produce as she said was her right, she came upon the ginger biscuits in the kitchen. She picked one up, sniffed it, then when Mrs Slope explained the tradition behind Mrs Esther's making them, she replaced it on the plate with an overly delicate show of distaste. Mrs Slope asked her not to put things to her face and then replace them, it was a dirty habit and might infect the children, and Lilian walked over and, virtually nose to nose with Mrs Slope, called her a mere servant, there to do her bidding.

When subsequently Beatrice decided on a huge roast of pork for the festive dinner that year, Lilian almost exploded. She stood in the kitchen, pushed out her not insignificant chest and yelled at the mother-in-law, in front of Mrs Slope and the Dodds girls and little Ralph who was looking for another biscuit, 'Is that another German custom of Esther's, Mil? Is it not our practice to have a goose or a traditional beef roast? Pig meat is favoured by the Germans, I believe, and predominates in all those spicy sausage things Esther brought with her. Wursts she calls them. The name suits!'

Unfortunately, Esther was within hearing of the remark but was mollified somewhat by Beatrice's icily composed response to her daughter-in-law, who was visibly diminished by its effectiveness. No bad humours would be allowed to spoil The Day.

Before the traditional midday dinner, the children were called together by Gran'papa and reminded that it was not only the birthday of Jesus but also the birthday of little Katherine Beatrice and, what's more, it was her very first! Alex and Aaron together gave the little girl a jigsaw puzzle they had fretworked with help from their dad, her Uncle George. Aunty Lilian had painted on it a picture of lovely farm animals – such a caring toy that Esther almost forgave Lilian her prejudices. Almost. Pre-warned, Susannah had embroidered a very pretty lace edge to a handkerchief with a yellow teddy bear in the corner. Little Rosalie had wrapped up a lovely doll's frock for her little cousin, who didn't realise till much later where it had to go. Ralph gave his sister a wooden wheelbarrow for when she goes in the garden, made by him as he said: 'I put the nails in!' Sitting in it was a teddy bear like the English king used to have and that was from Mumma and Dadda. Gran'mama and Gran'papa gave her a beautiful doll, dressed in a long dress and with shoes on her feet. The little girl, golden curls bobbing from her red ribbon, was clearly almost overwhelmed and sat on the big, well-worn sofa not knowing which to play with first.

It was a heart-warming start to the Christmas celebrations and Esther was so very pleased, after all, that they had come to Cumquats. This dinner, the Double As sat on the extended bench and Ralph and

Rosalie occupied the children's high chairs. Susannah was placed next to William and Esther shared the wide foot end of the table with her mother. Little Katherine was so overcome with her presents that she spent most of the meal sitting on a cushion on the carpet near her mumma, having already eaten some coddled egg in the kitchen. Rosalie was concerned that Kathy was not at the table and needed no encouragement to eat her meal so that she could finish earlier. Lilian allowed her to clamber down to join Katherine on the cushions. Esther found herself glowing with magnanimity even towards Lilian and her noisy husband, brother George, who seemed always to shout a point of view when his mouth was full of something.

She managed to enjoy quite a chat with William. His legal qualifications were to be updated and adapted to encompass certain points of Australian law that differed from the English but Rauf, now Ralph, Schulze was taking him under his wing and, with his sponsorship, William had already managed a few attendances at a magistrates' court. Esther was pleased that he seemed to be finding his niche.

Arthur of course said his customary few words at the head of the table. His traditional countdown of the farm's events and fortunes were tempered with only a minimal mention of the world political situation. Little Rosalie was fast becoming a favourite of her Aunt Esther, not only for her care in playing with little Katherine, but also for her quick intelligence and eagerness to please.

Rosalie was obviously a favourite also with the Dodds girls, now quite self-possessed young lasses of twelve and ten, who ensured that she had a big fat blob of her favourite lemon jelly on her tray. She had to clamber back up to eat it, which she did with her almost-four-year-old alacrity.

While the family ate their dessert – *thank you, Mama, it's not that rich and fruity pudding this time* – the elder girl, Anna, quietly moved to the piano and started to play a medley of simple Christmassy songs, perfectly. Esther turned to her mother in surprise, but her mother's attention was on Anna and she was keeping a careful rhythm with her fingers.

Mama, you are the dark horse! What a lovely start for the youngsters.

Susannah stepped up and added a few numbers from the *Pirates of Penzance*, recently performed in the city. That was a surprise and a popular one; even Lilian tapped her fingers. Then with an enquiring look at Beatrice, Anna slid onto the stool alongside Susannah and the two girls burst into a vigorous round of 'Chopsticks' for fun.

Although women had begun to achieve a measure of recognition and independence once thought unlikely, Esther realised it was still to a young girl's advantage to display some drawing room abilities and behaviours. In her professional opinion, Mrs Dodd was a wise parent in allowing her girls to take advantage of the resources available at Cumquats and Susannah had obviously had some musical schooling. Esther's educational aspirations were always to the fore and she was delighted her mama had been teaching the little girls here at Cumquats. If Lilian allowed, no doubt Rosalie was already practising chords under her mother's supervision. Lilian didn't play but had a lovely contralto singing voice she was always ready to demonstrate.

When dinner was finished, little Anna gave a curtsey and started to clear the plates. Esther gave her a beaming smile of acknowledgement. An admirable exchange of abilities.

Beatrice noted the smile with pleasure. 'Esther, do play us something, please.'

George asked for 'Deck the Halls' and began to sing it loudly and with enthusiasm. Lilian joined in with a delightful counterpoint and that set the mood for another session. Little Ralph started to sing and hum with his uncles and Rosalie, not to be outdone, also made an attempt with Susannah's encouragement. That session ended in indulgent laughter. By this time, little Katherine was fast asleep on her cushion hugging the teddy bear and the doll.

Later, sitting out in the garden enjoying a cooling breeze, uncles William and George chasing a football with Susannah, Maisie from the dairy with her loyal boyfriend, and whichever youngster wanted to join them in a riotous game, Beatrice, Esther and Lilian sat in the wicker chairs drinking lemon tea and supervising a game of building castles with wooden bricks by the younger ones. Katherine was still snoozing but now on her mumma's knee. The bricks game was a favourite with Ralph, his mother noticed; not so much the building up but the catastrophic kicking down. However, when one energetic kick flung a wooden brick to hit Rosalie's face, he laughed, showing no sign of concern. Unfortunately, before Esther could move Katherine to remonstrate with him, Lilian was quick to call him a nasty little fellow to hurt his darling cousin. Despite sharing a modicum of concern at Ralph's attitude, Esther replied that it was an accident, only to have Lilian retort, 'That boy is a little Hun.'

Arthur had come to join them, heard her remark and swung into a sudden rage. 'You're speaking of my grandson, Lilian. You insult my fine son-in-law and my beautiful daughter by your crass prejudice. I suggest you retire…'

George had also heard the remark. He disapproved of it but also of his father's chastising Lilian. 'Papa, that's enough if you please. Lilian, I cannot approve of your ugly behaviour towards a mere child. I agree that you should return to our room to calm down. Rosalie and the boys can stay here with me and continue to enjoy the day.'

Biting her lip, Lilian ran indoors.

George turned to his sister. 'Esther, please forgive her. Since losing the child, although time has passed, she has changed. She's far less tolerant. Dr Erica assures me it is a nervous disorder and won't last. Truthfully, I had thought things were improving. However, it has not helped to have her younger brother join the naval services. He was recently in a battle over in the Indian Ocean. He served in the *Sydney*.'

'The *Sydney*? I don't think I know…'

'The *Sydney* was sent to the Cocos Islands to save the wireless station there from an attack by the German ship *Emden*. Actually, the Germans planned to cut the undersea cable, one of only two that links Australia with the rest of the world. The *Sydney* engaged the *Emden* and battled for about two hours and the *Emden* had to beach on one of the islands to avoid sinking. Her brother was wounded – badly. Her mother was, and still is, distraught and she's constantly crying with worry to Lilian over the telephone, which is of no help to her, or to anyone.'

'I didn't know of her brother, George. I hope he recovers fully and perhaps may have some shore leave and visit his family to reassure them.'

She placed her arm on her father's sleeve. 'It's just a spat, Papa. However, Ralph's attitude needs some correcting, and I'll see to it. I'll go and see Lilian later and all will be well. You mustn't let yourself fly into rages like this. It is not good for you.'

Beatrice had taken note of the incident and took Arthur's hand, asking him to come with her into the kitchen. 'Mrs Dodd and Mrs Slope are in cahoots, Arthur, and want me to talk with you. They want us to have a new stove fitted. One like Esther's perhaps.' She led him back towards the house. 'It seems today's dinner tested our stove's effectiveness to the limit. Let's strike while the iron is hot, as you like to say, and see for ourselves…'

20

After the 1915 New Year, Esther was wondering why she hadn't had a letter. or even a telephone call, from Frank. She hoped that the news items about anti-German feeling would not worry him as he sat at home alone in the evenings. If he could write to her, in much the same conversational way they had exchanged confidences before their marriage, she was sure she could be a voice of reason should there be a matter causing him any distress.

A particular concern of hers sprang from an item in one of Arthur's newspapers featuring a Senate motion from a certain John Verran to attack or harass Australians with a German name or background. This would upset Frank, she knew, and as she was away in Renmark, he had no moderating voice to balance his concerns over a coffee conversation. She thought of telephoning him, but her parents would have to pay the cost. She remembered how she had thought him pessimistic when, even before the war talk, Frank had changed his name from Flach to Flack. Then he explained to her how most Britishers or Englander/Australians pronounced the name with a 'ch' as in church.

'At this end of the town they called me Mr Flatch. My father doesn't mind – he has been where he is for years now. But when I put up the business sign, I realised I wanted it to sound as it should, or nearly. And in the writing there is very little difference as a "k" can be painted to look like an "h"'. So you see, it wasn't because of a coming war.' He shrugged. 'Now I think it was maybe a good thing, even so.'

According to one of Arthur's newspapers, one of the first prominent victims of the prevalent dislike of anything German was, among others, Hermann Robert Homburg, the Attorney-General of South Australia. He had that very week resigned his position. Born in South Australia, but of German parents, Homburg had always been held in high esteem. In 1914, though, his office had been raided by soldiers with fixed bayonets. Esther knew that this would upset Frank, as he admired the man. On that occasion, Frank said it was because Homburg was a straight talker, and outspoken.

As Arthur Symonds stated, 'He was an able and efficient minister and he'll be a loss to justice in this state.'

To Esther's relief, that very evening Lilian came running to tell her a telephone call had been put through from Frank.

'Go and talk to him, Esther. I'll finish bathing little Katherine.'

Frank was obviously distressed, his voice was breaking with emotion. Just as she had suspected, he had read about Hermann Homburg. 'If they can hurt such a man as high up as that, Liebchen, what will they do to ordinary men? In the *Mt Barker Courier* there's a coroner's report just released of a man in his sixties drowning himself in the Murray River after the railways sacked him some weeks ago. You know what he'd done wrong? Nothing. He was sacked for being of enemy origin. Vati is so upset. He knew the man, I know the family. Oh, Ess! Everywhere there are stories of unpleasantness. I go out and about with the business and stories of such victimisations come to my ears too often…'

'Calm down, my Francis. I think every incident is exaggerated by the press to make it more sensational. Of course they're nasty, but I dislike the way the papers make the most of everything. Know yourself, my Francis, as you are known by others as a good and honest man. Rest easy, do.'

'Oh, Ess, you should know I was told to register at the police station today. I did and your friendly constable said all I had to do was to sign in whenever I go by. Then he spoke about some restrictions for voting. Do you know I may not be allowed to vote?'

'Those are newspaper rumours, I'm sure, Frank.'

'But Ess, it's also said I may have to sign a declaration of loyalty document if I want to quote for a job or if I want to do the job. I feel a stranger in my country, Esther.'

Frank's list went of concerns was a lengthy one. Some strength of will was called for.

'Oh, my Francis, keep calm. I'll come home as soon as possible after little Rosalie's birthday – that's 25 January. We've promised to stay for that and she and Ralph are such good friends they are making plans.'

She was hopefully able to be the voice of reason, as she later confided to her papa. 'It's not easy, Papa. I seem to be involved in wars within my walls as well as in the wider world. Lilian's attitude unfortunately reflects the growing dissension in Hahndorf – those of German heritage against Britishers as well as vice versa –' she hesitated '– and at times, I'm at war with myself.'

Arthur had to admit even he had been approached by some local councillors to lead a branch of what they called the All-British-League. He had declined, stating that as far as he was concerned such an organisation would, with its regular meetings and notices in the papers, only serve to heighten tensions and poison the atmosphere in the state. He told his daughter not to worry her mother but he knew that, as a result, he had to recognise he would now be on the receiving end of more hate mail of his own. He pushed his greying hair off his face with an impatient hand and a sigh of exasperation.

Esther took his hand. 'Papa, I'm concerned for you. Today you exploded. I didn't expect you to lose your calm and shout as you did. Yes, I know it was an unpleasant remark but Papa, your face went so red in anger it was nearly purple. Would you please, for me, pay a visit to the doctor and see how you're faring for a hard-working country man of sixty-five? I'd be happier, living so far away, knowing you're hale and hearty.' She kissed his right ear, like she did when a little girl.

He hugged her tightly. 'I promise, Esther. But it's only that I'm growing less patient, a little crotchety perhaps, as your mama tells me. Now let us also choose to ignore the newspapers for the next few days, shall we? If the world is at war, the Symondses are not!'

*

Whether or not George had spoken more to Lilian, Esther never knew, but she suspected. Lilian was seriously trying a conciliatory approach; she even asked Esther what was that *stollen* bread Mrs Slope mentioned to her before Christmas, and would it be something to try and make for future occasions and perhaps Esther might show her how? Not once did she speak ill of William, who was, in her estimation, lacking many of the superior qualities of his twin, her dear George. Not that William would have cared, had he been present still at Cumquats and not back in Adelaide! Nevertheless, Esther thought it all a decided improvement in relations and if Lilian was trying to build bridges, so would she, if only for the children's sake. With Beatrice, she even demonstrated to Lilian a way of making cuttings from some of the best vines to transplant. And Lilian didn't once grumble about the mud on her boots.

As Rosalie's fourth birthday approached on 25 January, they all plotted some child-favourite foods for the table and Esther even helped complete some embroidered flowers on a new party dress for the little girl, embroidery from which Lilian had been distracted. As her mother admitted to her, knowing of the change of mood was helping Arthur calm down considerably.

'He's actually seeing the doctor tomorrow, Esther. Erica spoke of blood pressure and I'm uncertain. I don't really know what that means, but I'm happy to have him examined. He does drink too much, I know, and I even make the wine and that makes me feel guilty. He was never one for drinking our water, even the rain water, and I feel that's a pity. Ah well…'

Rosalie's party went well. They sang children's songs around the piano and the little girl had an amazing verse vocabulary, so Esther realised. They all had a lovely time. She was ecstatic about her presents of coloured chalks for drawing and her new dress. Ralph was impressed by parties and started planning his own – not due until July – and he was insistent that Rosalie would have to be there. *Oh dear*, thought his mother.

Time came to depart and Thursday 28 January brought another long ride in the car to the train. Tearful goodbyes from her mama, an unusually emotional one from Papa and a tearful exchange between Rosalie and Ralph set the scene for a solemn few miles. George was the driver this day, relishing the opportunity of driving the Talbot and trying hard to lighten the mood in the car with his atrociously weak jokes.

Susannah was met at the Adelaide railway station by her father. An emotional Frank, driving the trap, met Esther and the children at Bridgewater.

21

The weather in the Mt Barker hills, including the Hahndorf township, was more predictable from January into February – hot and even hotter according to Esther. By the Sunday, the last day of the month, there were signs of a future dry spell: no rain was in the wind of the wise ones who put their wet fingers windwards to tell the weather, in Frank's scornful description.

By other signs that Esther knew only too well and could not ignore as she had tried to do while at Cumquats, there would be another little Flack, possibly around the time of her own birthday. She didn't tell Frank. He was quite in the doldrums already about bringing two children into a world of war.

The other night after he tucked Ralph in bed and read him a story, the red tractor one again of course, he came downstairs in tears, berating the idiocy of politicians and governments, and anything else relating to the war and conflict of any kind. 'I have children! They are not to know war, never, *never*! This discrimination and all because they carry my blood, my foreign blood. Oh, Liebchen! What have I done to them?'

She jumped up and hugged him and he cried wetly into her shoulder before calming down. She was distressed to see him so devastated. 'Hush, my Francis. Our children will be strong and they will know they are loved by us and all our families, wherever they later make their mark in life. We will give them that, and teach them the skills to rationalise situations. They will be strong in every way, because we will help them, show them.'

'Oh, Esther, you're educated, you recognise goodness where my fears prevent me from knowing it. It is you who gives me strength, Liebchen.' He sat down, his head eventually resting on her knee as he condemned his birth, his world, his everything, or so it seemed.

Esther found herself welling up at his unashamed expressions of love for his children and…her too? She stirred, rested his head on the cushion and brought him a schnapps to console him. This was not the moment to tell him about another child. This was time for bed and quiet and…she gave a secret smile.

Over the next few days, she determined to wait until her increasing bulk could not be hidden. Or perhaps should there be a day of brighter news, on any front, be it worldwide or domestic.

She wasn't pleased when, early in March, wearing his hat and carrying the ominous clipboard, the local constable came to the workshop. He asked for her husband, so she directed him out to the back lot where Frank and Willem were operating the steam saw.

Oh my! Please God it's nothing bad. Frank's too old, I think, to take away…

The front gate creaked; he'd exited around the front. She ran to the window to see the constable marching down the path, with young Willem, a dejected young fellow, coat over his arm, following behind him.

'What?' The back door flung open and Frank stood there, face black as thunderclouds.

'He asked for Willem Ils – that is, ILS – said his pa was a German seaman and a deserter from a coastal freighter. Had his picture in the police station – the father's, that is. His previous master had some papers and the wife sent them in – dobbed him in, Liebchen, as enemy!'

'Willem? He's not old enough, is he, Frank? Sixteen?'

'The constable says his old school attendance record says he's eighteen, late in April. Soon enough, said the constable, and he's taken the boy to the police station. Some others are there already waiting for tomorrow when the district commandant is coming. They'll all be interviewed and if I go there tomorrow afternoon and swear for him and he swears he'll stay loyal to Australia and me, they'll probably let him work out his apprenticeship with me. No question, Ess, I'll be there – nothing would keep me away. This poor lad had an awful start in his life. We're the best that's happened to him, so he told Bertie, and he just doesn't understand,

Esther. I was so hot and angry that I said to the constable, what about me? He said he knows my father was born German but knows he's loyal and so am I and they don't bother about me. But they wouldn't let me be a soldier, though. You know what? I never thought seriously of joining. Wouldn't now, wouldn't beg. If I'm not Australian enough for them now, I won't be ever. That's it, Ess.'

'I know what you need, Francis. Sit down.' She plonked a mug of coffee next to him and a doting Ralphy upon his father's knee.

Kathy came running over to Dadda, not to be outdone.

'Look to the future, my lovely man, and here it is, on your lap.'

*

Willem came home the next day. Flacks had guaranteed his full-time employment with permanent accommodation until he was twenty-one. On the way home, Frank had stopped at Baumanns and outfitted the lad with work trousers and good boots.

He said later to Esther, 'The Baumann boys were able to enlist with the AIF to fight the Germans. They aren't worried at all, they feel Australian, they sound Australian. That's how it should be, no? Mind you, they anglicised their names, or one did anyway. Brave lads.'

'Sensible move. Did you not change your name to Flack instead of Flach?'

'Hrmmph, I've explained that. Bertie's pleased. He likes the lad. I shall make sure his little hut is fitted out and comfortable. He's offered to share with the lad. Would you approve, my Esther? '

'Oh, indeed I would. And…well, perhaps now is the moment to say we may need to do some adjustments to our own accommodation, my love. You bade me a very fond farewell when I left for Renmark last December, did you not?' She smiled. 'We'll have another mouth to feed and space to provide for after about the middle of August.' Hands over her chest, she waited to see how he would react, given his recent despondency.

He hugged her so tightly she said her bones would crack. He was exultant. 'I'm so overwhelmed, Liebchen. This is wonderful news you give me. And this child, like Ralph and Katherine, will feel themselves Australian. We will make sure of that.'

The very next day, Esther telephoned her mother at the same time as Frank set off to tell his mother the baby news.

'Oh, Esther. I'm so pleased for you. You say Augustish? Goodness, you do seem to be born to reproduce – that will be three in as many years. You must take life easy, my dear. Promise? First, let me pass the telephone to your papa. The news will brighten him up. He's been in the vineyard and it's so hot and sultry today, he came in with a headache. ARTHUR!'

'Hello, my darling girl. No, no, I'm quite all right. Things are going well and growing at Cumquats and we've all been busy. Oh, congratulations to you both. Another wee Flack. Wonder if this boy will be like me, blond and grey-eyed?'

She laughed. 'Papa, you're so vain! It may be another little girl. Papa, on a serious note, are you keeping well? No more purple complexions?'

His turn to chortle. 'No, no, my lovely one. Your doctor Erica told me to eat less meat and drink less wine. I've been good and I didn't know vegetables could taste so well without gravy.'

'Oh, Papa!'

'I'd better go, darling girl, or this call will cost you a year's labour! Love you. Bless you and the baby.'

Esther came off the machine. 'Oh, Frank, what a wonderful invention the telephone is. I know my parents grumble about listeners learning their business, but for me, that call was almost as pleasant as chatting over one of his coffees.'

22

Esther was not quite so appreciative a few weeks later when the telephone's strident call awoke her in the middle of the night.

Frank was first out of bed. 'That could be the Bowmans. Walter may be in trouble. His father was... Hello?' He listened on the telephone.

A few notes of his responses penetrated Esther's drowsiness and she grabbed a shawl and ran downstairs.

He was holding the telephone with both hands... 'Oh no, my God...I am so, so sorry. I will... ESTHER! Here! Your mama...'

'Hello, Mama. What is it?' She listened for another few moments, the telephone to her ear, her hand down at her side, seeking Frank's.

She swallowed, choked on a sob. 'Oh, not Papa! What...when...?' then put the phone down without further comment and stared, speechless, at Frank.

'Frank, you heard? Oh, woe...Papa died tonight after dinner. He suddenly tipped over off his chair, Mama said, and she couldn't bring him back to life and it was a monstrous apoplexy and Doctor Erica had warned him so he knew but she's there and Mama says she's a comfort but she's devastated and can't think straight and can't imagine life without him... Frank, oh my Francis! This is not possible!'

He gathered her to him. 'Shush, Liebchen, yes, your papa knew he was in trouble. You and I have talked of this. He was being careful and trying to avoid it but he had the warning. Remember this, my dear, most of all you were there for his last birthday and he was so pleased to have the Christmas with you as well. He told me so only recently.'

Her knees were wobbling, she was collapsing. He helped her back onto the bed. 'Ess, he knew of this baby, and was delighted. If a boy, he will be called Arthur Francis. I'm Francis after your papa, you know that.

So he will be doubly blessed. Now, sleep with me, my love, and we will talk in the morning.'

A week later, Arthur was buried in one of the back paddocks at Cumquats, under a lone pencil pine. It was a spot with a thin pencil-line glimpse of the distant river; a river that had played such a role in his life. William attended the funeral and rang Esther to tell her who had been there. It was a long call and the operator actually told him to terminate as others wanted the line. She cried as she listened and, without much luck, tried to suppress her sobs for a time after. She walked around nursing the photograph taken of her parents at her wedding and wetting the frame with her tears.

Frank brought her a cup of chocolate, thinking to restore her.

'Oh, Frank, it seems most of Renmark were there. I was not. Papa was held in high esteem for his work all around the district with pumps and water, irrigation and things like that. Oh, I used to tease him shamelessly. I should be ashamed of myself. And so many flowers, William said. He has taken photographs and will post some to me. Oh, Papa…'

*

The weeks moved on. Esther grew more and more plump and decided she was sprouting – in her gardening terms – another big baby boy. Mrs Alphonso, who was quite experienced in midwifery, gave in her notice because her husband had a new job in Adelaide and they would all go. She would be hard to replace.

Frank was adamant. 'I am not going to let you do things like the laundry and washing floors, my Esther. Not only because you're expecting but later, too, you'll have three children on your hands and you're always busy with them. They're very lucky children. So if you want my help to find someone, let me know, but otherwise I'll leave it all to you. There are people, so make it quick please.'

However, Mrs Alphonso knew of a replacement, one Magda Blum. 'She is widow, not old, maybe only fifties, Australian with mother born in Hungary. No children borned, Missus.'

So Magda Blum was invited and declared she liked the house and the family and would think about it. Frank thought her hilarious. At her own insistence, she cooked some pastry to try out the kitchen stove and filled little tarts with some lemony concoction from their own tree. Frank was convinced, as was young Ralphy, who enjoyed all sweet foods. So was Esther; this lady, so it seemed, had talents as well as energy.

Beatrice rang Esther every week and sometimes quite late at night. 'She depends upon me, Frank. Lilian is no company for her and, you know, I swear I hear breathing on the party line when Mama and I are speaking. Whoever's listening in will know all about how Mama feels about losing Papa – and my pregnancy and everything else we talk about. I say very little about anything else. You just don't know who might start pointing the finger again.'

Frank also scanned the newspapers eagerly each day. They noted the progress, or otherwise, of the Allied forces, hating the accounts of the battles at Ypres, then the Gallipoli campaign. That was apparently planned to last for months. Frank commented that he had never known of most of these places; the war was showing him geography and how to learn to be optimistic. Esther wasn't sure about the validity of that last remark.

Then in May, that soldier medic who had become a hero at Gallipoli for carrying injured men on his donkey, Private Kirkpatrick by name, was shot in the heart, in action.

'This really cuts to the quick, Esther. A good man like that.'

'And in this paper, Frank, it says that the commander of the first Australian Imperial Force, Major General Bridges, has also died "from wounds sustained, et cetera." Apparently when he knew he'd die, he said he was proud he'd commanded an Australian division. Oh, such bravery, such good men lost, and the war isn't a year old. When will it end, Frank? They said by Christmas. Huh.'

Little Ralph was very curious about all the things Mumma and Dadda read in the papers; he wanted to read as well. He would sit on his dadda's knee trying to follow the lines of words with his finger – a little action which reaffirmed for the former teacher, his mother, that he was right-handed and that he could instinctively follow lines horizontally and from left to right, moving to a lower line for left to right also. She explained these things to Frank but despite his having mixed feelings due to the little boy's tender age, her love of teaching came to the fore; she started teaching little Ralph his alphabet. After all, with her increasing girth, it was something she could do while sitting down. He was an apt pupil for not quite three years old. She had to laugh, though, when 'm' meant 'Mog' and not 'Mumma' and shared with Frank that it seemed she was lower down her son's list of favourites than the family cat.

Frank had to laugh at her comment. 'Oh, my Esther the Educator! He's only three years old and you wish him to be a prodigy?' Nevertheless, he was proud that she was so obviously in control of the little boy's development.

She was also in touch with the higher end of schooling; it was brought regularly into focus when Susannah telephoned Esther, not infrequently, while struggling with her matriculation.

As Esther reported to Frank, 'One at the end of her education I can help and the other at the very beginning. Goodness me, my brain is being stretched! Your little niece Susannah has a solid grip on maths, though she lacks confidence in the equations and algebra. However, she should walk all over the English literacy topics.'

Frank was still keen for Susannah to achieve her goal. 'Esther, you've helped her with her school work in gaining good grades. I know this from Eloise when she telephoned the other day. Did you know that Susannah has been bullied at school by a group of Britisher girls for being German. How distressing is that? She's made of sterner stuff, though. She wrote an article about world peace in the school newspaper. I've asked her to bring you a copy when she comes next to visit her Oma. Eloise was so upset but a little brighter when she told me her Paul has been promoted to manager in his shop, with extra pay. They have three other children to feed: a family of four – that's what you always wanted, was it not? In the city they cost money, but I understand Paul keeps a good vegetable garden.'

A family of four became less appealing to Esther as month succeeded month and she grew in size. Her legs ached, she felt enormous – as she proclaimed after every short foray down the High Street. Friends wanted to feel the baby kicking and particularly if Ralph was with her he told everyone with great glee, 'Mumma cross 'cos her tummy hurts.'

'It's so embarrassing, Frank. Even our friendly mounted constable was down the street and he called me over and asked how I was feeling. He also asked me if Willem was still with us but that was his only reference to the war situation. Thankfully. It seems he knows Mrs Blum, Frank. Do you think that's a problem? Perhaps despite the dreadful war, and the way Hahndorf is enduring all of the nastiness, is it me growing unreasonably suspicious of what is not suspicious at all? I feel I'm at war with everyone and the world as well!'

'Ess, all pregnant women have fantasies. Mrs Blum said so.'

'Frank, I'm not growing silly because I'm expecting. I tell you this will be my last baby – I feel so big and clumsy and you imagine my brain is going to mush! If you must know, nothing's easy to do. I'm fighting my own war, I think! Expecting is no fun. And why does Mrs Blum insist on being called by that title? I like the name Magda. I sometimes think you'd rather have her here than me!'

Frank's reaction was to laugh so heartily he nearly choked. *Serve him right.*

Mama Kate often telephoned to see how Esther was feeling. She had noticed the frequent presence of the mounted constable in town. 'He's a decent man, that one, only doing what he's ordered to do, yet he exercises his common sense. We've known his family for years. He called in yesterday and said that the authorities have received letters declaring that the Germans are all armed and it's a grave threat to Australia's security. Absolute balderdash, Esther, but he must investigate such complaints.'

That very night, there was a terrible smashing of glass from around the workshop. Frank flung some trews over his nightshirt and ran out. It was the big, wide and high display window. It had been a most expensive expanse of glass. On the remaining unbroken piece near the roof was rudely scrawled in green paint the word 'HUN'. Frank was stupefied, stood there transfixed by the ugliness of the action. By the time he shook away the shock and absorbed what had happened, Mrs Blum, clad only in an old jacket over her white cotton nightshirt, was striding towards him over the lower window frame, dragging a young man whose hands were securely bound by one of Gemini's halters.

'Mrs Blum! However did you…? And that boy is but a child!'

Frank telephoned the police station and Esther's constable friend came within a quarter of an hour. Esther had come downstairs but when she knew things were in hand she went back upstairs to the children. Ralph was full of questions. Of course, he would be. She started shaking in shock and found it impossible to steady herself for quite some time; it was good to be back upstairs and not in public view.

Mrs Blum had proved her worth and that meant a lot to Esther. Where did that woman get her energy to run after and catch the young fellow? Yet she had. Esther learned later that Mrs Blum recognised him and called his name, and he stopped automatically to respond – his undoing.

The young perpetrator was one of a gang, according to the constable. He admitted to Frank, 'There've been other incidents and we think a rebel element is reacting to a newspaper announcement about a supposed rising among the Germans today.'

Frank slept in the workshop that night and Willem kept him company, at his own insistence.

It was a most unsettling experience. Then with bad timing, Mama Kate rang next morning to say, 'Have you seen the paper today? The big liner the *Lusitania* has been sunk by the Germans. It's absolutely horrible – all those poor innocent travellers and many of them Americans. Oh, Esther. And what's more, the rubbish I heard today you would not believe. Apparently, a few weeks ago, the constable was informed from Adelaide that the military authorities expect a rising among the Germans here tomorrow and they're taking necessary precautions. He told me he carefully informed them of the true situation in Hahndorf, that nothing like that is in the air. Apparently the authorities have been advised of a

German secret society. He says he put them right about that also. Then a Senator complained about the German Arms Hotel having a German coat of arms – it has nothing of the sort, it's even changed its name! And he claimed that the woollen factory was displaying a coat of arms. The constable was quite rightly offended that he'd be so slack as to allow such an obvious act of disloyalty to go unchallenged. It's all so dreadful!'

Kate was obviously taking things to heart but knew nothing of the Flack's Joinery window, so Esther told her the story.

'Oh, my dear girl. Are you all right?'

'We'll cope, Mama Kate.'

'Oh, this is a sorry business, all of it. I feel for you and Frank. I thought our family would be above all that… Do tell me if I can do anything to help. What of cleaning up the glass? Tell Frank to let Joshua know… Do say if so, won't you.'

<h1 style="text-align:center">23</h1>

By the beginning of July, Esther was growing concerned about her pregnancy. Despite Dr Elena's assurances, when lying down she sensed she heard two hearts beating. She certainly thought there seemed to be a fair number of limbs moving about. Her imagination ran riot when it was in the local paper about a calf born with two heads!

Frank was indulgent, but scoffed that all pregnant women have vivid imaginations. He was becoming impatient as she complained of her size and clumsiness and told her to visit Dr Elena. Elena admitted it seemed there was a possibility of twins, though perhaps not a probability.

'Oh, Elena, what kind of an answer is that!'

A persistent concern for Esther at the moment was Ralph's third birthday. It was coming up fast and he was certain his little friend Rosalie would come to celebrate. Esther was trying to work out ways of distracting him and not disappointing him too much. Then, wonder of wonders, Frank came up with the idea of taking the boy for a birthday ride on the tractor in Mr Lumberger's big paddock. Ralph absolutely revered the big red tractor he often saw as he looked over their rear fence.

'Oh, a brilliant idea, Frank. Wednesday is his day. I've made him a cake and Molly Simms is bringing little Dottie to play with Katherine. If Mr Lumberger could let it happen that day, Kathy will be busy with Dottie and content not to interfere. Do you think it could happen on Wednesday? Then if we let him know, the expectation should lessen his worries about Rosalie not being here.'

So it proved, and the little boy could barely wait until the day, and was quite accepting about Rosalie not being able to come. As he rationalised it to his father, 'Dadda, girls don't like tractors, do they?'

Esther didn't argue. Her little boy was happy; that was what mattered.

On 9 August, Esther walked down to Dr Elena's surgery. It was a pleasant walk, the children were left at home, so she enjoyed a little shopping. Then as she was about to cross the High Street, a woman approached her, one she didn't know.

'Hey, you! Is yer husband fighting in the war yet?'

Esther tried to ignore her and walked on, the woman now following at her heels.

'Mr Joseph Cook – know him, dearie? Leader of the opposition. He says we have to punish the maiming, murdering and poisoning Huns an' send our good brave boys to avenge their mates killed in Gallipoli! Wha'd'ya think on that, eh?'

Esther tried to break into a run but couldn't. The woman was sweaty-faced, her hair bedraggled and with a body odour like an overwhelming miasma. She spat at Esther as they reached the surgery door. The door opened. The nurse pulled Esther in, sat her down and brought a cold flannel for her face.

Elena led her into the surgery. 'Betty here saw what happened. Do sit down, Esther. Take a few deep breaths. I'm afraid we see this kind of unpleasantness. It's becoming a common sight now. One or two of the shops have had bricks thrown through the windows with paper messages wrapped round, saying the most awful things, name-calling and such.'

Esther put her hands over her face. 'When Frank went to enlist, he wasn't good enough. They wouldn't accept him. Now they spit at me!'

She took a few long breaths and felt better, remembering why she had come. Kate had said go with your instincts. So Esther was determined. 'Dr Elena, my brothers are twins and one has twin sons. Francis is also a twin. I feel I'm carrying twins. At times I feel I have half a dozen inside me, and all so energetic. Please, is there a way we can determine this? I was reading of a radiography technique being suggested for soldiers' war injuries where they can see under the skin and mark the bones. It would show…'

Elena held up a finger in caution. 'Esther. You're speaking of the electromagnetic radiation discovered by Röntgen in Bavaria. Many years ago now, but development has been slow. It's radical theory and yet to be tested properly. Yes, it's surely wonderful work and I'm fascinated. However, radiation has many unknown dangers and it's still very experimental. To be tried out on poor soldiers for whom there's no alternative, that is perhaps considered worthwhile, but not when nothing is wrong with healthy people. Certainly I would not subject your baby – or babies – to radiation. If you *are* having twins, as you firmly believe, we will try to find out in ways we know are safe. Esther, please, can you lie down on the gurney here? That's right…'

After some exhausting pummelling and use of the hearing trumpet, at a point when Esther was ready to cry 'Enough', Elena stood upright.

'Esther, I do believe you may be correct. Will you just sit up onto the edge of the bed for me? I do think you have two babies, one lying behind the other, making the heartbeat difficult to detect. I can feel also a limb around where a single one would not be. I'll check your blood pressure. Let me place this tape around your upper arm and I can measure using this device. It's one of the latest sphygmomanometers and I had it up from Adelaide only recently.'

'Oh, I think this is what Mama mentioned Dr Erica used on Papa when she was telling him to lose weight…'

'That would be right. I'll just put this cuff on your upper arm, quite tightly, bear with me. You can see it's connected to this column of mercury next to the graduated scale. That's the meter part. As I gradually tighten and release the pressure in the cuff, I can determine your systolic and diastolic blood pressure. Lie still now…'

'My goodness me… All right, Dr Elena, I'll stop talking.'

Elena squeezed and unsqueezed the cuff, watching the gauge, then finally released it. 'Your blood pressure's a little higher than recommended, Esther, but not critical. You planned for the last week of September, I believe? I think this is all going to happen before then, maybe two weeks or so from now, but I can only estimate. I do urge you to take rest as much as possible. Don't you have a birthday soon? Ah yes, the first day of September. Goodness me, you'll have had four children in three years and a month. My word, you will be kept busy! So, my friend and patient, you had better prepare for twins, earlier rather than later, continuing the family tradition! And do – this is important – take life a little more slowly. For instance…' She excused herself, telling Esther to remain sitting on the side of the gurney for a few moments, then in short time returned.

'I've taken the liberty of telephoning your house. Francis took the call and he'll be down here shortly with the trap to drive you home.'

'Elena, you shouldn't have done that. He's busy and…'

'He was drinking coffee. He'll leave the children with his mother, who turned up to visit after you left. So all is well. I can see you think it was a high-handed move, Esther. Please allow me. You're my patient. For you to walk home with your shopping baskets full, more than half a mile up the hill, is not a good idea. You've also had an upsetting incident. I didn't mention that to him, nor that you can expect two babies. That, my friend, is your news to break.'

Frank turned up and was most appreciative of Elena calling him. 'I'm glad you called, Dr Elena. This is a big baby. I've been watching her growing tired more easily and easy it is not! She has the other children now so active and she chases them all over. But me, she will not listen to. Come, Liebchen. I'll help you into the little trap and home we go. My Mutti waits to see you.'

Esther told him that it was not one baby but two. A wide smile broke but he seemed unsurprised. The horse missed not a step.

'I sensed it, knew it, Esther. I think we'll have to borrow Mutti's crib from out of her attic…'

Esther had to admit, it was rather pleasant not having to walk home.

24

It was late morning on Friday 27 August when Francis was up in Lobethal with Willem that Esther asked Mrs Blum to telephone Dr Elena, then Kate, and let Bertie know he must watch for customers. That done, she immersed herself in a refreshing warm bath.

Mrs Blum was now the acknowledged replacement for Mrs Alphonso and possessed of many surprising qualities. She admitted to being in her late forties, was tall, muscular and openly pleased, despite her chosen title, to have fled from marriage – a curiosity Esther was determined to pursue one day because dear old Mrs Alphonso had claimed she was a widow. However, in Esther's books, a person's secret life was to be respected these days and it was performance that counted.

Mrs Blum helped Esther out of the bath and into the little box room. Dr Elena arrived first. She introduced her midwifery nurse, who explained how she had been trained in the new obstetrics.

The doctor spoke first to Mrs Blum about what would be needed then inspected the hard single bed, made ready for the birth. She chuckled and couldn't resist commenting with a smile, 'This will no doubt have to be turned into another bedroom now, my friend!'

Kate arrived and made up the two cribs, lovingly stroking the timber rails of the one in which her own children, including Frank, had been soothed to sleep. She kissed Esther on the forehead and asked if she should phone Frank.

'I thought not, Mama Kate. He's due home this evening anyway and I wanted him to really finish this job, not leave early and it unfinished, as I wanted him home all day tomorrow. Importantly, he's not one to wait around not being able to do anything and he'd be over-anxious.'

Kate pulled a face and escaped downstairs to check on the other children. *Esther is often just too independent. However, she has the right…* *Hmm.*

Esther walked around upstairs, all over, in each room, but was not allowed to venture down the stairs; she accepted that. Her pains came rapidly. *Good, I can get it over with early.*

Despite the lack of space, Kate came back, sat on a little stool and held Esther's hand and mopped her brow. Then after only about two hours or twenty, depending on whether one measured time as Elena or Kate, a little boy as black-haired as his older brother made a noisy appearance.

'Another black-haired son, my goodness me! Hair so long it's waving above his brow. Oh, lovely boy!'

Elena handed the baby to her nurse. 'Now, rest time, Esther. Take advantage of it to relax a minute or two, until the next baby's ready to come.'

Kate peeked over the nurse's shoulder.

The nurse wrote, then called out, 'Seven pounds twelve ounces and all fingers and toes on this first one.'

Esther smiled then groaned. 'Oweeoh, Elena, this one's different and…'

Elena examined her then stood upright and rubbed her own back. 'Esther, I believe this one is breech. Put simply, he's coming feet first. Ah, I see my examination has started things happening. I must help this one.' Even as she spoke she kneeled down on a cushion at the foot of the bed issuing directions to Esther. 'It will be all right, but yes, just a little bit different. I must find…' She looked up at Kate. 'Hold Esther tight for me if I ask, please…'

The pains quickened and Elena winced as her arm was caught in the contraction. 'I have the feet together, that's good. Now I'll watch for the cord. Esther, stay awake, I need you to work… Mrs Kate, a cold cloth to her face please.'

Then it happened, the legs, the body, a shoulder, Dr Elena checking the cord, then, 'Whoops! Here she is, a little girl! Oh, my goodness, look at that red hair!'

It was too much for Esther; she didn't know whether to cry or to laugh and had energy for neither. 'Red hair! Did you say red?'

Thankfully, Dr Elena handed the baby over to the young nurse. Already, as if in protest at her handling, the little mite was yelling vigorously and that started off her big brother crying in empathy.

'Six pounds and four ounces for this second one, doctor.'

Elena smiled. 'Excellent weights, Esther. And both have good lungs. A good job well done, my friend. Now you can rest and admire your babies.' She looked at the clock. 'And two hours to midnight, Esther. Both can have the same birthday after all. But who in any of your families has red hair?'

*

Frank had not returned. Mrs Blum said he had rung earlier to say he would be home the next morning as he wanted to finish the job. Bertie took the call.

'Tell Missus Esther I didden tell him of baby coming. Not good to drive back through the dark too fast and all worried.'

Esther accepted that, especially when Mrs Blum described the awful weather.

'It's all rain and winds like we haven't seen for a long time. Much better Mr Frank come home in daylight and, perhaps, no sense of urgency, hey? Bertie did right thing, mum. Specially Mister Frank in that noisy old van thing. Gives you time to cuddle your babies and have a sleep. No?'

Esther was gratefully enjoying a hot cup of China tea with Dr Elena and Kate. 'This is lovely, Mrs Blum, and thank you for the sandwiches. I'm positively ravenous. Mama Kate, have you anyone in your family background with such red hair? It's so quaint that they're twins but not alike at all. And now I have two black-haired boys, a girl with very pale hair that Mama calls blonde and another little girl with this glorious colour.'

The question led into a discussion on heredity and it all became too involved for a weary Esther. She told them how the boy would be called Arthur Francis – that had been promised by Frank.

Kate was delighted to hear that. 'What of your little girl? Now you have that to puzzle. But there's plenty of time for thinking of that – and hair colours. You need rest now, my dear.'

'Mama Kate, Frank's not here and you are such a friend of Mama's. Will you please telephone her for me from the machine downstairs?'

'Happy to, my dear, but will she be happy to have such news over the machine? You have told me…'

'Mama Kate, I think she'd object more if she didn't know and I think any listener would only be pleased for me. Mama does call late sometimes so the time isn't a problem.'

Esther was falling asleep, so Kate rescued her dish before it fell off the bed, then made her way downstairs. The nurse was kept busy giving each baby a sip of cool boiled water from one of the new banana-shaped baby bottles with pinholed rubber nipples. The glass bottles were made by the Australian Glassware Company in Melbourne and had a graduated measurement marked on the sides so that the baby received the correct amount. The nipples were rubber and made in Ohio to suit the bottles. Dr Elena hadn't seen them before and marvelled at Australian ingenuity.

Then Elena left Esther and the two babies under the eye of the nurse until morning. Joshua would be driving over to collect his mother soon and they would give the doctor a ride back home too.

Kate reported that Beatrice had been surprised – in a delightful way – by the news of a red-haired granddaughter. 'She was so pleased for Esther that it's all over. Said she thinks now Esther has the four she wanted, she'll come to a stop! Especially as they're so close together. I do understand her concern because I had five and seemed always to be chasing one or the other. However, it's not for grandparents to say – Beattie or me! I didn't tell her of the breech birth either. I'll leave that to Esther.'

They laughed together until Elena yawned.

'Sorry, Kate. I feel quite ready for my bed. It's been a long, long day but a wonderful one.'

'I'm so thrilled, Elena. Two more delightful grandchildren – twins, and one another boy! Herbert will be thrilled and opening his schnapps, I know!'

25

Surprise visitors a few days later were Mrs Alphonso with young Al. Frank was delighted to see them and even more delighted with their congratulations. According to Esther, he was still reeling in surprise – mainly about the little girl's red hair.

'That is a mystery, my Esther. Red? Or orange? Heredity is a wonderful quirk of nature, is it not?'

He was pleased to see young Al and took him out into the garden to find Bertie. Mrs Alphonso had brought a shiny penny for each of the babies as a measure of good fortune. She also asked to see Ralph and Katherine and gave them each a child's picture story book made of cloth, all brightly painted. Both children immediately fell quiet, turning the pages and exclaiming to each other.

Mrs Alphonso had a beautiful round pot with her, in which could be seen only the tips of four sprouting plants. 'I grow these. They are favourite in my people's home country Spain. Here they are called hyacinth. They grow tall with deep blue, nearly purple-blue flowers, many little petals making big flower, Mrs Esther. They grow from bulb, like here in pot, and as they die down can be put in ground if you like, but old Bertie, he know them well and can fix for you. But lovely flower so you remember me an' Alphonso. Now tell me, if new baby boy is Arthur, what of your lovely red-head girl-baby, what is her name?'

'Oh, Mrs Alphonso, we're stumped. I want something unusual and glorious, like her hair will be.'

'Yes, problem. You have used other family names. Hmm… My hyacinths…perhaps…I wonder. Hyacinths are from Greek islands, I think, but are many in my country, an' we say name as hya-cint-a. An' in Inglese, we write as jacinta because your J sound we say as H. Jacinta. Is pretty name, no?'

Esther laughed and slapped her thighs. 'Oh, what linguistic intricacies! Mrs Alphonso, I have so missed you! And what a lovely sounding name is Jacinta. I know the flowers too – they're beautiful. I shall look forward to these flowering. I'm sure Frank will like it too. Jacinta she will be.'

*

Sunday 25 September, the twins' christening day, dawned dry and windy. It was almost a month since their birth and they were both well behaved and sleeping in their wraps. Little Ralph and Katherine were literally struck dumb by the ceremony. Arthur Francis began to yell at the shock of the holy water but little Jacinta Marjorie, though she opened her eyes wide, stayed quiet. *Thank the heavens! And Mama is so pleased I took her mother's name, Marjorie, and Frank likes it too.*

They each had the one godparent – as most of the family and friends were either of different religions or too far away. Beatrice was unable to come but planned to spend Christmas with them. She had quite forgotten her concern about the telephone broadcasting her private information to all her party line listeners – until her excitement eases somewhat, thought her daughter. However, Uncle William was pleased to drive up from Adelaide to stand for Arthur Francis the Second (as the poor little boy was being labelled).

Dr Elena, who as a child refugee had a deficient history, as she explained it, and didn't know if she had been baptised into any religion, said she would be honoured to be a sponsor for Jacinta. 'After all, I birthed her like a baby lamb, did I not? Legs first?' That was her quiet joke to Esther.

William stayed with them for a week and Esther enjoyed hearing all the news from home. Even though Will now lived in Adelaide, he said George was often on the telephone, and Beatrice had stayed with the Schulzes for a few days after Arthur died. Esther felt torn; she missed her noisy Renmark family and wished she could travel around more freely than she did. Every little bit of news about Cumquats and how her mother was coping, and even about Lilian, warmed her cockles, as Mrs Blum would say.

William had one piece of cheerful news that had her hoping. 'I'm seeing quite a lot of Dr Erica, Ess. She's an intelligent and such a caring woman and we can talk about anything at all for hours! Dr Roberts has taken her on as his partner in the practice and she's very popular. Actually,' he lowered his voice, 'I know you'll keep it to yourself, but she's so popular it's a problem, because I want to ask her to come to the city, to marry me, Ess.'

Esther squealed and flung her arms round his neck. 'Oh, Will, that's wonderful!'

He disentangled himself. 'Esther, big sister, think a minute. Not so fast – she's built up a flourishing career in Renmark. She's loved and admired there. My work is building up in the city. How can I ask her to leave it all and come and live with me?'

Esther cocked her head sideways. 'William Symonds, why not consider becoming a country lawyer? I do know they need one – Papa always bemoaned the lack – and as your career is the one that's building, not settled, why don't you move to the Riverland?'

That had not occurred to William. She wondered to herself if he would give it some thought, but decided planting the idea was enough for now. He would think about it, later, when back in the city.

The war news intervened of course. They commented on the battle of Loos that apparently started on the days of the twins' christening. It had been described as an autumn offensive, yet here of course it was spring. The French in the Champagne and the British in Flanders had, according to the newspaper, opened up with a massive blow against the German forces around Loos in Flanders. It was intended that the campaigns would cut deep into the German approaches in the heart of France, forcing the Germans into a retreat. However, the outcome seemed less favourable than anticipated and William saw casualty lists as quoted in the British papers.

He read out some figures. 'Horrible, actually. And it's all still going on at the Dardanelles – the Gallipoli campaign. So many deaths. I had thought to enlist, do my bit, as they say. I went along for an interview but when they knew I was a family lawyer, and that I couldn't even shoot, I was turned down. I can't think those are the reasons, though. I think I'm considered too old to start any training – they like young blood. Oh, sorry – not meant that way, sounds crass. But I think they want youngsters who won't question orders. I later heard that when they knew I'd graduated from Oxford, I was considered overqualified to be a soldier – I'd need to be given a commission and yet I was too ignorant of things military to lead men wisely. However, Ess, in my work I'm helping a lot of wives gain their rights after a husband dies. Sometimes a husband is from a family with property or if the property's in his name and not including his wife's and he was killed in the war, unless there are children who may have a claim, some of the young widows are turned from their homes by the family.'

At Esther's gasp, he smiled wryly. 'There are rotters in this world, Ess. Many of them live within our own borders. And, increasingly, if men are taken into camps because they're of German family, not all the wives can receive money from the government, despite the government having taken the breadwinner away. The most the government pays to the wife in these circumstances is twelve shillings and sixpence a week with an optional half-crown per week for each child. That money's not an automatic entitlement either. My services are usually pro bono but at least I'm gaining experience. I do feel I'm fighting a cause in my own way.'

26

The children grew, as did the business. There was a short break for the Christmas holiday. Beatrice didn't come after all, because she had badly injured her ankle. She was quick to say it was in a cast and recovering well under Erica's care, but awkward for travel. She was bitterly disappointed not to come and see the new little ones. Esther was concerned for her mama who, she knew, would not be happy sitting in a chair or even playing the piano to while away the time. It was a busy time in the orchards. However, she knew Dr Erica would look after her.

Nevertheless, at Flack's Joinery it was still an energetic Christmas with four small children to watch and of course it was Kathy's second birthday. Frank and Willem were kept busier than they had expected. Simple carpentry building work such as barns seemed to proliferate. Frank theorised that people were storing grains and even stock against hard times. Barns for all kinds of purposes were sprouting like mushrooms and one aspect he found unsettling.

'You know, Ess, it seems barns are to have locks on them, too. Nobody trusts anybody any more.'

Sometimes Joshua came to help. They devised a means of using the steam saw to cut the nine or ten feet lengths generally required under a sloping roof. Those lengths were manageable for the three men. Then they devised a lifting system for loading and raising them.

'Your papa taught us much about the power of steam, Ess. God bless him.'

As the war continued, there was little demand for corbels and decorative balustrades. Frank had no time for carving the little figurines which had proved an income boost before the war, nor did he have many suitable wood scraps for the purpose. However, he theorised that as long as they kept busy and were obviously doing acceptable work, they would be left alone by the authorities' alien hunters.

Then in the autumn of 1916, a Monday in May as Frank later recalled, a hammering on the front door at earliest daylight revealed two constables. Frank knew the police area of Mount Barker had extended and had recruited new officers. He didn't recognise this pair.

The plump one spoke. 'Willem Ils?'

Frank explained who he was and that Willem was his contracted apprentice.

'Not any longer, Mr Flack. Our documents show him as turned twenty-one. He's an adult an' him an' his brothers have been spreading sedition...'

'What?'

'Treason, Mr Flack. He's under arrest. Will you get him, please?'

Bertie and Willem had already heard the dogs and the conversation. Willem was readying to run but Bertie calmed him down.

'Pack a few things in this old case o' mine, lad, and go along. Best way. You'll be back soon enough.'

Bertie helped the lad to the gate of the property. He whispered to Frank. 'Mister, sir, the lad's coming quiet but he says his brothers, half-brothers that they are, are saying a lot of rot that he doesn't join in with. I told him just to tell the truth if they ask 'im an' I'm sure he'll be back home soon.'

Frank couldn't share that optimism and said he'd be down at the watch house to put things right as soon as he'd had breakfast.

Indoors, he opened up to Esther. 'I didn't know the lad was already twenty-one! Pity is, I don't think he knew either. They're going by those old school records, I reckon. I'll get on down as soon as Mrs Blum can make us breakfast. Bertie, come and join us, man, an' tell us what we don't know.'

'Mister Frank. Willem told me t'other day his brother – one of 'em, dunno which – was saying in the pub he was glad he had cousins over in Germany fighting for their country.'

Frank was furious and shouted at the man. 'Bertie, you *dummkopf.* Why didn't you tell me this?'

'Erm…sorry, Mister Flack, but I didn't give it no mind. Them brothers o' his are allus in trouble an' I thought it just summat o' the same.'

'Did you know he'd turned twenty-one, Bertie?'

'No, sir, an' I don't think he knows hissen. Like so many as come here to make a life, they don' have documents behind 'em. His mam, sir, was born here, I think, but not the kind to get any paper when he come along – if yer unnerstan me. Whatever, to me the lad's a hard worker an' honest as the day is long an' I'd like to tell the constable so.'

'You can come with me later today, Bertie. We'll find out what's what. Firstly, Esther Liebchen, can you please help me to draft a character reference for Willem? I'll take it with me. It may help…'

It took them more than two hours to draft and complete, Frank growing increasingly concerned that the lad would be put on a train before they arrived. He signed it then asked Esther to add her signature too. They managed to see the sergeant in charge but he decried the reference as being not relevant to the case.

'Mr Flack, you may be a respected citizen of this place but your sympathies might well be with your German forebears. It would seem that the previous reportings of the situation in this town are a little biased and the former mounted constable has been recalled. His was the bias.'

'I am a loyal Australian and my wife…'

'We know all about your wife, Mr Flack. Willem Ils will be taken by train tomorrow to the military at Fort Largs. You can make a case for his services in your business should you wish but we cannot allow such apparent disloyalty to our country to prevail.'

In the end, the sergeant reluctantly took the reference, placing it in a cardboard folder with Willem's name on the front. Frank took comfort from the act, hoping it might later be put forward in Willem's defence at any hearing of his case.

One of the other constables, as they were leaving, told Frank he would be notified of any further action; to ask for him, if he had any worries.

Frank recognised him – he had fixed a twisted window frame at his house not long ago – and took a measure of comfort from his reassurance.

After two weeks, Frank visited the watch house and the friendly constable showed him a list sent from Fort Largs. It listed some detainees who had been given a conditional reprieve and allowed to go home, Willem was not among them. On another page it listed detainees transferred to 'longer-term detention'.

'Oh no, Bertie, look at this. He's been sent to Holsworthy Internment Camp. It says it's at Liverpool, west of Sydney. That's more than what…a thousand miles away.'

The constable said his apprentice would be allowed letters but they would be censored before he could read them. 'The lad can write back, just that rules apply. Dunno how long he'll be there but yer know, now that the Torrens Island place is closed, I've 'eard tell that Holsworthy is not a bad place to be.' He bent close, speaking quietly. 'They were treated brutal like at Torrens Island and the government got scared an' now the camps have ter stick to the rules. Still restricted o'course, but I've 'eard they can swim and play tennis, learn to make tools, work at what they're used ter. The gov'ment wants 'em to come out better'n they went in.'

Frank felt more hopeful after hearing that and they drove home debating whether Willem could write letters or even read well enough if they wrote. Bertie said the lad could do as well as him at either one or the other.

'Maybe so, Bertie, but Mrs Esther's good at doing that. She'll write and we'll put our names.'

It was agreed that telling news and stuff like that in a letter was woman's stuff.

27

Frank needed a replacement for Willem. Herbert and Joshua had a fourteen-year-old applying for an apprenticeship in their cooperage. After interviewing the lad and his parents, seeing some specimens in timber made by the lad for the interview, Joshua realised the lad's talent for timbers was a natural not so much for the Flachs' business as for the Flacks'. Also, Frank was still lacking a helper.

He contacted his elder brother. 'This lad's called Michael Todman and his family are British for generations back. Local family. Struck me the lad's aptitude for carpentry might be a good fit for your business, brother. Shall I send him round?'

The lad was keen, and he had brought an example of dovetail and half-lap joints – this last one used widely in Frank's stair and balcony rails commissions – that had been precisely matched and fitted. As Frank told Esther later, the samples settled the matter for him but he felt obliged to test the lad on some attitude questions too.

'He's only young but I like him, Ess. Seems he's nearer to fifteen. Taken him on for a month's trial first off, then if he suits it'll be organising the paperwork. I'd like you to talk to him at times – on anything – to suss out his reactions to, well everything, such as the war, loyalties…all that you do so well.'

So Michael filled the hole left by Willem and showed every sign of being good value for the firm. At almost fifteen, he was well built, strong, and listened to whatever he was told and seemed to remember. On a personal level, he was polite to Esther, watchful should the children be in the garden or the yard, not afraid to chase them nicely out of harm's way – especially Ralph, who wanted to know what everybody was doing at any one time! The Todmans came to look over the firm and liked what they saw.

Michael's mother confessed to Esther she had no prejudice about German influences though she did find some of the sniping from a number of her own compatriots distressing at times. 'Some of our friends didn't take too kindly to my saying Michael wanted to join a German firm…'

'Mrs Todman, we're not a German firm, we're an Australian firm. Both Frank and I were born in this state. My parents are both English. Frank's mother is English and his father was a child refugee from an oppressive Prussian-German oligarchy that murdered his natural parents.'

'But you are Lutherans, aren't you? Ordered by your church to swear loyalty to Germany? And send your children to Lutheran schools where they're taught in the German language? What of those Germans recently caught in Adelaide, sitting and drinking by the river and singing songs about a wonderful Germany? The newspaper reported they said, "*Gott strafe Englanders*" whenever they met up, and stuff like that.'

'Oh my…yes, I read it too. They were very drunk, were they not? They denied next day saying anything like that, and one sensible constable dismissed that claim as vicious rumour. He denied he heard anything like that when he arrested the group. We do have to be careful, don't you think, to separate fact from fiction? As for my beliefs, I attend St Paul's Church of England – our children were baptised there – and Frank goes along either to his parents' church on special occasions if they ask him, or comes with me, but not often. I have close friends from Spain who are Catholics. Each to his or her own, I feel. I cannot agree that religion is a barrier between peoples. Now come and let us have a cup of coffee – do you drink coffee? And if you'll just watch the kettle on this hob for me, I'll go and quickly check on my children.'

So Michael joined the Flacks' work team. His mother Julianne soon became a staunch friend of Esther. Both women were plain-speaking, independent; they came from differing backgrounds but the more they spoke, the more they found in common. Julianne had been born in Adelaide city; she was three years older than Esther and had married at only eighteen to a man the same age who came selling ribbons, laces and such fripperies at the door. Her father had been against her marrying a gypsy, so they ran away. David was no gypsy; he was brought up as a Jew and his family were prominent in their religious community. However, they were both cut off entirely by their fathers as soon as they learned of the relationship; David's non-Jewish wife was not considered acceptable; her children would never be considered Jewish. They were determined to have a shared future, so put together their brief savings and bought a market table and a site.

'To cut a long story short, Esther, the ribbons became fabrics and patterns and fitments. David's a clever tailor, learned from his father, and we gradually bought the scissors and what we needed and I bought a sewing machine and sewed children's clothes to sell in a friendly draper's shop. Then David was asked for a suit and, well, we moved on. He had one supposed customer who cancelled his order when he saw David's scissors were German-made! So we understand stupidity. We have two daughters too but they're still at school. That's us, the Todmans, in a nutshell. So you see, we understand prejudice, we detest it. David and I both believe in taking people and situations at face value. We live down the Mount Barker Road, by the way. We now have a sign in the front about David's tailoring and we work from home.'

Esther recounted this to Frank at dinnertime. 'You know, Frank, I sensed an affinity between me and Julie, as she likes to be called. I thought after she left I hope we can become friends because, though I get on with people, I don't have another real woman friend. Even your Evelyn is now away so much teaching her art. Julie and I were even talking about what we were all doing over Christmas and – a sign of the times and its influences – her husband's Jewishness crossed my mind. Their beliefs are their own and are based in his Judaism but she said they would not bow to any organised religion telling them what's right or not right. She says they've learnt to live day by day. Hmm.

'What's more, Frank, they do the Christmas tree! For them it's tradition only – intriguing. You know, a small pine tree in the house decorated with candles and sweet things, all bright and shiny. Julie's mother adopted the custom after Queen Victoria encouraged it. It was, after all, a German custom – Prince Albert brought the idea to England. Victoria used to have one put in a drawing room each Christmas and theirs was one brought specially from his part of Germany every year.

'Julie is a very pleasant and intelligent individual, Frank. And one of her girls, the eldest one, has started only this year at the Grote Street school that Susannah went to. She must be bright. They drive her down on Sundays and bring her back on Fridays. She stays with a friend near the school. I'm not so sure I'd like that if she were mine...'

Frank was pleased that Esther, after all this time, seemed to have found a real friend. He knew she was determined for their partnership to be a success in all ways but sometimes he felt she locked herself in, as he put it, and was too critical of herself.

He had talked over with Kate how it worried him at times that Esther was not a woman to cuddle the children much. 'She once told me she had never felt what she calls maternal, Mutti. I know she loves the children, but she just doesn't always show it too much. She lets Ralph get away with mischief and the same mischief enacted by Kathy will make her chastise the little girl. It seems that she wants her girls to be perfect and that the boys do not need the discipline to help them along.'

'Frank, you've hit the proverbial nail on the head. She's told me herself how girls have to succeed in life to be recognised, that it happens to boys more easily because they are male. And it is a man's world, my son. But never fear that she doesn't love her children – her love is quite fiercely protective. She and I were talking recently about the differences in hair colour and eyes in families, and how it happens. Your Ralph has black hair and grey-blue eyes like his grandfather, Arthur, you say. Katherine has lovely golden hair and the same coloured eyes, that blue-grey. Yet your twins, one black-haired with light brown eyes like Esther, Jacinta with red hair and eyes like her mumma too, yet in some lights they look green! Beautiful babies all of them and we have shared some wonderings, she and I. I love Esther like my own daughter but I wonder if her children have not taken over her thinking entirely – that happens so easily. I love it when she talks to me, but I'm not her generation.

'Which makes me ask, as it's June, is it her mama's sixtieth birthday coming up? I've been trying to calculate. Will you please ask Esther and let me know if indeed it is Beatrice's sixtieth. It's a good age for a woman still so busy and active as she is and I'd like to make a special telephone call to my friend. We were once so close, you know.

'Back to Esther: if she and this Julie form a relationship in which they can each exchange problems and worries and such things, like I have with Annie Spiers, it cannot be a bad thing. Let's face it, Doctor Elena is so busy she can't be an ever present confidante and this Julie might. Rest easy, my son, concentrate on the business and leave the household to Esther. She's a good woman. Just make sure she knows you love her.'

That word 'love' again. It worried Frank. He did share with Esther his immediate rapport with David, Michael's father. He could talk with her; she always listened and seemed to understand how he felt about things, sometimes better than he did himself. 'David's all right, Ess. He told me openly he wanted the boy to become a bespoke tailor but always the boy wanted to build and chip away at wood. That's what he said. When he realised Michael's dedication to his goal and his obvious aptitude was demonstrated in school woodwork classes – like that – he knew to give way. Like me, he's learned the hard way about prejudice, though he's suffered more, I think. Nice fellow, Esther, as I can just imagine your papa saying.'

Papa. Esther knew her mother would miss him more on the days of celebration that he always made special. She had remembered Beatrice's sixtieth birthday early enough to send her a snug, crocheted hat and some warm gloves with a crochet backing; ones she hoped would be suitable for her when pruning the vines. *Though she has workers employed now to do most of those tasks.* Her mother actually telephoned to thank her. She loved the gloves. It was another late night call, though, when her listeners were presumably thought to be too busy going to bed to listen!

That August, they celebrated Arthur and Jacinta's first birthday with a little party at home, the only non-family child being young Dottie, Katherine's friend. Ralph's fourth birthday had recently passed too and he had a big chocolate cake, his choice. They didn't buy any expensive presents for him or the twins because they were not short of such things; in fact, in their mother's occasional estimation, they had too much! Jacinta was already a confident toddler and her favourite toy was Katherine's little wheelbarrow that she pushed everywhere with a soft knitted dolly reposing in it, knitted by one of Esther's church group lady friends. Julie came to the teatime celebration; she had knitted a little shawl for the dolly so Susannah's well-used hanky gift could have a wash! Arthur was still a tentative walker but a competent crawler – with lightning speed, as his mother had long discovered. Favourite with both children was a huge number of oddly shaped wooden blocks made over time by Bertie and carefully shaved and sanded until smooth. They built them into houses and barns and garages and tall towers to knock over. Dadda built the biggest tower and it fell down over Mumma's feet, making them all laugh. The resultant mess, laughed Julie, demonstrated what a happy celebration it had been.

As darkness fell, Julie's husband turned up to take her home in the car so she wouldn't get wet. The rain had hardly eased all day – which pleased Bertie in his garden because the rainwater tank was filling nicely, so he said. Esther was pleased that the other big tank that fed the house was also filling. Her childhood in the Riverland had taught her about water, its being as necessary as bees for growing things. Then and there, the water supplies and irrigation allocations were constantly a concern, so her water-saving methods had long been part of her housekeeping. However, a lovely warm bath for the children after they'd played outside for a large part of the day was a necessity, she felt. Even indoors, as they had been today, they were sticky-faced and -fingered enough in her estimation to receive a dip.

David Todman was invited to stay for coffee. Mrs Blum offered to put the children to bed that evening. Bertie volunteered to collect some beer and a bottle of wine so the adults could enjoy a party day late supper – and that was eagerly agreed. Once called The German Arms, the hotel had been renamed The Hahndorf and was shortly to be changed again to The Ambleside. David Todman thought the change ridiculous.

They spoke about the war and the ways in which their lifestyles were being challenged by prejudice, although the Todmans' experiences were slightly different from the Flacks'. Then to cheer themselves up they played cards until it was almost midnight. The women won!

As they went to bed that night, Esther was happy to notice how relaxed Frank seemed; he'd been so worried about the war, about Willem, about his township that he loved and the implications for the business, even the future costs of schools for the children! *He's turning into such a worrier but right now he's more relaxed than I've seen for ages. Ohoh…I haven't seen that look for a long time…*

He scrambled under the heavy duck-down quilt. 'I really enjoyed this evening, Liebchen. We must do it more often…have people in and…this too…'

She chuckled and pulled his head down for a kiss, a long one and not their usual kiss goodnight. 'Oh, Frank, we may be an old married couple but…married we are…'

It was his turn to chuckle as he stood to pull off his nightshirt. He posed with his arms upright over his head and a vivid shaft of lightning knifed into the room causing his hair to stand on end like a broom between his upright arms. His eyes opened wide in astonishment, as did Esther's. His knees folded and the bed's legs jumped on the floorboards as Frank collapsed, laughing, on top of her.

She was shaking with laughter. 'Oh, Frank, your pose – it was almost biblical!'

A heavenly response – a cacophonous crash of thunder – seemed to shake the very foundations of the building and they shook the bed again with their laughter.

Frank's face was buried in his pillow, his shoulders shaking, his skin glistening in the light of the lamp. She reached to stroke his shoulder muscles… Mmm…

Their door opened and a loud squeal heralded a very little body that jumped on Esther. 'Mumma, it's the war, isn't it? It's guns…an' Dadda, you'll get cold, you all bare!' It was Katherine; little Miss-conscientious-and-scared-of-thunder-storms-Kathy.

Her parents convulsed as Esther pulled the little girl under the covers and Frank pulled on his nightshirt to protect his modesty.

He was crying with laughing. 'Yes, love, we must do *it* again…!'

<h1 style="text-align:center">28</h1>

Unfortunately, the newspapers the following day were less than pleasant. At the beginning of the month, a long-prepared offensive in Picardy had started over the River Somme. It was the biggest British force sent yet into battle: twenty-six divisions, and every man a volunteer, on a fifteen-mile front. Field Marshall Haig had ordered them to reclaim four thousand yards of territory from the Germans.

'Frank, I remember reading of this about a week ago. Now I think of the Baumans, the Hinkes, the Smiths and the other families we know who have sons still away at this war and it's already more than halfway through 1916. It seems we're gaining another point of view after the event, and what actually happened. Oh my, the French had promised forty divisions, it says here, but could only manage eighteen because of that attack back in when…the start of this year? At Verdun, they had appalling casualties.

'It makes me feel quite ill reading this. It says every man is carrying seventy pounds weight of equipment, and because of the weight they couldn't run – "traversed slowly", it says – through dreadfully muddy conditions. Oh my goodness, here's a photograph of troops making their way through a muddy swamp that was once a forest.

'It says that "Now the news can be released that in the first five minutes of the battle, thousands were cut down by relentless enemy fire and on every side there were dead and wounded." These are such young men – some only sixteen, they say. Sixteen-year-olds are not fully grown men with muscles to carry such a load in such hellish conditions. Oh my God!

'Oh and goodness me, they suspended the attack at midday to resume at four o'clock and the Germans during that time allowed stretcher-bearers to work in no-man's-land. There were later truces also and a padre behind the lines said, "The dying and wounded were being brought in non-stop but were all cheerful, saying it was a glorious success." Huh Didn't Churchill say he wanted to report the action again, after they wouldn't let him take part in the war cabinet? Do you think he's doing this reporting? It's certainly more descriptive than much of what I've read earlier. But, Frank, I'm not too sure I want to read all the fine detail. The paper should let the photograph do the telling. It does, quite clearly.

'Ahah, there's a footnote to this. The first day, 1 July, I think, they only made a few miles yet the casualty list was dreadful, Frank.' She looked up from the paper. 'We do seem to have reports a lot later than the action, don't you think? But the British took two thousand prisoners and they had sixty thousand casualties. The rate among officers was sixty per cent and forty per cent among other ranks. I bet Field Marshall Haig wasn't among the officers in the field. It all makes me feel quite sick.'

Frank had been listening and could not resist commenting, 'Esther, all the rampant pro-British, anti-German groups here will hit out at this one, wanting to know why more Australians aren't in that fight. They conveniently forget about Fromelles. Remember that report last week?'

Esther shook her head. 'No…so many, lately.'

'Not much was written, Ess, but it was the British 6th Division with the 5th Australian against a Bavarian division with supporting artillery divisions. And that was, if I remember right, my Ess, from 19 July – I need to find the article again. It was near the town of Fromelles and, I think it said, was intended somehow to support the British army in their battle somewhere else but it was part of the terrible Somme offensive. I do remember that and it was a daytime attack with no proper trenches for defence and our troops were bombarded by German artillery on both flanks. Australia lost 5,533 men on that one day alone. That figure stuck in my mind, and it included some of the so-called German-background Australians – those who were allowed to join!'

<h1 style="text-align:center">29</h1>

As 1916 drew towards its end, it seemed to Esther that while at home her children grew, the business prospered and young Michael was a great help to Frank, she had so much to be thankful for. The trouble was that, in knowing of other troubles around the world, she felt she was selfish to be so thankful.

She felt she hadn't aged, as people spoke of ageing. Standing before her mirror – that Mama still called a looking glass, bless her – it was now a regular routine to smooth Pond's Cream on her face each morning. As she tilted the side glasses to throw the daylight onto her skin, she was satisfied it hadn't roughened.

'I know it's supposed to be only oil and water sweetened with rose petals, Esther of the Mirror, but I do like the feel of it on my skin. My hair seems to have lost some of its lustre, but Mama's tip of combing through some filtered cold tea in the mornings seems to help it keep its shine. I don't have any noticeable grey hairs yet, either. I could perhaps have it cut at the ends, though. I'll ask Evie if she could trim it for me – she has a wonderful knack with hair.'

She did a twirl and smoothed her hands over her hips. 'I seem to have lost my narrow waist, Mog – and may I ask how you got into our bedroom? I'm still quite trim, despite giving birth to four children over three years, as Mama never fails to remind me, and I think I'm pretty fortunate, in many ways. I've just turned thirty-five, been married more than five years, and I have four lovely children. I just wonder what kind of a world we're bringing them into. Well, whatever eventuates, I'm in good condition to keep them safe, I feel. Now Mog, you skedaddle!'

Her mother telephoned her for her birthday. As usual, she wanted to hear all about the children. She was quite delighted to know how Ralphy, at only just four, was starting to read simple words and develop words into stories, and to hear that Katherine loved to play with the beautiful doll given her by Gan'ma Beatrice on her first birthday. Esther described how, after seeing her baby brother and sister tucked up in a shawl when tiny, Kathy guarded Dolly assiduously from the eager fingers of little Jacinta. She wasn't very tidy, though; she was too easily distracted and left her toys all over the place. However, Dolly survived various energetic ministrations and was, as they were speaking, tucked up in the shawl knitted by Julie. Kathy liked to try to read, speedily recognising the individual sounds of the alphabet. Esther thought she might soon take things further with the children's reading and perhaps start to teach Ralphy his numbers, and how they were written.

After replacing the telephone, and repeating her children's achievements, she felt her earlier self-congratulatory twirl in front of the mirror had been quite justifiable.

Yet despite all her planning, at the back of her mind was always the thought that Frank might be called to enlist, be conscripted, despite his being nearly thirty-six. Then she read a report one fine, warm October day that the prime minister had lost his referendum! *Oh, the good Lord has heard my prayers! Happiness, happiness!* Billy Hughes had wanted conscription for, so she thought, all men under forty years of age. His thinking was that Australians should serve with Britain in the war against Germany.

Dr Elena came for coffee one morning and to check on the twins, saying there was a case of measles in the town. 'Fortunately it's being isolated, Esther, but best to keep the little ones at home for a week until I know.'

Esther commented how Elena must feel overpowered by illness at times. 'You see so much of the unhappier side of life. And just when I thought things were settling down in the town it seems that even the Heysens – you know, that lovely painter family – have been accused of all kinds of things because they're from Germany originally. Frank's sister, Evelyn, has been taking art lessons from his wife Sallie and getting advice on her works for some time now. Evie is so upset – not helped of course by being herself the daughter of a German-Australian. It's just so unpleasant what's happening, and so unwarranted. I feel angry, Elena, really angry and upset for them too.'

'I couldn't agree more with you, Esther. Such ignorance and in the so-called leaders of our state! Yesterday, in the bakery, they were talking of that All-British League visiting the Heysens recently on the excuse that they were checking allegations that Hans was circulating stories about the late king. How ridiculous is that? It's preposterous, reprehensible and nothing less, that such a good man has to defend himself against their accusations, including that he had no hidden wireless sets for transmitting signals. And he has painted such wonderful pictures of our Australian trees and scenery that so surely declare his love for the country.'

'I notice in the newspapers, Elena, that there are letters from many moderate South Australians deploring that attitude and many declare that not all British Australians support the objectives of the All-British League. The other day one writer noted that the entire British royal family would fail the proposed parentage test required to join the league due to all their intermarrying with other European royalty. And we know only too well, do we not, that there are already Australians of German parentage being killed or injured in this war while fighting for the British side.'

Elena sighed and shook her head in despair. 'I can also tell you, Esther, but don't pass it around, please, that I've had people refuse my services. One told me that my name was foreign and therefore so was I, so I could not be loyal to our country. I was calling at her home to warn against the possibility of measles and she wouldn't let me over her step when she knew my name.'

'Oh dear, my friend, at times I do despair. Do feel you can come and knock on our door any time for a schnapps to revive you – I know that you share Frank's preference for its bitey flavour! And it is cheering.'

Elena smiled, then spoke of needing help in the practice; perhaps by taking on a student doctor as an intern. 'One with a less startling spelling to their surname might help!' She shrugged as she smiled. 'It does seem that I'm not seen by the authorities as completely Australian. However, I will persist. I'll need to for certain if the measles spreads.'

She then mentioned a friend of hers, a professional theatre nurse with the Australian Army Nursing Service who had written from Egypt. 'She writes to me as a fellow practitioner. She has treated some dreadful injuries to our soldiers from the Gallipoli campaign, Esther. I won't tell you the details She does say there's a friendly rivalry between the Australian nurses and the British – more a matter of who's been trained, who's cleverer, if that's a word. How silly is that! She's very friendly with one of the English nurses in the same billet, however, and they speak of visiting each other after the war. They both see the most dreadful injuries and wish they could operate and treat them in ideal conditions. But Margaret longs each day for a hot shower under which she can linger in complete privacy. She says it's the little successes that keep them going. On two occasions she had to do a surgery. Speed was necessary and both doctors were overwhelmed by the number of wounded. Now she's talking of studying to be a doctor when she comes home. She has a name more foreign even than mine. I hope by then some order and sanity will once again prevail. You know, one of her English friends drives an ambulance – this is in France – and at the sites of battles she helps load the injured as well as unloading them when they need treatment. She says it's strange the way the wounded accept nurses to be women, but an ambulance driver is supposed to be a big gruff soldier type.'

She sipped her coffee. 'You know, Esther, on another tack: there'll be a great change in the way men look upon women after this war. Here, women are doing the jobs of the men even in the factories in Adelaide. I think it will be interesting to see how society might change.' She tilted her coffee cup. 'Here's to us women, Esther.'

*

Herbert, Frank's father, was delighted with the result of the referendum on conscription. He invited Frank on one visit to share a schnapps with him to celebrate Billy Hughes getting one in the eye.

Frank often went round to see his parents, not only because their businesses collaborated in some projects, but also to see that they were well and not being harassed again. Herbert, being German-born and proud to say so, especially after his beer, had somehow fallen foul of one of the additional constables posted to the town. A city auxiliary, he was one of the kind who hated the Hun and walked around the township slapping his long boots with a whip. 'Hope he's sent back to the city soon because if he can't find trouble, he invents it, builds it up.' So became the general consensus.

'Frank, my son, I love this place I have come to. I remember Pastor Wilhelm from the old settlement, but I remember little of my early childhood. It was you asking me about black hair because of the babies – it made me dig deep into memories. My parents were killed, I know, in the upsets over in my country at the time. I didn't see it happen because I was staying with my cousin Friedrich's family. His parents were taken away and a man his father worked for got us onto the ship to come here. It is sadness, I think, that at times makes me have little minutes of memory. I remember I was loved and had schooling but not much else. My cousin died soon after we arrived here, from phthisis, that's what the doctor wrote. I know he just went thinner and weaker when we first landed here. I didn't speak any English but one of the men in an office at Port Adelaide took me to a Lutheran church where he knew he could be translated and the church pastor took me in. I think I was about ten or eleven years old. I had more schooling there, then later I was put to work with a carpenter and I married his daughter. Helga was sixteen. Then one day she was run over by the brewery cart. My employer was grief-stricken and I was sent to the Lutheran settlement near here, and Pastor Wilhelm, lovely man and lovelier wife, treated me like family. But deep down I feel I owe my mother and father some loyalty, and when I have the beer it washes out. It was not their fault they were persecuted, and they brought me up well as a boy. I know they loved me when I remember my mother's hair...'

He broke off. 'I was wrong to remark on being proud, but I am proud of what I have done and made of this life my parents and my family gave me in those sad early years. They loved me and I owe them respect. Not their country that betrayed them, but them and the hundreds like them. Can you understand?'

'Vati, that is a long story for you and one I should have known long ago – you do not tell it enough. Yes, you can be proud but now, be proud of me and Eloise and Josh – not forgetting Inga, who you hardly ever see, and Evelyn, who you see often – proud of creating us as responsible citizens of this state. And our children. I'll come with you next time you see our friendly constable and your reasons for what you said, whatever it was, will make sense with him. He's a reasonable man and he'll put a stop to any nastiness concerning you. Of that I'm sure.'

Frank had also wanted to chat with Evie. All this talk of friendship and sharing thoughts, and the mysterious love, was playing on his mind. He also wanted to talk to his sister about things – she was another female of Esther's generation, after all. He had also wanted to ask her to sketch a dragon for him so he could draft a design requested by a customer on a newel post. No luck on either issue, so he drove home again, his brain whirling with sadness for his father – a man with memories…

Esther was reading to the children, so he settled to do some designing. His mind wasn't on the task; he was trying to think up ways to ensure that he was making Esther happy. So he hadn't spoken to his sister this evening; at least he could try her tomorrow. He knew Esther envied his comparative ease to visit his parental home. His own mother, Kate, argued, 'I see you as being quite close. Esther loves her children, her life and you, not necessarily in that order. She is her mother all over again.' Mutti first knew Beatrice when they were young women together, living in Bridgewater, so she should know.

And yet…perhaps that was what was missing? Esther could not see her mother; she missed having her mother around to speak with. She had said she wished her mama could see the children. They had all spoken on the telephone, when her mother was happy to do so; her dislike of the instrument, the machine as she sometimes called it, seemed occasionally to him to be unnatural. This year had been her mama's sixtieth birthday and though she had spoken as long as Mama permitted on the telephone on her day, it was not the same as chattering – his word – over a coffee. Esther had sent her mama some present she had made, he knew that, and also some photographs. However, it wasn't as if any photographs could show Jacinta's hair in its glorious colour. Also, since that last Christmas together, her beloved Papa had died and he knew Esther wanted to find out, really find out, how Beatrice was managing. However, for Esther to travel that distance with four young children – with all the arrangements there and on the way, travel was a formidable problem.

Since talking with his mother, he realised he needed to be more perceptive of how Esther really felt. He always thought of her…yes, as a partner, but almost as a business partner; one who shared his ideas; was level-headed and commonsensical. He consoled himself with the assurance that they had achieved much of what they planned deliberately during all those letter-writing months before they married; they had their family, their way ahead seemed certain. Yet somehow he knew it could be a rocky one unless she knew he really appreciated her, or so it seemed whenever he read the women's pages in the paper. He wasn't one for fancy words and realised now and again that an occasion had presented itself when he could have expressed his feelings, but he generally thought of those things after the event; things he should have said and he'd missed his chance. He worried; did he always think of things practical when he should appreciate her more? Surely she was the more practical one?

Is it appreciation I'm thinking? All the things I feel for her, is it love? Is love more than making a family, providing for it and caring for it? How do we know if we have the love that's supposed to make rocky paths become smooth. What is it Vati says in the old language? Erm… 'Liebe ist nicht etwas, was man findet. Liebe ist etwas, was dich findet.' *He says it means love isn't something you find; love is something that finds you. Hmm. So is what I feel for Ess true love and I just don't know it? It has found me, grown upon me? Vati tells me things when we meet, things that make me think. And we can meet quite often. I do see that my Esther has miles between her and her mother.*

Next time, he mentioned to his father how he felt it had been hard on Esther being married to a Lutheran German husband, in that she had been challenged a couple of times in the street; that incident of a woman spitting at her in the street just before the twins were born still made him flare with anger.

Herbert understood but reminded him of Esther's common sense, her inner strengths. 'She knew something of the awkward community feelings before you were wed, my Francis. She must have done, because there were mutterings for a while before. She still chose to marry you. Give her credit for her special qualities. She is naturally and professionally an educator, Frank. She has an eye and an ear for whatever needs to be done, that other people can miss. I have heard gossips and know, because my friend the constable tells me, how highly she is regarded, and not only among our Lutheran community. Your children are taken down the street with her, and sometimes with Mrs Blum, and are always admired and so well behaved. Your Mutti tells me of a pair of bed quilts that Esther and her friends in her church needlework have made for the good doctor Elena's surgery rooms, where there are six beds for sick children too ill to be moved or need to be taken from their house. Those beds are used by Hahndorf children from any family – any family – who needs help. And she knits woollen hats for our church soup-kitchen men – you bring them to your mother – things like that. And of course all that jam she gives to the kitchen for bread sandwiches, as she calls them. You have a good woman for a wife, Frank.'

Frank felt foolish standing there listening; how could his father know more of what Esther did than he, her husband? Yes, he knew of the quilts; he hadn't thought about the woollen things and the jams. He knew that for her church club she knitted soldiers' socks and made jams for trading tables. He was obviously too busy to notice other things. That was not good enough. And he knew she liked to help Elena with all surgery matters, and so some of her church friends also helped – he had not realised. He also knew of Elena's problems with a minority of her patients refusing her help because she was foreign. To him it was a further demonstration of the hypocrisy, the bigotry still prevalent, and an added confusion to occupy his thoughts and prevent his sleep.

Then one afternoon, he found Evie at home and asked her how he could show Esther what he felt for her. She came up with an idea straight away. *Obvious really, why did I not think of it?*

He thought it through on the short drive home and ventured the topic almost as soon as he walked in the door. 'Liebchen, why not write or telephone your mama and invite her to come here for Christmas time. You know, she may like that.'

Esther was delighted at the thought. 'Oh, that would be wonderful! Her ankle's been healed for ages!'

Her mama was delighted. After working things out with George and Lilian, she telephoned to say she would like to travel on Monday 18 December and return on Thursday 18 January in time for Rosalie's sixth birthday on the 25th.

'Oh Esther, it will be lovely to see you again and this time, no injured ankle! It will be simply wonderful to see your children, especially before they enter the world of school. What a lovely idea of Frank's. Rosie is to start school at the beginning of February. I've promised to go shopping with Lilian beforehand. I'll be back in time. They have a colourful uniform at that level and not much to buy initially but it will be fun to choose. The school here seems to be a happy and efficient one, says Lilian. Aaron and Alexander enjoy their days there and she's pleased with the teachers, who maintain discipline with understanding, so she says. Rosie knows a number of the children already and some are starting at the same time.'

So that was settled. Esther was happy that her children's grandmother would get to know them better and that they would get to know grandmama.

She and Frank chatted in bed that night. It was the one place where, usually, they could be alone. Frank remembered his mother's advice: 'Stay close.'

'Oh, I'm looking forward to seeing her again. Thank you for thinking of it, my Frank, and of me.'

He smiled happily. That had been a good move. He turned over and moved closer. 'Esther, Liebchen, does lightning ever strike twice?'

'Huh? What?' She giggled. 'Lock the door then, Frank, and we may find out...'

*

So Rosie was starting school after Christmas. Schools were a topic of concern and conflict at Hahndorf. As a result of the passing of the amendment to the Education Act in November 1916, the Lutheran school on Main Street was to close mid-year in 1917. Ralph was due to begin at the start of 1918. She did know from Dr Elena that the highly thought of head teacher at the public school to which all the Lutherans would be transferred, a Lutheran described and accepted as a German Australian, planned to remain in the role. It was rumoured that he would anglicise his name to keep the position. Like Elena, Esther thought it was wrong that he might have to do that. But anything could happen before Ralphy started school; maybe even this terrible war would end.

Esther and Frank had already talked about which school the children should attend. Because the Hahndorf Academy had closed a few years previously and now the Lutheran school would be doing the same, there was only one viable option, the public school in Church Street. Esther was quite accepting of this, but did wonder if it would be over-crowded.

The ruling about the Lutheran schools being censored, closed and at all levels throughout the state criticised for not teaching in the English language was an emotive one among the staunchly Lutheran communities. Some were accused of taking down royal pictures and – worse still – refusing to fly the Union Jack; accusations bitterly debated and in many cases refuted. However, the Act was affirmed and, hoped Esther, 'It will all settle down before our children are affected.'

However, she did share the Flachs' unhappiness about changing the name of the township in accordance with the 1917 Nomenclature Act.

'Says here,' she flicked the page with her finger, 'Hahndorf is to be

Ambleside, so that's why the hotel is changing its name. That's next year, Frank, yet we read this in the paper already. When do the changes begin?'

It seemed to her that the industry and energy of Captain Hahn, in settling his ship's load of emigrants here in the original settlement, a mere two years after the British colony of South Australia was declared, was a momentous achievement deserving of honour. To have the town named after him seemed to her a small but just reward.

'Now tell me this, Frank. Our capital city is Adelaide, named after King William's wife. All right, but her name was actually Adelheid and she was German, from Saxe-Meiningen. How convenient that her name was anglicised when the state began. Is there not a measure of hypocrisy in all this? What do you think, Frank?'

'I know it sounds odd, Ess, but I feel mainly a twisted sense of pride. People like my father who fled the tyrannies in Europe and came to this country were able to found sixty-nine townships here – living, busy townships. That's an achievement that will outlast the senseless name changing ordered by this silly Nomenclature Act. Whatever they have to be named, I bet some, most, will revert eventually to their original names. What's more to the point, Esther, is that only a few months ago we, the Flacks, changed the name of our little industry to a joinery and paid all that money for the signwriter to paint the new workshop sign. Lovely big lettering that has the name of our town proudly in big letters in the corner! Do I have to have that painted out? I protest, I really do. Do these senseless war-mongering parliamentarians understand the costs involved in changing large signboards, letterhead and all the other things…street names even and – *and* – they want to change even the names for the bakery! And my favourite *Berliner Pfannkuchen* is now to be called a Kitchener bun.'

Later, as he read another article, he looked about to explode. 'You know how Hermann Homburg, our past Attorney General, was forced to resign? A good man, him. But here's some more about the towns and districts with names indicating a German influence: the district of Homburg is to become the Hundred of Haig. That is just insulting,

Esther. Haig ignored a lot of sound advice against his plans for the Somme conflict. I know many blame that man for the slaughter at the Somme, or so I feel.'

Esther was explaining all about the nomenclature changes to her mother on the telephone. It was late at night and Beatrice felt that most of the party line listeners would be getting ready for bed; she actually welcomed calls at such a late hour, feeling free of curious listeners.

Beatrice paused for thought, then asked, 'Esther, do you have a large lake near to your town?'

'Haha, Mama, the lack of water is a problem here. Why do you ask?'

'Because near Kendal where I grew up, where I lived on the farm until I married, there was a very pretty town called Ambleside. It's still there, at the head of England's largest body of water, Lake Windermere, which isn't a lake at all really, it's a mere, as the name correctly demonstrates. No, it's a pretty name to have if you have a lake on whose sides you can amble. However, for a Hills town, I think that shows a rather confused reasoning. Altogether confused, my dear. But oh, I am so looking forward to seeing you all again and only a couple of weeks now until I arrive.'

30

Beatrice's arrival in church on her first Sunday – the last in Advent – caused a ripple of interest in the congregation; some wanted to meet her, others to renew their acquaintance. It seemed that Arthur Symonds's aptitude for steam machinery, that Beatrice had never really understood, had somehow been recognised by the family who owned the original mill in Main Street. There were links with the church community and Beatrice had to listen closely to determine, as she said, the 'whiches and wheres' of the connection. Back in the early days of the township, the mill had operated by steam. It had a colourful history, started off as a watermill then became steam-operated under one of the sons. The boiler had exploded many years before, in 1853, and later the mill was restored by a son of the family. The correspondence with Arthur seemingly eventuated because of an enquiry just after the turn of the century as to whether it was sensible to restore the steam operation for the processing of wattle bark. Not only that connection, of which Beatrice had been totally ignorant, but also one of Esther's church friends from the knitting and quilting group was from the family of Mr J.C.F. Faehrmann, whose carpentry expertise had erected the huge red gum pillars of the restored mill back in the 1850s and in the 1880s helped build the St Paul's Church of England – the church of this friendly group of ladies.

As the ever-practical Dr Elena later commented, 'All this recognition of your father, Esther, not to put too fine a point on it, will only do your family's standing good in the township. Whether we like it or not, distinctions still exist. It's good when barriers are broken down.'

Esther was just pleased her dear papa was known so well. As Beatrice summarised when she and Esther walked home afterwards, 'To have that kind of history would have thrilled your papa. We came to Renmark, to Cumquats, before the town was established. Its history is much more recent. To be able to make these connections, to grasp the whole concept of local heritage here around Hahndorf, of the German families, Lutheran and non-Lutheran, I find really heart-warming, Esther. Your children will grow here, and it's a good place.'

Kate and Herbert with Evelyn and Joshua were expected for lunch that day and Mrs Blum had done them proud. Earlier in the week while Beatrice was out somewhere with Kate, Esther had made fruit pies, meat pies, cold pork pies and two huge fruit cakes. For today's beef roast, Mrs Blum had conjured up what she called Yorkshire pudding, to serve under the gravy.

Both Kate and Beatrice were stunned by these; both had memories of the pancakey pudding being served, soaked in gravy, before the meats.

Kate laughed. 'In the orphanage, the idea was to take the edge off our appetites before the expensive meat was served.'

Beatrice commented, 'Certainly this Hahndorf is a mix of cultures!'

It was a most enjoyable meal. Afterwards, the men retired to the workshop to smoke the new cheroots, which all the women despised, and drink the schnapps made by Herbert.

Joshua took advantage of the relaxed mood to confess to his father and brother that he would be getting married.

'About time,' said his brother.

'An' who's the *mädchen*, my Joshua?' asked his father.

'Her name is Miriam and she's the daughter of one of the mounted constables, Vati.'

There was silence for a moment or two. Herbert's face was a picture, like a moving sea of expression. 'She is a Britisher?'

'No, Vati. She is of French blood, Miriam de Ville.'

'She is not of our Lutheran church, she is Catholic? Is she truly a maid, my Joshua? Or perhaps a widow or…? Why have we not seen her with you?'

Frank thought it was time to intervene. 'About time, my dear brother. May you have many sons to carry the dynasty forward. Now we have to meet her.' He turned to his father, who still had his cheroot poised in front of his face, reflecting his surprise. 'Vati, we must arrange for her to come to a meal with us. How about Christmas, or afterwards perhaps? It's only days away. Will you speak with my mother?'

Herbert's thoughts were spoken aloud. 'Another not of my church. What is wrong with my children that they do this to me? Inga married someone who doesn't believe in anything and we hardly ever see her or hear from her. Evelyn does not wish to marry at all, just to paint and make friends of all those arty people. As to my sons, Francis marries an Anglican and Joshua now a… What religion is your lady friend, Joshua?'

Josh was a little nervous after his father's outburst. 'Her family are Baptist. They're Protestant, Vati. Their church is in Tynte Street, North Adelaide. Miriam believes, but has opinions different from her family. Her God is our God, though, Vati. And yes, she is a good woman. She's twenty-seven years old, tall as me and with lovely gold hair. She smiles and laughs a lot at life, maintains that life is what we make of it.'

Frank excused himself and went into the other room. He came back a few minutes later with a plate of ginger biscuits. 'Mrs Blum sent these in to us. Josh, I mentioned Miriam to Mutti. She was surprised but only a little. She said she knew you were seeing someone and was only waiting to find out!'

That brought a smile from Herbert. 'That is my Katerin. You cannot put one over on her.'

Frank blinked at his father's unusual use of slang and said to Josh, 'Mutti says if Miriam would like to share your Christmas, she's welcome. I know she'll also be welcome here at our house.'

Herbert looked down at his cold cheroot. 'I didn't really like this thing anyway. Tastes like ash in a cold fire grate.' He looked up at his second son. 'My Joshua, I am not an unreasonable man but my faith has been the essence of my living for many years now. Forgive me if I am a little disappointed but I am sensible, I think. I do know the world is changing and if your mother thinks she will welcome this Miriam to our table, then so will I. I have seen how happy Frank is with his Esther, who is of a different church. His was a wise decision and I am sure yours will be too. You are of a good age to know your own mind, my son, and I will be content if you are. Now, excuse me, I will go to check the stars before we go home.' He walked out of the other door and into the garden.

Joshua exhaled, slowly. 'Phew. I've been so nervous, Frank. You'll like Miriam and so will Mutti. Evie has met her from the painting classes and likes her well enough to be my wife – she told me I should ask her and not shilly-shally. You see, I've known Miriam for almost a year now. She lives at Lobethal – to be known as Tweedvale to Mutti's amusement.'

Frank didn't understand. 'Why is Mutti amused? I thought she despaired of all this Nomenclature Act business.'

Josh pulled a face. 'Come on, Frank. What was Mutti's name before she married, huh? Was it not Tweed?'

They both chortled. It had been a tense few moments but now the hard bit, as Frank said later to Esther, was over.

*

Esther was so thrilled to have her children getting to know their grandmother. Oma Kate of course was familiar to them; this new grandmother Esther thought would have been forgotten by the elder two, but Ralph remembered playing on the piano with her. Not so little Katherine, who had celebrated her first birthday at Cumquats, yet an affinity now sprang up between her and Ganma from the first hug.

'It's because you're both blondes, Mama!'

Beatrice was intrigued by the twins. 'Oh, my darling girl, they could be taken so easily for being of a different family…well, until you look at their eyes. Alexander and Aaron, for instance, both with dark blond hair and Arthur's smoky-grey eyes…well, that's my name for them. Certainly not a cold grey. But your twins: little Arthur is so dark-haired like Ralph and with your hazel eyes, like Jacinta too, but Ralph has his Grandpa Arthur's eyes, as does Kathy. Kathy's hair is such a delicate blonde. It's beautiful. As to Jacinta's hair – oh, I love her name – her hair is so, so what? Auburn, copper, titian…well, I think so. I believe titian hair is supposedly a brownish shade of red hair, auburn hair is a brownish shade of hair encompassing the actual colour red. Hard to say, take your pick! I'll settle for glorious!'

The twins accepted their new grandmama quite readily. They called her Ganma and Esther was sure the name would stick. She was Mumma's mumma. Dadda's mumma had long been called Oma and Herbert was Opa. They were accustomed to people coming and going; it was one of those homes, as Beatrice later wrote in her diary, where people called all the time. 'Just a knock on the door and they enter, that's if Mrs Blum isn't around to guard the perimeter! I rather like the easy way of it, actually, but I think at Cumquats it wouldn't work with all the acreage… Hahndorf is a friendlier place now than it was at the start of the war panics. However, I don't live here.'

Frank spoke of a former customer of Herbert's who had driven over from Melbourne and decided to break his return trip at Hahndorf to renew their friendship. He was staying at the Flachs' overnight. 'He's an interesting fellow, says he's an engineer of sorts and he's really interested in the new Model T Ford. In fact, he wants one. They're apparently very tough and versatile and cost about two hundred and ten pounds.'

This fellow had obviously infected Frank with his enthusiasm. Beatrice had to admit life was so much easier for them on Cumquats using Arthur's Talbot to get into the town or anywhere distant. 'We had a Ford before the Talbot. I didn't know the Model T could be built in bits and pieces. What is it William called it? That's right, they can be bought in kit form and assembled by any person with only a basic knowledge of mechanics. So William said. Would you really have use for one, though, Frank? Maybe later they're going to make one with a space on the back to carry things, like the American pick-up trucks. Do you not see one of those as being useful for your business?'

31

The three women were sipping one of the Cumquats wines and nibbling cheese biscuits. Julie was expected and was looking forward to meeting Esther's mother. Little Katherine was hoping for help with her jigsaw. Esther was brandishing the daily newspaper and tutting to herself and her friends as she read. It seemed that the coming year was to be opened with a flourish of newspaper columns and posters calling young men to the colours.

'At this late stage? Recruitment's dropped off alarmingly and Victoria's apparently unable to raise its quota for the month.'

'Quota? I thought it was all voluntary since Billy Hughes lost his referendum. So how could they impose quotas?'

'Goodness knows, Mama, but they need an indication, I suppose. Says here some recruitment committees are no longer properly organised and fewer men are coming forward. Hardly surprising, in my opinion. They recognise the futility of it all.'

Elena agreed, nodding. 'I've seen some of the damage caused by the hatred, the sheer bigotry of some of the so-called best people in this town. I've protested to patients on occasion and so many say they're sure this year will mark the end. Here, we're a close-knit community, which makes some of the incidents all the harder to bear. You agree, Esther?'

'Certainly do.'

'Oh look, you two, this goes over the page. They're appealing to those eligible to consider enlisting as a matter of duty and honour.'

'Fiddlesticks, Mama. People here have lived through it. Duty and honour can be laid at different doors nowadays. We need to keep safe and healthy the young men and women we have left. In war, quickly trained and ill-prepared, they're mere cannon fodder. And the republicans are calling louder than ever and striking a welcome chord with many. Sorry, Mama, but I empathise with that too.'

'Goodness, your papa would be shocked to the core to hear you say that.'

'No, he would not, Mama. No denying his patriotism but in that core of which you speak was bedded pure common sense. He'd be glad beyond measure that his own sons and grandsons have not added to the loss of all our future generations. If I remember correctly, back in 1910, that Christmas Will and I came home, after the old king died and Will recounted the mourning in England, didn't Papa say something about him – the old king – being, as he put it, a little removed from our Australian reality? That was quite a concession from an avowed monarchist. Anyway, there's another angle. Since the *Lusitania* was sunk, I read that America is arming itself with new ships, aircraft and things. Perhaps they feel vulnerable and angry but if, if, they enter the war, there'll be men – and women – enough to add to our numbers, I'm sure.'

Mrs Blum came into the room. 'Mrs Todman here, mum. Sorry Missus Symonds, but that Lilian is on the telephone for you. Again.'

'Oops. I wonder what it is this time, Esther. I must say, though I shouldn't, that Lilian seems unable to make a decision on her own. And yet, as I keep reminding myself, she's very good at the accounts and at forecasting expenditure.' Beatrice unwound from the cushions and headed out to the telephone.

'Oh Julie, hello. I'll introduce you to Mama when she comes back.'

'Julie chuckled. 'Not to worry, Ess. I believe she may know who I am! We'll talk when she comes back.'

'Mumma? This jiggle-saw is broked. I have a blue sky piece here with a yellow flower and no yellow flower to put it in. I fink it's really Ralphy's jiggle-saw wiv a steam train an' Ralphy's outside wiv Bertie, looking after the little baby chickens.' Katherine handed the piece to her mother then sat back on the rug, cross-legged, to concentrate on her jigglesaw.

Julie leaned over to help place a fat red hen piece and somehow the conversation resumed among the other women about the virtues of keeping hens and the possible inclusion of duck eggs for baking…

Beatrice returned, smiling. 'Sorry to be so long. As soon as I put the telephone down from Lilian, it rang again and I'm sure I sounded impatient as I answered. But it was William, Esther. He wants to know if he can come here over New Year, to celebrate the coming of the last year of the war, so he says. Always hopeful, is William.'

'Lovely, Mama. Of course! We'll fit him in somewhere.'

'He's bringing someone with him, Esther. Be here on the 29th. You'll never guess…it's Erica!'

'Well, well, Mama. We have the two sofas…we'll fit them in. Mama, I confess Will spoke to me about his liking Erica when he came up for the twins' christening. He said he was hopeful. However, time has gone by, over a year now. I'd heard nothing so I've said nothing! And Mama, I'm sorry not to have introduced you, but you know of Julie…?'

Beatrice leaned down, put out her hand. 'Hello, Julie. Esther's spoken of you of course and it's so good to meet you. I do enjoy meeting her friends.'

Esther mentioned how plans were being made for Christmas and Katherine's birthday. She was concerned that the little girl had only one celebration a year when other children had two. 'Poor little girl. Sharing her birthday with Christmas makes it too easy to overlook. We shall have to ensure she knows it's her special day too! Now, how can we separate the two events? All ideas welcomed!'

Ideas flowed along with another plate of crackers and a sip or three of the wine.

Beatrice sat back, feeling quite at home among her daughter's friends. 'How about a birthday pancake breakfast…?

A chorus of hand clapping greeted the suggestion.

Elena sat down on the carpet to help Katherine complete the jigsaw. 'Back to your extra visitor – Erica can have a bed at my place, Esther. I should be delighted to meet her, another female doctor. We could swap notes! She'd be very welcome. Even if you or your brother take her round the countryside all day, as I'll have to be on duty for much of it, she can sleep at my place.'

'That's very good of you, Elena. I'm sure Erica and you will get on –
you have so much in common. Goodness, what's that row? Is it Ralph?
He's positively howling!'

A very red-faced and muddy-booted Bertie marched into the room
regardless of the scattered rugs. He was dragging a most reluctant and
rowdy Ralph by the arm. 'This boy 'as put the baby chicks, Ma'am, only
two days old, they are, in the 'orse trough to swim!'

'Oh my goodness, Ralphy! Bertie, have any survived?' Ever the
practical Esther.

'Ralph! Those poor little chickens!' That was Ganma.

Elena's shoulders shook a little as she exchanged a grin with Julie and
they both earnestly tried to complete the jig saw with Katherine.

'I've told 'im he can't come out with me any more these holidays,
Missus Esther. He's allus up to tricks. He knows them's chickens not
ducks, Missus. Only one drownded, so could be worse, providin' the
others Mrs Blum 'as dried in the towel don't catch cold. 'E're 'e is, Missus.'

The young perpetrator looked wide-eyed at his mother. 'Mumma, the
baby ducks wanna swim. They said so to me…'

'Upstairs, young man. With me.' Esther sighed. 'Elena, Julie, Mama,
I'll sort this out then see you back here. Now, come with me, young man,
and we'll decide what to do with you. I know one thing: you always liked
being out with Bertie and I know he's taught you lots of things, but not
this. I think you'll have to stay indoors now and play with Katherine.'

The other women smiled as they heard the boy protesting to his
mother as they climbed the stairs. 'Oh no, Mumma, that's not fair – she's
a girl…'

32

It was certainly a busy Christmas Day that year. Later in the day, other family and friends were to join them but very early in the morning the growing Flack family all awoke to a pancake breakfast, Little Miss Three's favourite food. Then a game of pass the parcel in which she caught her birthday presents.

Beatrice was pleased to see how Esther, the very commonsensical Mumma, was giggling in delight as with her little daughter and Ralphy, she and Frank and the others played the simple games and had fun. It was good to see her enjoying the children and not deliberately assessing behaviours and developmental traits. *Why does being a mother have to be such a challenge for her? She's actually doing a marvellous job with this four but it's rare to see her shedding that schoolmarm skin. One day, maybe…*

David and Julie came along for lunch – Christmas dinner, as Mrs Blum proudly called it – their son Michael choosing to share Bertie's feast in his little chalet, ostensibly so he could help watch out for a stray fox that had been threatening the young chickens. Elena came but had left messages at the surgery if she were needed. Mrs Blum excelled herself at the dinner which, to everyone's delight, included tiny copies of her Yorkshire puddings. She declined to sit with them at the table, though, but they all helped to clear plates and put out the dessert. Today it was a chilled chocolate custard with preserved pears, a favourite of Frank's. Beatrice and Julie talked for ages about the individualism of sons, a conversation shared riotously by Kate.

Evelyn vigorously defended what she called the independence of young women, which invited a few comments from her father. Yet Herbert himself enjoyed an earnest discussion with David on the follies of organised religions. Joshua was spending the day with his new fianceé in

Adelaide; Kate hoped this was a hopeful sign for Miriam's family accepting Joshua. She did wish that her middle daughter Inga and her husband lived nearer. However, now they had the telephone installed, she heard from them more than before, and Evie and Inga had always connected, in the way sisters can.

The four children had a square table put to one side of the room and were being thoroughly spoiled by everyone. At one stage, they all four broke into giggles, even the two eighteen-month-old toddlers. Frank looked at his four offspring in wonder – such beautiful children, how could they be his? Yet little Arthur had his Opa's nose with its distinctive broad bridge and little Katherine two dimples just like her Oma namesake. Her hair was the nearest in colour to his own, but his had always been like straw in his estimation, whereas hers was sleek, shiny and so pale it could look silver not gold. Esther's hair was a dark brown with red glints to catch the sun – that must be where Jacinta's glorious flame-coloured hair came from, and the boys' beautifully drawn black eyebrows from her too.

He sat back into the cushions while the conversations went to and fro around him. *My Vati says their black hair is from his mother, the midnight maiden. It gives me a warm feeling to know something so good can carry from all that long-ago badness. Ralph's a bit of a mischief, says Ess and we have to keep him occupied. She feels he is almost ready for school. Well, he can read and he's starting to write – and Kathy's not far behind him. But he's not five years old until the middle of winter and I don't believe he's yet old enough to mix with strange children. Nor does Esther, but she worries he has an overactive imagination. My girls will also have a good education, I'm resolved on that. Look at what Susannah has achieved – gaining excellent marks already at university. She's dedicated but would have found it harder without Esther's help. Ralph? Well, we're just going to have to keep him interested in things – though perhaps not minding day-old chickens! Bertie slapped his legs. I'm glad I didn't have to. What can we do with the boy. Fishing? Swimming? I don't want him to have a knife for whittling. Not yet. Oh dear, I'll have to think...*

'Francis!' The cry broke into his musing.

'Yes, Mutti?'

'We're saying goodbyes now. Your father wants to check on that boiler. He loves having the steam, but oh, it worries him too much, I feel. Joshua called on the telephone to say he's coming home. I'm hoping things went well for him.'

*

Kisses and handshakes all round and not too much later, the Flack's Joinery household was its usual chaotic number. Esther and Mrs Blum were clanging and chinking in the kitchen, Ralph was sulking, the little ones were stretched out on the carpet building with the wooden blocks. Little Katherine was stomping around declaring it was her special day and her father and grandmother poured another drink and flopped onto the long sofa. Frank had to smile at the way Kathy flicked her shoulder-length hair around her shoulders and casually ran her hands through its layers.

Beatrice smiled. 'My word, she'll be a beauty one day, Frank. Those long black eyelashes are used to effect too, have you noticed?' She chuckled. 'You'll be worn out worrying over her when she's grown and being chased by the boys. I wonder how Jacinta will turn out? With that glorious red hair and pale skin, she's a smiley little girl but I wonder if she'll develop into a firebrand? Have you noticed how, toddler that she is, there are signs of determination there? I've noticed how those flexibly coloured eyes, so like her mother's, can also grow quite green when her temper flares. It'll be fascinating watching her grow. I hope I shall still be around.'

'Mama Beatrice! You're only the same age as my mother and, like her, you're young and active. You'll be around for many years yet.'

'I know, Frank, but losing Arthur so suddenly made so much seem pointless afterwards, no matter how I reminded myself I had so much to live for. And the war: the newspapers are full of battles, skirmishes and political angst. And on a personal level, the house can be so empty with George and his men in the fields, Lilian out with her friends or in the study. And now with George's encouragement she's doing more of the planting and gardening, and in her way, not mine. William seems to spend a lot of time in Adelaide and he's very reticent about whether he and Erica will marry. They're so good together but it's where they'll live, I think, that holds up their planning. To put it simply, I'm not needed there, really, not any more. It's so depressing. There are days I feel old age galloping up to me at a rate of knots, as Arthur used to say.'

That night in bed, Esther dismissed her husband's concerns about her mother. 'Papa used to call her quixotic, my Francis. She was going on to me about being surplus to requirements like that article about the old guns our soldiers are using. Yet in many ways she can be quite determined. And so can I,' she chuckled. 'It's Christmas and I notice you're wearing your new nightshirt. Does it fit you well? Shall we...?'

Needing no further encouragement, he jumped from the bed and ran over to lock the bedroom door...

*

William and Erica drove up from Adelaide, William driving a Ford Model T on trial.

'It's a superb little car, Esther, and we love it, don't we, Erica? To think the journey only took three hours. Mind you, we did stop and park on the grass at the side of the road overlooking the city below.'

'Yes, we saw right over to the sea, didn't we, William? Almost unbelievable, then we got to the point when the hills block the view. But it's all so beautiful.'

'Hello, Mama. It's so good to see you here too. I bet you like being here with all these little grandchildren, don't you? Is Esther bossing you around...?'

'William, you are dreadful! Mama, let's introduce him to the little people he won't recognise...'

'And I'd like to have a talk with Frank, Esther. Haven't seen him since Arty's christening. Is he working at home?'

'Arty? Is that what you call my little Arthur Francis, Uncle William!' Esther had to laugh. 'I rather like it. I find it hard calling such a little fellow such an awe-inspiring name – like his grandpa! We'll call it a godfather's privilege! Come on, let's go inside.'

She called the children. Ralph scrambled first down the stairs, closely followed by a tentative Katherine.

'Looks like the other two littlies are upstairs with Mrs Blum. Ralph, Kathy, say hello to Uncle William and Aunt Erica.'

William grinned. 'Factual title, my big sister, and true. Erica finally consented to be my wife.'

'Oh, lovely. Give me a hug!'

William pushed her off in a friendly way. 'I won't let her get away, Esther. We'll get it all fixed as soon as we can.'

'Oh, Will, Erica, I'm so very thrilled. You're so right for each other.'

Esther claimed a hug from each of them.

Frank had heard the car and came indoors, boots and all. He was quickly informed and was soon pumping William's hand and kissing Erica's outstretched one. 'Erica, how good to see you again. I'm glad to know you'll be joining this mad family! Now, Will, show me the motor vehicle.'

Beatrice laughed as Esther grimaced. 'Men are the mad ones. It's all about these new motorcars. And Erica, Elena wanted to be here to meet you but she was called out. She'll not be long, I'm sure. Fairly routine call, she said.'

'Oh, Esther, I'm looking forward to meeting her, I really am. You know, gaining new insights into her work and sharing some of mine. We'll enjoy each other's company, I'm sure.'

33

1917 had turned into a busy year, a complicated one, in Esther's opinion. Yet contradictory, because when she looked back, she found it hard to realise what happened when. As she asked Frank, 'Where did 1917 go? I think it's because all the things that happened seemed to speed the time along more quickly, it just flew along. Mama with us that first month, then the business grew busy. Dear old Opa Herbert fell ill and thankfully recovered – you were so worried. The children grew, developed new habits but each night I went to bed and then when the next morning broke I found the year was moving on and on, and…'

He looked up from his morning coffee and shook his head in amusement.

'Oh, Frank. It's already 1918, it's Monday 28 January and my oldest child is this day starting school. Like the *Advertiser* calls it, a red-letter day.'

Later, she stood in the playground as Ralph headed in a line with the other newbies into the school front door. At home he looked so tall, strong and stubborn; in this classroom line, he was neither the tallest nor the bravest boy. He was trying desperately to stop his bottom lip from trembling.

Yet despite thinking the past year had flown, when she looked at Ralph it was to realise that this day had been a long time arriving. How paradoxical was that? Since his escapade with the chickens a year ago, Ralph's tricks and antics had grown even more of a headache, and were too frequent. He needed greater challenges and she had been looking forward to his being kept busy at school. Now the day had come and she was in two minds to run and pick him up and take him home again!

She turned. Two of her friends from the quilting and sewing club were also watching their offspring take the first steps.

Jean called her over. 'Mildred and I are going into the café to lick our wounds. Coming?'

'Oh yes. Just what I need!'

They found a small table in the bakery shop, where Mildred promptly broke into tears.

'Sorry, you two. She looked so small…'

Jean forced a smile and they all broke into tentative laughter.

'Seems incongruous, really, yet isn't it so deliciously normal that we three mums are farewelling our children into school when in the wise world all around us the wars are raging.'

Mildred agreed with Jean. She bent over and whispered, 'Here we are having lovely coffee in a favourite shop and we wouldn't have dared come in here only a couple of years ago when the nastiness was at its height, simply because it's owned by the so-called enemies.'

Esther nodded. 'The silliness and the nastiness of war is still with us but somehow I think it's coming to an end, at least I hope so. Is that silly of me?'

'No, Esther, I feel the same. My husband feels that desperate acts by the Germans are defying the wishes of President Wilson in America. Not a good move on their part and John feels it's the beginning of the end. I do hope so. I have English cousins fighting in the British Army and my old mum is worried for her sister's boys. There are so many sad tales and you know what – it's on all sides.'

Jean said she had relatives too. 'My parents are still in England and they're old now. I have a younger brother somewhere in France at the moment with his regiment, a sister who was a nurse before enlisting and is now goodness knows where and two nephews in the navy. I so hope, for their sakes, that they manage to get home alive when the war ends. My Philip says Germany can't win it now the Americans are involved and they should recognise the fact.'

The young bakery girl came over for their order. Esther suggested they all indulge in a warm pastry to start the day and, laughing about their waistlines, they agreed.

Esther sipped her hot coffee. 'Frank feels much the same way as your Philip. Being of English extraction, I used to find it hard to understand how he felt because of his German heritage and the way he felt beleaguered at times. I learned how many Australians of German backgrounds are as loyal as any of us because their parents, or the previous generation anyway, fled from the most brutal suppression at the hands of their own countrymen. They had even more grounds for hating the Kaiser and when their own Australian-born children were blamed by others simply for being of German blood, like the nastinesses we know of around our own town, it was very painful for them. My Frank felt at times he was being wrongly judged and blamed, yet he was born here and his mother's English.'

Jean fished in her purse for a handkerchief. 'I have no German connections, so I didn't suffer any of the insults and other things. I just kept away – so how about that for selfishness! I didn't like the behaviour of some other anti-German types, though – certainly not all that rock throwing at the shop windows when it all started. That horrified me. I'm so glad a lot of that quietened down. At least it did for me and mine. Mind you, I hated it when a man came to the door harassing my husband to join a league for Britishers – I can't remember its name. My Philip was absolutely furious. He almost threw the man out of the door! I won't forget in a hurry.'

Mildred put down her cup. 'You know Mr Tognarelli in the ice cream shop? He came here after Italy opted out of its treaty with Austria and Germany – the Treaty of London, wasn't it, back in the beginning? Italy was promised rewards by Russia and England if they too declared war on Germany, though Germany had been their ally for years. Mr Tognarelli told me he's never been happier. He loves living here. He believes we should all be Australians like the Federation promised at the start of the century and not make differences. Certainly not for our children. Nice fellow when you get to know him, and I do because I love his new ice cream – he calls it *gelato*. He has a lovely big family and, unless I'm wrong, wasn't that his little Anna in the girl's line at the school this morning?'

Esther picked up her purse. 'That pastry was so delicious and running with plum jam, oh my. You know, my mother would commend Mr Tognarelli on his common sense. I certainly do. We all love his gelato! Well now, I'd better get back to the other children. Frank will be impatient to know how Ralph behaved – sad or happy, you know. But I have so enjoyed this coffee break – it's what we needed, I suspect! Let's try to meet here again. But I don't think I'd better indulge too often in these pastries!'

*

Esther walked home, her mind still on the café chat with her friends. The past year had been busy; no doubt that was why it seemed to have flown. Yet the bigger events weren't on her doorstep, so to speak. Her mother had returned to Cumquats after a lovely Christmas and New Year with them all, including Will with Erica. Elena and Erica had become firm friends. Opa Herbert's shingles had meant extra work for Josh and consequently Frank had given him a hand a few times. One huge surprise was that Josh went to Lobethal (now Tweedvale) to visit Miriam then came home on the Tuesday, married. Secretly, he and Miriam had arranged everything and even attended the North Adelaide Baptist Church, with her mother to be called forward, and made husband and wife. Because of Herbert's illness, Kate declined, although she gave the young couple her blessing, and when Herbert learned that Miriam's father's illness prevented him attending, he was more philosophical about his own absence.

At the moment, the young couple were living at the cooperage, where Josh's extensive bedroom had been converted to accommodate them. Herbert was happy with all this, particularly when the pastor had visited and blessed the young couple. His Katerin was happy to have them both around for a while, especially as Evelyn had joined an artists' group and went away for weeks in the country to paint and draw.

Soon after getting back to Cumquats, William had received a note from some British solicitors. Mrs Fletcher the Second (Beatrice's stepmother) had died at the start of the year. 'Those Gibsons didn't even let me know.

Now they're contesting the will saying that with her years of residency, as her family they have prior interests, as they phrased it.'

The residency referred to was the house bequeathed to William by Beatrice's father with provision for Mrs Fletcher to live there until her death. The surprise upshot was that William took ship for England, taking Erica with him. They were married on board ship by the captain! Beatrice recounted her concerns to Esther that their ship would be sunk by the German submarines. Nevertheless, their news had excited and worried Mama in equal doses. She was rarely off the telephone – her late evening calls were now almost routine.

William had written to her of the restrictions on board ship due to some wounded troops collected from Gibraltar to be shipped to England. 'There were so many of the poor blokes, Mama, and if their bodies were whole, most were mentally shot to pieces. A couple of their own doctors were looking after them and we were restricted which decks we could go onto. They slept up on the decks, because some, as one of the doctors told Erica, would go mad if they were confined. Mama, we grumbled about unpleasant incidents in our lives but nothing can equal the horrors they had endured.'

Some weeks later he wrote, as Beatrice recounted on the telephone to Esther, that he and Erica had taken up residency themselves in the Kendal property. 'Should be a straight forward case, Mama. Lots of your stepmama's personal things were taken by her family, the Gibsons. After that, we decided to make it our home for the moment. It's a very pleasant property, high up on a hill overlooking the town.'

Beatrice was keeping Esther apprised of it all as developments ensued. She even telephoned with some of the news but only after about ten o'clock in the evening, when she felt most of her party line listeners would be readying for bed. Those developments filled up what gaps existed in the otherwise busy year for the Flack's Joinery cohort.

Esther knew her mother was ambivalent about William's prospects; she heard all about it on the telephone. 'Mama loves the expediency and immediacy of the telephone, Frank, but she carries on in a histrionic way about possible listeners knowing her private business. Gets a bit annoying, in truth – especially when she calls late at night because she thinks most people are in bed! She's certain many of the Cumquats neighbours on the party line will know of William's plans, Frank. Rather than ringing so late at night, I wish Mama would put pen to paper more often. She says that things do seem to be moving towards William looking for a position in that Lake District. He writes that the matter of the inheritance has been cleared up. It seems they're living in the house. Also, he likes it there, and she says when he was over there living with her father, it was the area of his growing years. And he did gain a reputable degree from Oxford. He did some clerking there and here, so he's well qualified. Erica has relatives over there, too, so Mama's rather afraid Renmark may lose a good doctor and she her son.'

Then a letter came: Lilian had miscarried again. 'I'm writing because I can't risk this being heard. It's sad for Cumquats. I know she's a lot younger than George, but there comes a time to stop testing Nature. So I doubt I'll have any more Symonds grandchildren running around Cumquats, Esther.'

Esther read it to Frank. 'I'm sorry for Lilian and George, Frank, but even I feel glad Mama didn't relay that news over the party line.'

Remembering all these snippets as she walked home that first school day, Esther realised how lucky she had been in her own life. *George is say, thirty-five or so, and Lilian about twenty-nine. She was married too young. I think personally she never grew up. No, Esther, stop being mean: Mama says she is very clever at the accounting. That's good, because George isn't, nor is Mama.*

She looked up to the clouds, fluffy white ones tinted gold on the edges. 'Such a beautiful sight. If you are indeed listening, God, do thank your Mother Nature for me. I wanted four children and I have four children, four healthy and beautiful children, if a little naughty at times. I was a teacher and I wanted to have children I could teach, teach well and feel a sense of accomplishment. No matter how good the reports and the thanks of the parents of my pupils at school, my teaching of them was never acknowledged, no matter the level of potential I unleashed and excellence I achieved. I can now look at my own children, girls and boys, and know I am good at doing just that. By whatever means, I am blessed. Frank realises that, Susannah knows that, and I can be content. So thank you.'

She walked up the hill. 'God, do you know I was perhaps rather calculating in encouraging Frank, but time was running away from me. Teaching has its downsides. One is, as Mama constantly tells me, a tendency to put into practice in one's own home the theories that are brought to one's desk at school about children's development. She always told me to rely on my instincts at times when the rule book said one thing and I felt another. Yet I put those theories to good use in my teaching days.'

Two magpies carolled from the grass by the lane side, prompting a smile.

'Lovely birds… Also, God, being a teacher, with all the preparations and marking and other necessary tasks, does lock one away from entertainments and socialising. I needed a man in my life. The only other man I might have wanted did not want me. Frank is a good and decent person who also worked hard to build a business of his own. Neither of us had someone else in mind when we knew it was the right time. Also, no doubt about it, we both knew from our own parents' examples that mutual respect and liking were a good start for a relationship. Love grows anyway…if encouraged, does it not? So why, when everything is so beautiful and working as it should, do I feel that I'm doing something wrong, or not doing enough? Papa used to tell me I was often at war with myself.'

It was with a thoughtful expression on her face that she met her husband and elder daughter at the door.

'Oh, Ess, how was the boy?'

'Mumma, was Ralphy good at marching in a line? And why you got jam on your face?'

34

'This letter is grubby but still sealed, though it looks like somebody read it first, Esther. I do believe it may be from Willem in Holsworthy... Oh, joy of joys, he's all right...'

Not only all right, Esther thought as Frank handed it to her. The young man had filled a page with small, neat writing and it was full of news.

'Frank, he even writes the date at the top in full, 14 April 1918. It's taken more than a month to get here. Ahah...he has been working with a group, a class in metal work and they've made a lathe, made all the steel parts of it, every nut, ratchet and bolt. He started off making a spade to dig in the vegetable garden and he plays football and goes swimming and he's in a diving team! Oh, Frank, the young man has had a charmed life, it would seem. He's learning a special craft. Oh, my goodness! This writing is neater than mine, Frank. He must have had some schooling of the usual sort, too.'

'You know Ess, it's heartening to feel that some goodness can come from his arrest. But he doesn't say if and when he may be released, or where they'll send him. We'll reply and let him know he can come back here to work if he wishes.'

'Hold it there, my Francis. Michael's becoming a very talented timber worker. How will he feel being replaced?'

'Not even thinking of that, Esther. Michael is a good carpenter, yes, but he's also very good with the carving and the twists and curls on the veranda posts. And you know what? A lathe would be most welcome here, one day. But if Willem comes back, he can help me with all the stairways and structural work, he was always good at that, and Michael can help when necessary but perhaps concentrate on what your mama calls the fiddly bits. We've done pretty well over the last couple of years. Mind you,

I still feel guilty when I know how many window frames we made after all those broken window episodes. I still feel I shouldn't have charged for making them.'

'Francis! Don't talk such nonsense. You're a businessman. Did we not pay for our broken workshop display window? Its replacement glass wasn't offered for nothing, despite all the protestations of sympathy. Nor did we expect it to be – we, like all others, have our pride, Frank. You belittle your heritage talking that way. However, it is just so good to hear from Willem. You must let Bertie know and, yes, I'll write back from us all, so any messages…?'

She picked up the day's *Advertiser*. 'Dame Nellie Melba's in the United States and she's raised £75,000 for the war effort. Hmm – our war effort or theirs?'

'Esther, we're on the same side now, you know! More to my interest, turn to the next page. The original ANZACS are returning home – they're in Sydney, and they're receiving no official reception. Oh, how penny-pinching is that! How badly we treat so many good men…' He stormed back to his workshop.

Goodness, poor Frank. He takes everything so personally.

*

It was a dreadfully wet and windy June day when Mrs Blum ushered an equally wet Julie Todman into the warmth of the living room after announcing her in her usual hearty way. 'I'll put on the pot, Mrs Flack. Coffee, is it not?'

Julie was excited and had brought a copy of the *Chronicle* from the day before. 'Sir John Monash has been put in charge of the AIF! Is that not wonderful? David feels that if he had been the commander way back, the war would be over by now. Instead, they gave command to those fuddy-duddies whose warmongering was back in the last century. Well, so said David!' She smiled, a little embarrassed. 'You see, he's Jewish – a Jew from a Prussian background, no less. It's so difficult in these times to be…well, different. And to be so acknowledged. David feels so proud, almost as if he's a relation or a friend. His wife was a friend of David's cousin's mother, so there is a vague connection.' She sat down with a self-conscious shrug. 'You must think me childish but now, above all, David feels there will be a significant turn in our fortunes.'

Esther looked heavenwards. 'Oh, I do hope so, Julie. I worry for my children. Will we ever feel free again to say as we feel, do as we want without penalty, imagined or otherwise?'

'I know how you mean. My Patricia's now in her second year at the Mount Barker High School, and Irene will follow in the new year. I'm not sorry we moved them from the Grote Street school – I didn't like Patricia being away from home all week. They've had their own difficulties but none to fill them with dread and David and I try not to emphasise the war theatres and losses, and all the awful stuff, when they're home. However, I know they all follow the various battles at school, so I just let them get on with it and we try to talk things through. And now that General Monash is at the helm we should see the end of things this year. Of that I'm convinced. He's a genius with mathematics, you know. To David, that means the man can organise tactics. Oh, Esther, this coffee of yours is lovely and mellow. Where did you buy it?'

The conversation developed into a cosy country chat, particularly when Elena dropped in. She had received a letter from Erica. 'Esther, you're to be an aunt! I'm to be sure and tell you. Your William is to be a father. She says they had a celebration over there for something last Easter and…'

The three women rolled in laughter on the cushions.

Esther was delighted. 'Goodness, it must be very early days. Easter Sunday was…when? The 5th of April.' No more needed to be said.

Then as if on cue, Mrs Blum announced a telephone call for Mrs Esther. 'It's Mrs Beatrice, mum.'

'Goodness me, a call in the morning!'

Esther didn't care for the 'mum' form of address but Mrs Blum said it was now the done thing for responsible housekeepers. She had agreed it could run its course and told Frank, who really didn't care one way or the other, 'Our Magda has fits and starts with enthusiasms and something else will take its place soon.'

'Mama, hello! What's so urgent that you aren't waiting until all your listeners are in bed?'

'Oh, Esther, don't tease! William's to be a father, Esther, I'm to be a grandmama again. Isn't that wonderful? The pity is that he's staying there for a while, at least for the next four or five years, to see how things work out and maybe have a second infant and then, when school looms, they shall come home.'

'It's lovely news, Mama. He said "home". He's obviously not thinking of becoming English again. Relax, Mama. Start embroidering some lovely baby clothes such as you made for all my babies.'

Elena raised her eyebrows at the implication and made her point when Esther returned. 'Esther, you can't assume they'll have the two at once. Yes, William's a twin but Erica isn't, so there's no guarantee their family of two children will be completed in less time than your mama fears.'

'William's twin George has twins — well, Lilian more correctly and she didn't know of twins in her family. This whole business of heredity has fascinated me ever since I gave birth to Jacinta with that flame-coloured mop of hers. You know, speaking of Jassy, she has requested a new hairbrush for her birthday! That's only a few weeks away — where does the time go! And she'll only be three. Arty has asked for — you'll never guess — some coloured pencils!'

Julie chuckled. 'His nick name suits him, Esther — Arty the artist.'

Esther nodded. 'For one so young, he really does have an eye. Well, that's what Evie Flach tells me. I'll show you something.' She left the room for a moment and came back with a cardboard folder. 'He drew this recently. It's in chalk, hence the cover. You'll get it all over your fingers.'

'Goodness, Esther. It's Mr Blumberg's red tractor, and recognisably so. Look at the detail on those huge black tyres — all the ridges.'

Esther smiled. 'And underneath,' she carefully lifted the tractor picture to reveal one of a huge tabby cat smiling. 'And look what he wrote: "M O G". Our old cat, Mog, is preserved for ever in chalky chalk! He does like his drawing. Jacinta loves to write the letters of the alphabet but if it takes too long she gives up. She doesn't have her twin's patience. Funnily enough, Katherine seldom draws but when she does it's really clever. She likes to read now and, yes, she tries to write the letters as they sound to her. I think I should teach her to write music. She'll be just five when she starts school next year. I'm a bit concerned because when I was speaking to one of the teachers about Ralph and I mentioned she was to start there, though not for another year, the teacher said I shouldn't have taught her to read. He went on to say that Ralph's reading's already a problem – he's way ahead of the primer they use. That's why the boy gets bored, he said.

'Thinking of my own teaching years, I asked if Ralph, and another little girl who's a competent reader in his class, could be given a primer at a suitable level. He looked at me in horror, telling me he has thirty-seven children in his class and they learn the same things at the same rate. "Six years old to start learning letters is policy!" So he shouted at me. He was at the end of his tether, I think, after a year of change. The basic problem is that they became so overcrowded after the closure of the church school.'

Elena looked at her friend. 'I've known you for quite some time now, Esther. You're an intelligent woman, a professional educator who taught, latterly, in a private school, a prestigious one, one where resources were plentiful and expectations high, yours included. No, don't pull a face at me, my friend, just ask yourself if you're expecting too much from a little school that's recently been turned into one from three, that's had its curriculum upturned. It has only four teachers, one of whom is still struggling to teach in English to conform. They're good people, intelligent too, but fighting their own war. Have you thought that you might be able to help? And how?'

'I understand, Elena. But there's no way I could step into that school. Yes, I'm a teacher but I haven't taught little children, new pupils, for a long time.'

'Think of it, Esther. You've taught your little toddlers to beyond anyone else's expectations, yet you've done it gently, persuasively – they're not under tension. So why not take your children from the school for maybe a couple of years until things settle down, sort themselves out. Perhaps other children who've been put into unsuitable age classes because of all the upsets could join yours?'

'Oh, Elena, I value the way the school's central to the community. I think my children, all children, benefit from meeting and learning to be with other children. Ralph has made a friend, Peter Kirksch. His mother and I have decided it will be good for them to meet up in the holidays as well as at school. He has the best part of a year there yet and Kathy doesn't start till next year. I do have yet another two still at home who'll need my attention for another two, maybe three, years. I admit, Frank and I have wondered about sending the children to Mount Barker school. Yet I feel we can keep the children mentally challenged if needed. And would moving to another school not spread the over-crowding problem? Mount Barker school is only about four miles and with the car – yes, Frank's insistent on buying a motorcar – it would only be a short drive, though twice a day. Schooling at home isn't good – they need that contact with other children, we feel, though we're still thinking and talking about it. Now, my friends, are you still on the coffee or who would like a glass of Cumquats vineyard vino, to quote Mr Tognarelli, to drink to my young brother William and the lovely Erica?'

35

'Look, Ess! Here's a report of our Australian troops. Do you know how they celebrated ANZAC Day? It says here, with a victory in France! They surrounded the little town of Villers-Bretonneux that General Ludendorff's men had surrounded days before. Well, I hadn't known too many details but the battle to regain the town had been going for two or three weeks before two of our Australian brigades went in without any artillery cover and encircled the village in tough combat. The report says our troops were unflinching. Oh, Ess, I feel so proud.'

'Oh, my Francis! How could anyone ever think you're not a proud Australian!'

'Not so quick, Ess. It says we lost almost two thousand men. And it does touch us locally… You know the Friedrichs up near Lobethal, where I did that big staircase and carved the ornate newel post with a dragon? They lost a son in that battle and the father only found out recently about his death. He told me out in his barn so his wife wouldn't see him cry. I can't imagine… His lad was a young Australian-born bloke with a German-born father who had cousins in Germany on the other side, a most unhappy tangle. No one had heard from the lad for too long and they worried. It seems he'd anglicised his name totally to enlist – his family did not know of that – and when all the families were advised of casualties, the authorities didn't link a Frederick with a Friedrich. It was a friend in the city who chased up the story for him. He died for his country, Ess. This country. Only twenty years old. There's another brother in the thick of it all and he volunteered by putting his age up, like many of his mates. Yet some bigots out there call us traitors.'

'Oh, Frank, my love, it's been nasty. God bless those brave young men. Our own small battles seem insignificant when comparing, but we have fought in our way. However, the only way is to feel optimistic, to hope and trust as we look to the future for our children. And what did my papa always say? "We're turning the corner." We don't encounter so much of that nastiness now, do we? How long since a window was broken wilfully, or that awful HUN word painted on doors? How long since that abhorrent business of pig's heads and trotters being thrown onto family gardens? Not that I ever understood the reasoning behind that horrible gesture. No longer do you see people avoiding each other on the street. Here we walk down Main Street and see people we talk to, exchange a friendly comment. I take Ralphy to school, meet with other parents, all so natural now. I feel we're almost back to being normal, except for the dreadful war tally we face every day in the newspapers, and of course from stories you learn as you go about the business.

'You know what I think? We're obsessed with this war. No! Allow me, please…I understand, but think for a minute. The first thing we do is read the paper in the morning, for lists of wounded, for war-related happenings. It has affected us and our town and our state and our country, yes of course, but it seems to me we talk some days of little else! It's affecting our conversation, our business, our every thought.

'Talking of conversations, Mama is becoming greatly incensed by the way in which all her – and our – news passes down the party line. Another complaint: she met a woman in Renmark's High Street, someone whose face she vaguely recognised, who congratulated her on William's good fortune in having a house in England and being able to make the choice whether to live there a bit longer or not. Then she left with the comment, "It must be nice to be so rich." Mama's been peculiar about the telephone for a while, I know, but now declares she'll only write letters unless she wants a quick answer on something. My father always resented what he called the interference of telephone calls, so might it be an age thing? So if I don't have calls from her, I shall not fret, Francis, I'll look forward to an occasional letter instead – for non-urgent news and chatty stuff.'

Frank smiled, knowing his wife also despaired of having Hahndorf news passed around Renmark after talking with her mother. *Has Esther the time to sit and write letters?*

She more or less answered the unspoken question. 'So, Frank, I propose we stop buying a newspaper for a week or even two. Let's talk of other things, and it'll leave time for other tasks too. I do tend to read the papers from cover to cover. And Ralphy has a birthday coming up in July, the twins in August, I have one in September and you and Kathy in December. Happier celebrations. Let's indulge in happiness plans, my Francis! Small events they may be in comparison but they *do* matter!'

For six days, they indulged only in anecdotal gossip, mostly from Mrs Blum, an enthusiastic shopper and gossiper when she felt it advisable to be in the know.

Then a letter came from William with the postmark of Kendal, Westmorland.

'Frank, this has taken nearly five weeks since writing, according to the date inside. He says a few cases of Spanish flu have occurred in Kendal and the outlying district and they've quarantined some wards in the hospitals. Goodness, it must be worse than just taking an aspirin. Erica's been doctoring in the hospital in the children's wards and William's worried for her but says she claims to be immune because she's had her share of various illnesses due to her work over the years and she's always managed to get over them. He says this influenza is spreading all over Europe.

'And listen to this! Erica wants their baby to be born in Australia and, oh, Frank! She says it is babies, plural. They're expecting twins! Oh my goodness, was any other family so blessed! He says they must arrive here well before Christmas and he's written to Mama to see if they can stay at Cumquats as they have the space. Oh, that is such lovely news. Mama will be thrilled.

'He's been planting and organising the garden. He says it's pleasant gardening over there, not worrying about the sun drying out the soil. He never has to hose the flowerbeds. Hmm, I wonder what he's planted… Says they actually have more rain than he'd like and wishes he could send some to Mama, who's told him of their dry weather and the low river.

'He sends his love to everyone as he says goodbye. It's nice to hear from him. All seems well, though I think we should find out about this Spanish flu, don't you? I'll buy a newspaper tomorrow.'

*

Ralph had a wonderful day at school on his birthday. The little boy felt quite grown-up. Dadda had promised him a penknife for when he was six and at breakfast that morning he had unwrapped one. It had a red handle with his initials, RRF, carved along it.

'Oh, Dadda! Can I take it to school to show my friends?'

'No, Ralph. It's not allowed at school. I've spoken to Sir. Some boys aren't sensible with knives. I know you are – you've used one in my workshop and know all about how to hold it, how to carve with it. Other boys don't. When Peter comes round to see you, you may show him. You'll keep it high on the shelf above your bed or on your own bench in my workshop – and if ever, *ever*, you leave it somewhere else where your sisters and brother can find it, be warned that I will take it off you until you learn to be more responsible. Is that fair?'

'I s'pose so, Dadda, but can I tell my friends…?'

'Yes, and you can tell them how careful you have to be with it. Now you're six, I think you know how to be responsible. All right?'

Esther had no qualms about the penknife; it was she who had suggested it for Ralphy's sixth. Her brothers each had their first penknife at six. They had nicked their fingers at odd times as they whittled but nothing more. *All boys have penknives; whittling and carving, if they are good enough – and Ralph might take after his father – keeps restless fingers busy and occupied.*

Esther looked for news of the Spanish flu in the paper and learned little. 'Perhaps it's run its course, Frank.'

Frank was pleased to read of Germany's defeat at the battle of Amiens; they were pushed back to the Hindenburg line. 'Many prisoners were taken. The Germans had had enough, throwing down their helmets in surrender. This has to end soon, Esther. They must all of them be at the point of desperation.'

'Who can blame them, Frank? The battle was fought with tanks and low-flying planes and the Germans were battered, really battered, into submission. Tanks! Oh, how awful… According to the report, many of the Germans say they're simply fed up with the war and were glad to be taken. Oh, is this the beginning of the end, my Francis? With Arty and

Jassy having their birthday next week, it's all suddenly such a happier day today for looking forward.'

Mrs Blum made pancakes for breakfast on 27 August. Ralph enjoyed them before going off to school and aunty Elena came to share in the occasion with her little titian-haired special girl. Not that Arty was forgotten. She gave him a little box, called a pencil sharpener, to hold in his hand. As his new coloured pencils wore down and needed a new point, he could put one in and with a few twists – possibly with Mumma's fingers, he thought – it would sharpen to a new point and toss out the little bits of wood not needed.

Aunty Elena smiled. 'Safer for a three-year-old than a penknife, Esther!'

Esther's birthday was on a Sunday. Mama broke her new rule of not telephoning so that she could wish her a very pleasant day. After the service at church that morning, to which she'd taken Ralph and Katherine, some of her quilting ladies, as Frank called them, gave her a box of Haigh's chocolates.

'Oh, how wonderful. Thank you so much!'

'I was in the city, Esther,' said Elaine Featherstone, 'and simply could not resist a visit to their shop. You give me so much lovely fruit from your trees to make jam, this is just a little thank you and your birthday seemed opportune. Do take them home and share them with your husband, don't open them now!'

Ralph and Katherine were quite astonished that Mumma had a present.

Katherine muttered as much to Ralph as they walked home. 'Mumma always says she's happy with what she has already and gives us a hug, doesn't she, Ralphy?'

He thought so too but decided quietly to have a think.

Frank and Mrs Blum were delighted that Esther's friend had thought to bring her such a lovely gift up from the city especially when Esther assured them, 'We'll share them after dinner tonight with our coffee, Frank – and you Mrs Blum.'

Katherine asked Mrs Blum what she could do to make something special for Mumma and Ralph disappeared into his father's workshop, to his own little bench. He knew what he could do.

Oma turned up with Opa and Aunty Evelyn, who was immediately grabbed by Katherine to engage with her and Mrs Blum in some whispered conspiracy.

Frank broke open a bottle of Mama Beatrice's white wine: 'the last one left!' Esther was hustled onto a chair with a full glass, protesting that it was only lunchtime, just as Elena walked in, carrying a lovely tulip bulb in a pot for Esther. Oma revealed a bottle of White Opal to follow the Cumquats wine and they settled into a happy bunch on the sofas. Not long after, Julie and David turned up with Michael, whereupon Frank led his two mates out into his workshop, with Michael invited too.

'Women talk!' laughed Opa as they exited with alacrity. 'Your wife's a popular lady, Frank.'

In the workshop, Ralph was not too pleased to have his peace disturbed; they all wanted to know what he was doing.

Dadda came over, quickly got the unspoken message, put a hand on his son's shoulder, and steered his friends, with a surreptitious wink, over to the other big work table beyond the lathe. '*Meine Freunde*, my son is at his own bench and we have an agreement, he and I. He doesn't disturb me when I'm working, nor must I disturb him.'

They all sat around on a collection of simple three-legged stools and, exactly on cue, Mrs Blum rushed in with a cluster of stoneware steins and an impressive pile of cheese twists and homemade buttered teacakes.

'Mr Frank, Missus Esther says you probably want to tap your keg?'

Ralph looked over to them as Opa Herbert cheered and lifted an empty pot towards his son.

Mrs Blum turned to Ralph, winked, tapped her nose and put down a couple of fat teacakes and a tall mug of her lemonade near to his hand, with an assuring whisper, 'Not to worry, young fella.'

Very soon, the sounds of masculine merriment filtered through the plank walls of the workshop, causing Esther to laugh with her women friends.

'Mrs Blum says Ralph's up there too. I think he might be learning the beginnings of what it will be like to be male!'

She passed around the Haigh's chocolates to a chorus of 'oohs' and 'aahs'. When there were only four left in the box, she slipped them under a chair.

'You know, I don't like talking of the war but you probably all read the hopeful reports in the papers lately. I feel as if a huge load has been taken off my mind, that my children can grow up in a decent world free of war for their lifetimes. How about you all?'

There was a chorus of assent as Oma Kate broached the other bottle.

Esther lounged back in her chair and looked around at her chattering friends. 'You're all such wonderful people. I owe you so much for your friendship and your support and help when things went wrong…'

Kate threw a cushion at her, causing Esther to collapse into giggles. 'You're a wonderful daughter to me – is that not right, Evelyn? You're a good wife to my son and a caring and clever mother to my Flack grandchildren. Enjoy your day, my Esther, and with the war ending, enjoy your life!'

Elena clapped her hands and there was laughter and mirthful comments all round.

Mrs Blum knocked on the door and brought in almost-three-year-old Arty and Jacinta. They rushed to their mother, Jacinta claiming her lap and Arty sitting on her slippered feet.

'Missus Esther, I'm bringing in a pot of tea now and also little Katherine has a surprise.'

In came the tea. Cups were poured and then, with Mrs Blum's steadying hand to help, a tentative, nearly-five-year-old little blonde carried in a tray on which stood a sponge cake in three cream-filled tiers. On its top was printed, lovingly and laboriously with the icing pipe,

I LOV

MUMMA

'Oh! Ooh ah, my Kathy that is lovely, gorgeous. I'm so happy!' She put little Jacinta on the floor, stood and gave her elder daughter a huge hug. 'You are so clever! What a wonderful surprise!'

Mrs Blum cut a slice for everyone, whispering to Esther, 'I know you won't mind the spelling mistake. All her own work, mum.'

Arty got his cake all over the carpet instead of on his napkin but Esther didn't care. 'This has been the happiest of birthdays. Everyone, I'm blessed to have such wonderful children and such friends.' She looked around the room. 'But where is Ralph to have some cake?

There was a knock on the door and, as if he had heard, Mrs Blum issued in a hesitant Ralph.

He saw the cake but with great determination directed his eyes to his mother. He held out a piece of wood to her, a shape. It was recognisably a fox: a lean body, hugging the ground, tail extended and a lifelike dog sneer of determination beneath its screwed up eyes. 'This is for you, Mumma. I carved it with my new knife. 'Cos I remember you like the one Dadda made for you a long time ago so I copied it. It's a fox and it's looking for a chicken, Mumma.'

It was all too much for Esther. She burst into tears. 'I can't remember when I was last so happy! Look, I can see every whisker on the fox's tail – you're so clever, my Ralphy. Thank you.'

She looked at her friends, tears of happiness still on her cheeks. 'I have no worries about the war as it affects me and mine. Friends who give me such wonderful comfort and gifts, and my darling children… What more could I ever want?

*

In bed that night, Esther granted Frank two of the remaining chocolates.

'Oh my, oh Ess! Where does such inspiration come from? Our big boy has a talent – I'm so thrilled at that. And these chocolates are delicious! And you've had such a wonderful birthday, I'm so glad. You deserve it. Esther, my dear wife and mother of my wonderful children, come here, Liebchen…'

It was a long time before they fell asleep that night.

36

'It's all coming to an end, Esther!' Frank folded up his newspaper and gave a broad smile. 'It says here how the Allies are breaking through in so many places. This article says Flanders, where the whole horrible war began. Look here, on this page is about the heroic Arabs with that General Allenby in Palestine. They're slow in reporting, mind you – they date this 1 October. They mention that general again and, wait for it, Ess, "Patrols of the Australian Mounted Division of Allenby's army are also converging on Damascus." That division, they say, fought from Egypt to Gaza, captured Jerusalem and freed Palestine from the Ottoman rule. Ottoman must mean the Turks, Ess. You remember that English major who rode camels – Lawrence? It says here it was his tactical guidance that ensured the success of the Arab revolt. My, oh my…he rode his camel to fight the Turks all the way from Arabia with the son of Sheik Hussein and the son will now be the king of Syria. Oh, Ess, this is like reading to Ralphy at bedtime!'

Esther smiled, placed some folded linen on the table and picked up the other paper. 'Oh dear, here's a headline, Frank, about that Spanish flu William mentioned. It's not good news. However, William and Erica were to land in Melbourne yesterday, so they're well out of it now. I'm so eager for Mama to telephone to say they're safely at Cumquats. He might tell us something of the epidemic of flu as it's supposed to be over in Britain. Do you remember last week when there was a report of a steamer ship quarantined in Darwin with fifty people on board? It certainly seems a nasty infection but not necessarily a fatal one. Remember Erica's earlier comments from her hospital? I think it's good that Hahndorf's not one of the busiest places and we have the lovely clear, fresh air here.'

Mrs Blum came in. 'Your mama, mum, on the telephone.'

'Oh my, I wonder what's happened? Or perhaps it's William…'

It was only a quick call and she reported back. 'Mama just wanted to let me know William and Erica have arrived safely. She said she'd let him tell us all the news – he's already written a note and sent it to the post for me. She no longer feels safe talking too much on their party line, she says.'

Only three days later, she received William's letter. He had enclosed a photograph of the house and garden in Kendal.

'That looks a biggish house, Frank. Oh, look at the rows of planted vegetables – he must have been busy…well, I think they must be vegetables in such lines. They'd hardly be young vines over there! Frank, he writes – and this is just on arriving at Mama's – that they're so tired. They've had enough of travelling. They're staying a while at Cumquats.

'They had a very boring five weeks on the seas, because Erica insisted on them eating in their cabin as much as possible and they avoided all the get-togethers. She'd even brought masks to wear if necessary! There were a number of wounded soldiers travelling back and William says they looked exhausted even at the end of the trip. Importantly, no one on board contracted the flu. However, he had a cold because Erica said they had to get their fresh air when no one else was around, so it was usually getting dark and very cold when they prowled along the decks! But she's well, growing very big and, according to William, the ship's doctor was very cross that she was sailing so late in her condition. He says he had to argue with that doctor that Erica was not yet quite seven months. As if she didn't know, her a doctor!

'He says that Lilian has put together a package of all double stuff for them to use, and the pram the twins used, which has been well used since, is still there. Dr Roberts has asked to go round, though he's now officially retiring at the end of the year. He wants to see Erica.'

She flopped down among her cushions. 'I'm so envious of Mama being there, Frank, but William also says that after the babies are born he plans to drive over here to see us. Erica and Elena have been corresponding. She hadn't said, and I didn't know but it is so pleasant.'

The Armistice, signed at the eleventh hour of the eleventh day of the eleventh month, seemed almost an anticlimax. The morning paper later claimed that the end came almost at an unexpected speed.

'Listen, Ess! It was all signed in a railway carriage in a forest in Compiègne, in France. Marshall Foch was even last month planning a new offensive for 14 November – that's tomorrow! It says it was General Ludendorff who was panicking, begging the Kaiser to sound an immediate armistice before the front gave way.'

He read on. 'All politics, Ess. It reports that the generals refused to surrender, that High Command refused to be involved in surrender negotiations. It goes on, "Hindenburg and Ludendorff faded into the background and although Germany had officially admitted defeat, the generals would not enter into the surrender negotiations. It was a civilian, accompanied by two minor – though influential – army officers who came with a white flag." How can they admit defeat and yet not agree to negotiate a surrender, Ess?'

'It's all politics, as you say: politics and semantics, my Francis.' She sat back in her chair, frowning in contemplation. 'You know, this coffee tastes better than any I've had for a long time. So…it's over.' She carefully put her cup on the table then startled Frank by jumping to her feet, skipping over to him and pulling his paper away from him. 'We've done with the newspapers, Frank. Come, dance with me! The war is over, *yes*! And for all of us, a new beginning!'

Mrs Blum came to the door. 'I heard shouting… Oh yes! And Mrs Kate's on the telephone for you, mum. She asks if you've read the paper…'

Esther ran to the telephone but it must have been a short conversation. She returned to Frank, smiling. 'Mama Kate says that church bells are to ring out and the other Lutheran churches are to do the same thing, maybe all churches, like they used to call us to service. She's so excited! Funny, but no one else at the school gate this morning seemed to know of any developments but Mama Kate says two of the shops down their way have decorated the windows with the Union Jack and one has photographs of their two sons who were lost and a young cousin too. And some have put streamers up and Mr Tognarelli is giving away free gelato on Saturday… Oh, it's so pleasant to know it's over, Frank.'

'Liebchen, not many of my friends read of the world war happenings as you did. They're more interested in the price of the wursts, that we cannot use the pigs as we wish, that so much must go to the government. It's then made in the government factories into that tinned meat for sending to the troops, Ess, did you know? But it makes pigs expensive for a farmer to kill. But yes, they'll decorate when they think it's all over. And I heard there'll be big marches of all the troops when they return. You know, there are still many personal battles behind house doors – not all can come to a peaceful and happy conclusion. The luckier returning soldiers I would have thought to be too exhausted to blow up balloons and just pleased to be – what do they call it? – demobilised to go to their homes, embrace their families and close the doors on the world. Oh, who is that banging at the door?'

Mrs Blum came in, grinning from ear to ear and clutching the elbow of a stocky young man. He was dressed in what looked almost a military uniform, and was carrying a hessian bag with a stitched seam and handles. The young fellow had a worried look on his face.

She's caught him thieving, Frank thought, then he looked closer and grinned. 'Willem! They've released you. Oh, man, I am pleased.' Frank stepped forward and clasped the younger man's outstretched hand. 'Willem, how good to see you again, and looking so well. But we thought next year…'

'Missus Esther, we were released because it was better for us not to risk the Spanish flu. Or so one of the guards told me. I had to give address and, no, I don't have the sickness but I wonder do I have a job? If not, I…'

Frank was still clasping Willem's hands. 'You have, my friend, but we're different now, bigger, and you'll stay and we'll talk, yes?'

Another knock and in came Mrs Blum, being her usually forthright self. 'I brought Michael to meet Willem, mum. I knew you'd want this.'

'Did you now, Mrs Blum? You need not be concerned. Mr Frank will allow the two young men plenty of time to get to know each other. I'd like you, if you would, to prepare enough lunch for us all, including Bertie, say for an hour's time? Thank you.'

'We'll walk up to Bertie's hut, Willem.'

Frank nodded to Michael. No introductions were necessary, he knew of Willem's internment, so the lad smiled and shouldered Willem's bag. As they went through the door, Willem handed to Esther another newspaper, well creased, but a Sydney one, dated the previous day.

She read that before the Armistice, the Kaiser had abdicated his throne and fled Germany hoping for asylum in Holland. Seemingly, units of anti-revolutionary soldiers caused others in the German aristocracy, including King Louis of Bavaria and five other German kings, princes and grand dukes to be chased out of their castles. 'Oh goodness me! We didn't read of this. Apparently,' she read out loud to Mog the cat, 'the new German chancellor, Prince Max of Baden, is "of liberal persuasion" and he handed over to the president of the Social Democrats, Friedrich Ebert, a trade union official and a saddle maker! This Ebert stood up in the Reichstag, proclaimed a republic and announced that arms were to be distributed to workers' and soldiers' councils. Oh my, oh my, I do hope it won't go the same way as Russia… It reads on that the "socialists have taken their cue from the Bolsheviks". That will disturb Frank when he reads it but at least we have Willem back with us. We shall hear his tales over lunch.'

*

Bertie joined them for lunch and Mrs Blum kept popping in and out between giving the twins their lunch at the kitchen table – under Katherine's big-sisterly watchful eye! Bertie was delighted to have Willem back to share his hut, and they were busy planning how to rearrange it to how it was when Willem was with him before.

Willem said his mother and other family had disappeared; no one knew what had happened to them. He continued, 'So many of those who were in Holsworthy with me are to be deported. I thought I would be too but when I was called in to the guard hut, they showed me your reference, Mister Frank, that you and Bertie wrote for me so long ago. I'd also been active in the camp in the metalwork groups rather than the *Kamp Spiegel*, the camp paper – and apparently that was a good mark for me. But I must see the constable here before nightfall today and then perhaps I might have to report regularly – whatever the Hahndorf constabulary say. I have a release paper to show them. I'm very lucky, you know. Another one to be released is an old man whose name you'll know. He's Edmund Resch who makes beer – he has the big brewery.'

'Resch's beer!'

'Yes, he was more than seventy when they arrested him only about a year ago. I never knew him till I saw him at the camp police station. It wasn't really bad there if you kept away from the activists. At first I, too, was angry all the time. Then I found I could learn writing, reading and specially metalworking! Some men actually made a lathe – they made every bolt and ratchet and blade. *Wunderbar* stuff. I saw some of their work, and I learned a lot from them. I hoped if I learned it would help me when all the bad stuff came to an end. Our huts were small and they said basic but I shared with some good blokes and we were friends. They kept asking my name and my surname. "Ils", the guards said, isn't German but Norwegian. Then one read from a paper that although Norway was neutral in the war, it had given Britain control over their very big merchant fleet because of something called a tonnage agreement. They decided that was a very friendly act towards Britain. So I'm not an enemy!'

'Goodness, Willem! Your language is German. Was that then from your mother?'

'I suppose so. But in many ways have I been lucky. I was able to learn new things and also I belonged to an athletics club and kept fit. So now I look in the glass, see I'm a man and probably twenty-four or twenty-five years old, healthy and grateful for my new life and being able to come back to work for you, Mr Frank. And I see again my good friend Mr Bertie and meet my new friend Michael.'

37

Christmas 1918 would be a strange one, so forecast the newspapers, as they reported on the Spanish flu pandemic. The advice was comprehensive and challenging: avoid crowds, wear a mask in public places, wash hands and faces; sneeze and cough into handkerchiefs; wash bedlinen daily – well, certainly pillowcases; wash fruit and vegetables before eating; and at the first symptoms, see your doctor. At that stage no one knew of another local who had succumbed. However, it effectively halted the usual seasonal shopping excursions.

Poor Dr Elena was almost under siege. After all the colicky babies and runny-nosed schoolchildren with scratches that 'bled black blood', she tried to stem such hysterical panic and maintain what she called common sense. The other surgery in the town was similarly beleaguered and Elena took to putting notices out that listed possible, even probable, first symptoms, hoping to calm people's fears. However, she happily came to join the Flack's Joinery family for their Christmas dinner and to find out how her friend Erica's babies were faring, but Esther had heard no more and when she telephoned her mother on Christmas Eve, she spoke to Erica, who whispered that she had been having twinges for a week but nothing significant.

'Mama's obviously warned Erica about all the tattling and tale-telling that goes on after the party line chats, Frank. It can be so frustrating. I want to know more!'

Then, seemingly only hours after the last call, William rang. He actually shouted over the telephone, 'Esther! Boys – I have two sons! So alike they are too – peas in a pod! Lovely young chaps!'

Mama was pleased to complete the news more sensibly. It seemed the twins were born on Boxing Day and William teased that to be marvellous, applauding the skills of pugilism, a sport he had taken up at Oxford. As Erica later confessed to her, his attitude to boxing as a sport horrified his wife, to whom all violence was abhorrent. His argument that it was a game of skill and tactics and a healthy outlet for supposed male aggression bore no weight for Erica.

'Oh, goodness, Frank, that will delight those other ladies who listen into Mama's calls! It was unusual for Mama to be so candid but, do you know, I don't care and nor should she! This is all happy, happy news!'

A letter came a few days later from Erica, with annotations by William that sang on the page. 'The baby boys are true Symondses. Like me, blond hair and grey eyes. Choosing names was hard, Ess. Most of the best boy's names, to my mind, are taken. But the infants arrived on St Stephen's Day, so one will be Stephen. Erica remembers a name in her family – Pyotr, pronounced Peter – so another is Peter. I rather like Oxford and Fletcher as second names but she's not convinced.'

Nor am I, thought Esther.

Another letter, entirely from Erica, settled the matter. 'The first twin was arguably on the chime of midnight on the 25th, depending if one's clock was fast or slow, and the clocks in Cumquats do go crazy at times. So we plumped for St Stephen's Day and he'll be Stephen James. I had a dear friend called James who I found out recently was killed on the Somme – he's named for him. The lazier baby will be Nicholas Peter. You know, they're identical, absolutely, and I've put an anklet on each of them with their first name. Later, as they grow, we'll spot differences as with Rosalie's brothers, Alexander and Aaron, I hope.'

The comment made Esther call the double As to mind. 'You know, Frank, I couldn't distinguish Alex from Aaron when they were smaller. Now, if I remember correctly, they were born in December 1907. Goodness me, they'll be almost eleven and I simply don't remember their birthdays as I should. Now they'll be starting growing spurts so they may change in appearance, differ a little. Hopefully! When I went over for Katherine's first Christmas, they just looked like all little boys look. I know I still had trouble determining one from another. I wonder if I could ask Lilian to send me a photograph of them, and of Rosalie of course. Ralphy still talks of Rosalie, you know. Children never forget, do they?

'Well, Liebchen, why not have photographs taken of our four and send some over to Cumquats? That might start something.'

It took until almost the start of the new 1919 school year, but Esther took the children and her none-too-willing husband to the Mount Barker studio of a visiting Mr MacDougall, Photographer, from Adelaide. When the prints arrived, her favourite was undoubtedly the family one, with an immaculately clad Frank standing at the rear, his hand on the back of the chair on which Esther had been placed, Ralphy standing at his side, Katherine standing by her mother, and Arthur and Jacinta sitting cross-legged on the floor. They had photographs taken of the two girls with their mumma and the two boys with their dadda, and one of the four children as a group.

The photographer, when she collected the prints, stated repeatedly that colour photography was being developed in America and London and he could hardly wait. 'Imagine, Mr and Mrs Flack, a photograph of your two daughters with their absolutely gorgeous hair colouring, sitting together, and the two boys – so sooty-haired. Colour will surely be with us before many more years pass.'

Esther did find colour a tantalising prospect, even though his description of sooty-haired sons did not inspire. Frank told his parents he had done enough posing and dressing in a starchy collar, while admitting he was pleased it was done. His sister Evelyn did suggest they ask her friend Sallie to paint the children, rather than wait until whenever for colour photography But Esther didn't really care for that; she favoured leaving their friends undisturbed, like all others similarly affected, to get on with their lives at their own pace and preference.

Her mama actually telephoned to thank her for the photographs. She was so excited. 'Oh, they are growing into beautiful children, Esther. I do think Ralph has a look of Frank and yet that sideways smile reminds me of your papa.'

A letter from Beatrice spoke of Lilian planning a trip into Melbourne and wanting Beatrice to go with her. It was all a matter of finding a boarding school for the older twins, apparently. Not imminently, but for the following year perhaps when secondary school began for them.

'Apparently, Alex wants to be an engineer – irrigation and water, in all its behaviours. He takes after his grandpa. Aaron isn't sure. He talks of horticulture and viticulture. You know that includes my vines, so I hope! But I'm not really in favour of sending the boys away for a term at a time. What is your experience, Esther? Does absence from home alienate the children in any way from their home life? William says it didn't hurt him – and he was on the other side of the world, not just a train ride away.'

'Oh, I shall write back straight away. I'm more worried about her venturing into the city when they're in the throes of this flu pandemic. I'll ask if Erica doesn't have concerns. Mama could bring the virus, bacteria or whatever causes it, back to the children. And William and Erica's are vulnerable newborns too. I shall try and persuade them not to go. Surely, if this school's not for a few years, there's plenty of time.'

A few days later, there was a telephone call from Lilian. 'Esther, this doesn't concern you…well, yet for a while until your children are older, but it's necessary to get the boys' names down on a list as early as possible. That's why I want to go. And they do say the numbers of sick are falling somewhat. By the time we go next month perhaps, the statistics may be even better! So don't worry about your mother either. Don't dissuade her from coming. She's out in the vineyards at the moment, where she usually goes.'

Not a pleasant call and the fact that her mother was outdoors meant that no doubt Lilian had seized the opportunity, party line gossips or not.

Esther refused to allow Lilian to upset her. Anyway she was quite involved with settling her own children back to school, or, in Kathy's case, starting her for the first time. Ralph was eager to be back with his friends and play footy. Nor should she have worried about Kathy either. Her little friend since babyhood, Dottie, was also starting and was in her class.

Kathy didn't even want to kiss her mother goodbye at the school gates; in she marched, little cardboard case in her hand at the ready. Esther did notice there was an extra teacher and that the classes, or their lines, seemed smaller. Kathy had already warned Esther that she would learn her two times table that day and tell her at teatime!

As it eventuated, all she spoke about at teatime was that her name was Kathy at school. 'Like at home and not Katy or Katherine. And Dottie found a new friend called June and we're sharing her.'

Dr Elena was worried that the school was starting as scheduled. She would have preferred the school to have waited another month before returning and allowing the pupils to mix and mingle and congregate, as she described it. 'Measles was bad enough last year but this Spanish flu is nastier. If we can all avoid contact with the city and postpone a few community events so as to keep people separate as much as possible, we in Hahndorf and most other Hills towns with healthy lifestyles and good clean air…well, we might escape the worst.'

They were sitting that first schoolday afternoon in the Flacks' living room – Esther's sanctuary as Elena had called it during the war. Another of Katherine's drawings was being admired.

Julie had joined them as she was to collect Michael to drive him to a Mount Barker barber. She agreed with Elena. 'We're fortunate to live where we do. I don't miss Adelaide life at all, even though we don't have the theatres, cinemas and the other places. I have good neighbours, and even better friends.' She leaned over and took a hand of each of them. 'You two more than any. You know, I wouldn't be going to that barber with the boy but he has no other means of getting there. He won't let me or his father tackle it now and it has started to curl over his collar. You know, he's more man than boy, but in many ways he still needs caring for!'

Esther poured the coffee and offered one of Mrs Blum's oaty biscuits. 'You know what's so very enjoyable? We're sitting here discussing children's paintings, haircuts and fresh air instead of swapping notes from the papers on a battle's progress, who won, who lost and how many were killed and injured.' She sat down and curled her legs under her. 'The war – all that hatred, all that local prejudice – it dominated our lives yet now seems to have faded into the shadows. Long may it stay there.'

38

Then came a rare call from Esther's mother, whose first comment was, 'If my party line sharers are not cooking their teas, they jolly well should be! Now, my dear, discretion is the better part of valour. PARTY LINE LISTENERS, TAKE NOTE! I want to reassure you, dear, that I am not travelling into the city – Melbourne, that is. As you know, Lilian favours Melbourne over Adelaide, as her family's there. To put it simply, Victoria has closed its border all the way along the Murray – they're cautious about the Spanish flu. Also, the South Australian police are monitoring all the border gateways to keep travellers out of the state. At least that puts a hold on Lilian's eagerness.

'Lilian says the papers tell us not to panic, that strict procedures are already in place to limit its impact. But it's a ghastly disease, Esther. I simply didn't realise it can strike so swiftly, and apparently it causes victims' lungs to fill with blood and they drown! You can be healthy in the morning and dead by teatime and, so my paper says, young healthy adults are the ones attacked first, not the little ones and the very old. They're putting up an auxiliary hospital in Brighton, not far from the city, and probably in other places too. They're planning separate wards for male and female. They've appointed a matron to take charge. However, the whole state of Victoria is declared infected! They've closed the theatres and the schools. They only recognised the extent of it recently.'

Esther expressed her relief to Frank. 'She's not going. Thank goodness for that. She'll stay safe. But she's becoming quite angry with her neighbours on the party line. Erica said in her last letter that Mama is almost paranoid about listeners to her telephone calls since that woman spoke to her about William inheriting the house and all that. Perhaps that's a harsh word, paranoid. It's more related to mental instability and Mama is certainly not a candidate for that! However, since Papa died she's become, according to Erica, in some ways more volatile in her emotions, happy one day and depressed the next, though the babies keep her involved, she says. Apparently little Rosalie's quite close to Mama, and that's good too.

'Oh, Frank, I should have said earlier, Mama Kate rang me today too. Papa Herbert has come down with some spots or something that makes him scratch. He's worried about having shingles again, I think. He also has a business problem and wants your advice, someone or something you can help him with. Do you want to call over there this evening? Your tea can be ready in ten minutes if you want to go soon. I'll eat with the little ones and talk school stuff and baby chat.'

Elena came over that evening. She'd heard from Erica, so knew even more news of Cumquats than Beatrice had imparted to Esther. 'They're finding it hard living with Lilian. So is your mother, apparently. Lilian throws her weight around, saying the property was left to George and not William.' She gave a grimace. 'There's a lot of weight to throw around too, according to Erica. She says Lilian has grown so very fat.'

'Oh, has she now? Well, I know all about the legal arrangement, so do my brothers, as papa and mama held a conference with us all that Christmas time after William returned, and I was there. I also know that in law the property, all the bequests, if that's the word, were left subject to Mama's discretion. It all passed to Mama, in effect. I do know it's always been in her mind, as it was in Papa's, that George is the natural heir to Cumquats. There was an arrangement by which a substantial amount – regarded then as a fair share of the estate, I believe – was spent on William's travel, his board with my grandfather in England and his costs for his university education. I know it was all written down. Papa was meticulous in those regards.'

Elena continued, 'Erica tells me that William has only a sentimental attachment to Cumquats. He thinks of it as home but expects nothing more from it. As long as your mama is comfortable, that's his main concern. William and Erica have the Kendal property, currently it's being rented, and all he wants is to be made welcome when he stays at Cumquats.

Lilian is quite openly objectionable to Erica at times but she's also making snide remarks about your mama. Since she hurt that ankle, she suffers with rheumatism, according to Erica, and finds hobbling on rough earth around the vines…well, not the pleasure it was once. She's employed a local family – son and daughter-in-law of a friend – to help with pruning, picking, all of it. And she pays them. It's that which affronts Lilian, who has said openly that your mother has no right, that she's spending her and George's inheritance. William said your mother seems to have lost her fire recently – his words – and just sits and takes the insults. So William spoke to George and he was horrified that his wife is behaving like that. George spends much of his time outdoors of course, so he doesn't witness the unpleasantness.

'However, there was a huge argument between husband and wife in which her dislike of Erica, "that foreign woman", was screamed out. So William and Erica and their babies are wondering what to do, whether to go back to England or for him to return to his old chambers in Adelaide – apparently that's an option – and make a home in the city.'

There was a cry from upstairs and Esther ran to check.

She returned about ten minutes later. 'Kathy dreaming again. She has a vivid imagination, that child.'

But their time was over, it seemed. Elena had to leave; a baby was imminent and she wanted to visit.

Then Frank came home, relieved that the reason for his father's itches and spots was a new kerosene for cleaning. 'His doctor says he has an allergy to it – whatever that is. It's reacted on his skin anyway. He has some chalky stuff from that man doctor and rubs it on and it stops the itching. So it's nothing serious. Now, what has upset you, Liebchen?' He stubbed out his pipe and listened, then shook his head. 'I cannot imagine your mother just letting that happen, letting Lilian boss her about. As for George? Well, I only met him briefly, and I thought him an amiable fellow and, as your papa would have said, a true man of the soil. I know Lilian only from your comments. William and Erica I like. It's all an unhappy state of affairs.'

'I agree Frank and – oh, there's the telephone bell. Are you expecting a call?'

A knock and Mrs Blum was at the door. 'Telephone for you, mum. It's your mama. She says it's urgent.'

'Mama, hello!'

'Sorry to telephone, and so late, dear. One point: all those listeners are hopefully in bed! But…oh dear…I've had a row with Lilian and she was rather unpleasant. She actually says she can't live with me, because she's the lady of the house and there can't be two of us. You see, local people always ask for me, not her. She's asked if I'd rather live with you and Frank. Well,my dear, I want to tell you that it's not personal because I love visiting you all in Hahndorf, but this is my home that Arthur and I built up together back in whenever it was. That soil in which my grapes grow is my soil, Esther. I'm staying here and I've told William so. He may telephone you, that's why I'm telephoning so late. I wanted to tell you first.

'Don't be upset, Esther, for any reason. I'm not an old decrepit shred of humanity. I believe that's how she referred to me, screaming at the top of her voice. I'm apparently too big for my boots too. Yes, I am a little hurt that after so long here she seems to dislike me so strongly, but above all, I'm angry, dear girl. I will not tolerate such behaviour. If push comes to shove – as dear old Mary Lee used to say, bless her – I'm quite aware of my own powers of financial control here. George is very upset indeed at her attitude and he's said she should go to stay with her family for a while and assess her lifestyle and position at Cumquats, as he's not leaving and nor will I be. It's good that both my sons are conscious of my feelings, Esther, but I'm so sorry to be the reason for the unpleasantness.'

'Oh, Mama, you're not the reason, not at all. I – we – have an idea from William and Erica of what's going on. You'll come here any time if you wish to, but rest assured I also know of your love for Cumquats. I do feel that perhaps you should assert yourself a little more, Mama.'

After a few more comments, she hung up the instrument and collected her thoughts in order to pass on the main points to Frank, who had anxiously listened to one half of the conversation.

It was almost a fortnight before Esther heard again from Cumquats. She had been debating whether or not to telephone but knew her anxiety would transmit and that would upset her mama, so when William rang one mid-morning, she was relieved to hear his voice.

'Hello, Ess. I won't take up too much time – I'm calling from the post office. I know Mama told you of events. Well, Lilian's now at her parent's place and looking forward to a shopping spree with her mother in the next few days. That's the story we've put about. She may stay away a couple of weeks or so. The boys are still with us here, going to school and all the rest of it, as is Rosalie. Little Rosie and Erica have quite a bond, which is nice to see. And the lovely young Dodds girls have more or less grown up with Rosie and without Lilian interfering – she had the attitude that the Dodds were only servants and would thereby be a bad influence – Rosie's quite enjoying being taken under their wing, for girly stuff, you know what I mean.

'You know, Ess, I rather like this fatherhood thing. My two baby sons have had their ninth-week birthday and they're gaining weight rapidly. They had to go onto goats' milk, which has upset Erica a little, but they have voracious appetites and they're thriving on it. It's useful having a doctor as a mother! Mama's quite the Queen Bee again, and she's organising the household better than I remember for a long time – all to do with Lilian being away, I think. George is quite upset at how things have turned out but Lilian's mother has telephoned him and seemingly assured him she'll give Lilian a talking to. I'm not sure what that involves and frankly I don't care as long as she learns – and earns – her place in the team. On the plus side, Mama's grapes are coming along well for the end of February. She says they've defeated the drought.

'I've been asked to do some legal work on behalf of a farmer neighbour who was sold some inferior feed for his pigs. You know, I thought pigs ate only scraps and wallowed in mud. I'm learning, Ess!'

He chuckled, a pleasing sound to his big sister, for whom it implied a happier Cumquats environment. She returned the chuckle, relishing the rare, long chat with him.

*

Later, Esther carried an elevenses tray out to the workshop, Arty and Jacinta hopping and skipping after her but coming to a disciplined stop at the workshop door – they knew they were not allowed in. Frank had Michael monitoring the lathe as he turned some ornamental posts for a new hotel balcony. The design was a very fetching twist, a spiral; Esther fancied having some new table legs in that design. One day, perhaps! Willem was further over the small paddock cutting the lengths of timber. Esther loved the smell of timber being cut, sawn and worked; it had a lovely sawdusty smell like the butcher's floor. She grinned at her own simile; as if sawdust would not smell like timber!

Frank was pleased to hear that things at Cumquats seemed to be settling down, albeit temporarily. He hoped it meant Esther would be more relaxed about matters. He did feel she worried too much about her mother. Though his mother and hers were something of the same age, his mother's welfare seemed not to concern Evelyn at all. His Mutti did fuss over his father, Herbert, however. He wondered if it was the age group…

'Esther, Liebchen. This is a lovely cup of coffee. It's time we all had a break here, I think. The noise gets too much at times to talk.' He walked to the door, blew a long signal to Willem on his wooden whistle and plonked his stocky body on one of the stools. 'What does this day promise for you, my Esther?'

'A little bit of playing school time. Jacinta and Arty with Dottie's little sister are going to have some drawing with chalk and I'm trying their aptitude with letters. A for Arthur, J for Jacinta and D for Deborah. Then I'm going to see if they can draw dear old Mog, who spends most of his time asleep on a chair now so is a sedentary subject, and that will give us an M or a C. As much as anything, I want to teach them how to hold the chalk between thumb and index finger, properly, so later they'll hold pencils and be able to properly guide the point. So…fun all round! Come on, Arty and Jassy, let's have a bit of lunch before Debbie arrives.'

Frank smiled to himself. *Once a teacher, always a teacher, my Esther.*

39

'That telephone bell is so strident, Frank. Honest*ly*! Erm…right. Hello, Flack's Joinery…what! Hello… George is that you?'

'Oh, catastrophe, Esther. Oh dear God, what will I do?' His voice was broken by noisy wet sobs and Esther blanched.

'George, Georgie, please what is it? Not Mama?'

'Oh, Esther, it's Lilian, my Lily. She got this Spanish fever, this influenza. She died, Esther, died…'

'Oh, Georgie, oh NO!'

'…and it looks like her mother will too and it was her father who telephoned and he's so cut up that I couldn't understand him. Oh, Ess… Mama's upset too but she'll help me tell the boys and Rosalie when they get home from school. Oh, Ess, excuse me…here's Will.'

'Hello, Esther. Shocking news. She telephoned to say she, her mother and her father had the inoculation at their local community centre on the Monday so she waited until Wednesday, to see if there were any after effects, before going into the city. The border was open because the authorities said there was what they called a quiescent period of infection – fewer cases, I suppose. They shopped then stayed at the usual boarding house that night – that's when she telephoned Mama, I think – then planned another excursion on Thursday after breakfast. She intended to go home on the train and her father was to meet them at the station. He did. He said they were both very happy showing him their purchases. Lilian had bought presents for her three and our twins and for the two Dodd girls – it quite showed the more pleasant side of her personality, more the old Lilian, no?

'However, it seems by bedtime that night her mother was quite ill and the doctor was called. He was busy and came in the early hours, by which time her mother was fading fast and Lilian was, as he said, breathing like she was blowing through a bottle, then she bled through her nose and mouth and it was horrible! She died about ten o'clock this morning, her father said.

'George is in a dreadful state. We're none of us allowed to travel there – the border's closed again. I don't know about funerals, even if there can be one, the infection is now so rife. Oh, dear God, Ess, we're all on tenterhooks now. Lilian's father isn't apparently ill at all but the inoculation, so the newspaper says, that many Melburnians thought would give them immunity was flawed! It hadn't been tested long enough and the causative organism hadn't been isolated. So her father isn't entirely safe either.

'You know, Esther, there'll be a terrible brouhaha about all this. The legal fraternity will make a mint of money. No, before you ask, not me – too close to home, Ess, too close to home. We haven't yet discussed things, Erica and I, but as you know we had debated moving. However, I feel George needs me at the moment, and he is my twin, as Erica understands, and we'll probably stay on here now until…well, for as long as we're needed – sort of a voluntary quarantine. I'll keep you in the picture, dear sister, but meanwhile, please keep you and yours safe and well.'

Esther's legs felt weak and she flopped onto the stool Frank thoughtfully pushed behind her at her first exclamation.

'Oh, Frank, I couldn't like Lilian. I never felt close to her. Lately with all this business with Mama I was even feeling something close to hate and now, oh dear, I shouldn't have been so callous. Now I don't like myself.'

'Come here, my Esther, cry on me, and never blame yourself.'

'Oh, Francis, I feel that everywhere there's unhappiness and conflict. It's a consolation to realise we know of no one here in Hahndorf with symptoms of this awful sickness…well, Elena didn't when we spoke this morning. She and the other doctor keep their fingers on the pulse of things, or so she insists when we talk. It's hard for her. I shall make us a cup of chocolate then I'll get up to bed and hope to dream away all the nasty things that have happened.'

It seemed as if it might be a cold winter and a wet one. Old Bertie came down with a shocking cold and generously passed it onto Willem, who gave it to Michael, who passed it to his parents, and when Julie visited Esther one Saturday, it closed the circle. A couple of days later, Esther was feeling terribly off colour. Intuitively, children being children, they knew they had their mumma at a disadvantage and played up, until they too one by one succumbed. Mrs Blum was squeezing lemons and raiding the honey jar for, so it seemed, the whole household. At the back of everyone's mind was the thought that it might be the Spanish flu.

It was not. By the following Saturday, Esther was recovering and she and Frank were sitting at the kitchen table, Frank still finding relief for his sore throat with Mrs Blum's lemon tea and honey.

Esther was flipping through that day's paper. 'We don't scour the pages any more as soon as we buy the paper, do we? All those weeks of the war – we used to scour them for news and talk of what was being said and done to our friends here in our town. It dominated all our thinking, Frank. I used to worry and have nightmares. Sometimes – and this sounds quite shallow even as I say it – I feel that one way or another I'm at war with myself, with my feelings. Or, more to the point, how I feel compared to how it seems others think I should feel. Do you know how I mean?'

Frank lifted his head from the paper. 'I'm sorry, Ess, I was just reading. There are two items worth the telling. One is that the German chancellor has formally signed the Armistice after kicking up quite a fuss about the terms.'

'What? Can I see… So does that finally mean it's all officially over? Properly? So the German chancellor has given up some territory to Poland – that's an interesting turnabout, no? Oh, and another thing, our Australian war casualties – to date they say, so they're not complete – are given as 308,752. That's 58,201 dead, 166,617 wounded and 83,146 sick, with an unknown number missing or still prisoners. Oh my, oh my! What a terrible price to pay for peace – all those sons, brothers, fathers, cousins and…and Bavaria has declared itself a soviet republic – how will your father react to that? That's where he's from, no?'

Frank made as if to answer but the door flew open and Willem came running into the kitchen, soaking wet and muddy-footed. He was crying loudly, tears rolling down his face. 'Mr Bertie, our Mr Bertie! He coughed so bad then he looked at me, said, "Be good, Willem" and stopped breathing! He just died, Mr Frank, died. He's gone, oh Mr Bertie.'

'Oh *no*! Frank…!'

Frank pulled on this boots. 'Esther, telephone Elena, will you? I'll go with Willem. Can you tell my Mutti, please, Ess? Oh, I shall miss him so, my good friend Bertie.'

Esther rang Elena, who knew all the procedures to be followed, then managed to put the telephone down in its cradle before bursting into hot angry tears. 'Oh, dear old Bertie, you very dear man.'

A long time later, Frank climbed up to bed and didn't wake her. He could see she'd been crying.

The following morning, quite early, Esther was supervising the children's breakfast and wondering how to tell the children about Bertie and whether Kathy was getting over her cough, when she had a telephone call from Mrs Alphonso.

'Missus Esther. I speak to Doctor Elena and she tell me of my friend Bertie. He was Catholic, you know, like me. He was a friend. I would like to attend him. You know I did other times…'

Elena was quite happy with that arrangement, and said she would contact the Catholic priest from Mount Barker. 'Bertie once told me he liked to go to that church. It's not yet completed but it has a nave, a tower and…well, holds services. We talked when I collected the vegetables. He knew I come from a Catholic background and therefore I would like to go to his funeral, if you would not mind. You and Frank and the children with their coughs and sneezes are better kept away. Leave it all to me, Esther. It will be my pleasure for a lovely old friend.'

'We'll all be going, I think, Elena. Well, Mrs Blum will, I'm sure, watch the children. And Mrs Alphonso has telephoned – she'll be going.'

They all met up at the funeral and most of Bertie's friends came back to Flack's Joinery for drinks and biscuits.

Young Alphonso – Al – now a pleasant-faced, tall young man was sad but pleased to remember Bertie. 'Mr Bertie was a friend to me, Mrs Esther, when other boys tease me because of the way I spoke. I was sad to hear of him going, but pleased to go to his funeral earlier today.'

Mrs Alphonso presented Frank with a rather grubby envelope. 'These were his wishes, Mr Frank. I have opened to see he is buried as he wanted. It is all good. There is message of thanks to you.'

'Goodness, Ess, the old man thanks me for being his friend at a time he needed one. He's written down what he calls the correct way to cut and preserve the cabbages for sauerkraut. Me? Oh Bertie, old friend. You'll be badly missed.'

Esther was trying to suppress a laugh and ended up coughing instead. 'Oh, Bertie, you dear man, it was me spoiled your cabbages!'

The Alphonsos, mother and son, looked at each other and grinned. 'Oh, Missus Esther, me an' Al heard Bertie many times say you cut his cabbages wrong way and not good cook of German foods.'

Esther's eyebrows shot to the ceiling but she recognised the truth of the matter. All good friends together, their smiles stretched to laughter so infectious the room echoed with chortles and chuckles and the occasional strangled hoot from Esther. Frank slapped his thighs and started coughing he laughed so much and even the children started giggling.

It took some minutes before young Al could intervene. 'You know, we'll remember that dear old man as one who brought smiles and laughter to us all in his way. He would like us laughing like this. Even the priest called Bertie one of Nature's gentlemen. And with happiness is how we remember him. I like that.'

40

'Esther, Esther? Come see. I bought a paper while down the street. I saw the headlines and it's an answer to what you keep asking me. On 28 June in this Lord's Year of 1919, at ten minutes to four in the afternoon, in the Palace of Versailles, the Germans at last signed the Peace Treaty. Now it *is* over. All formally written down, documented, all that. Our flag was going up on the baker's window and Mr Tognarelli, the ice cream man, was playing on that old wind-up phonograph of his on a table under the street blind. It was lovely, Ess – that Peter Dawson singing "On the Road to Mandalay". It made prickles come on the back of my neck, Ess! Then as I came up the street, special notices were getting painted on the dairy's big gates and someone called out to me, "It's over!"'

'Oh, that is wonderful Frank! And listen, open the door. Isn't that the St Paul's bell? Dong dong, dong dong dong dong. Oh, joy of joys! Now it really is all behind us! Go call your mama!'

The telephone rang before he could pick it up and he handed it to Esther with a grin.

'Oh, Esther, isn't it wonderful. It's all over!' Her mother was crying down the telephone. 'I so wish your papa could be here to share the moment...'

'Mama, he would be so glad to know we're all able to celebrate this ending, or this new beginning – whichever you choose. Be brave, Mama. I'm sending you a great big fat hug over the lines. As you've always said, put your right hand on your left shoulder, your left hand on your right shoulder and snuggle down into them. That's a big hug from all of us for you.'

Beatrice laughed at that and they managed to speak of happier things for a minute or two before Esther apologised for needing to finish the call, saying Frank wanted to call his parents.

They too were absolutely delighted, saying they could hear the other churches joining in the bell ringing.

'So it is really over. The Armistice was misleading in a sense, wasn't it? This report continues, saying that the Germans have accepted terms that were imposed on them virtually without negotiation. That's what I understood – that they were refusing to negotiate. It says here they refused to sign for almost two months! They caved in only under the threat of military occupation by the allied forces. The treaty has two hundred pages, Ess, and it's taken more than five months to be drawn up at the Paris conference of the victorious allies. It says that even the English were aghast at the French demands, yet Lloyd George, the British prime minister, who was campaigning for an election, had promised to squeeze the German lemon until the pips squeak. Apparently the French wanted really tough terms against the Germans and Lloyd George said that, in his view, the terms demanded are so harsh we shall have to fight another war all over again in twenty-five years at three times the human cost.'

'Oh no, my Francis, let's hope that's not prophetic. This has been quite enough, this one. They did call it the war to end all wars, did they not?' She sat down on the arm of his chair. 'You know, it will be marvellous not to feel obliged to pick up the newspaper to learn of some tragic event or other. I feel I spent most of the war reading and worrying about it. Now all that's past. Or so I hope.

'At church and at the sewing group, a recent comment from one of the ladies summed it up, that even the Spanish flu seems to have receded into the past. Life is almost as it was before the war, before the animosity became an accepted way of life. I couldn't readily agree with the Spanish flu comment since Lilian…you know…but I hope she's correct.

'One of the new quilting group ladies commented that we women feel we can now walk where we want without fear of being spat on, or criticised or questioned, even by the constables. That was one all-encompassing opinion expressed at the last meeting. The mothers at the school gate mingle and talk quite freely. As Emily Strauss put it, "Who cares who's what, Britisher, Italian or German?"' She grinned. 'Grammar aside, a lovely sentiment. You know I repeated that to Julie and she said how she felt quite accepted now in the township but David still felt there was a prejudice against him for being Jewish. She assured him that no one of her acquaintance suggests that David's anything other than a responsible man, a good tailor and honourable husband and father. Paradoxically, it's his parents who make Julie feel inadequate that way and she tolerates that prejudice, though it angers her at times when they won't recognise her children as their bloodline. Other members of their synagogue are more accepting yet she's still reluctant to drive down to Adelaide, in case she feels obliged to call in to let her children know their grandparents, which she hates doing. Isn't that sad?'

Frank looked up at her, and folded the newspaper. 'Your family and mine seem to have settled down, Ess, but what of you personally? Has your life resumed a normality, my Esther? Are you happy? For instance, when is the last time you drove down to Adelaide? Even perhaps to see Susannah?'

'Oh, Frank, I went down to buy fabric for Kathy's school dress and brought a roll home for Mrs Tilley's shop – she paid me for it of course. I had a look around Charles Birk's – if you remember, I bought you that lanolin for your hands. Another time I bought some yards of fine linen for your nightshirts, remember? And Susannah, she comes up to see her Oma Kate now and again and I usually pop down to see her there or she comes here – you see her too, don't you? I went to Mount Barker with Mama Kate to see Evie's submissions in their art show. You know, the fact that we can have an art show in the area strikes a nice normal chord, does it not?'

She patted his knee. 'I must go and pick up Kathy and Ralph from school. I wonder if anything was said to them about the war ending, properly ending. It's homework night for them both tonight and they need to sit down quietly and get it completed before I let them out to play. Mrs Blum has taken the terrible twosome to play at Dottie's house with her little ones, and I'm to take Dottie home first to meet them there, so I'd better make a move. You know, Frank. Life is now going to be so ordinary, so pleasant. I have a huge contentment feel – does that make sense? My days are quite full here in our own town and I have you and the children to care for and chase after.' She smiled. 'Mama and everyone at Cumquats will be recovering so, unless I have an unavoidable reason to go to Adelaide, or anywhere else, I really don't bother to go.'

*

One evening later in July, watching the twins – restless sleepers both – toss, turn and mutter in their sleep, she sat in the nursery chair, their latest picture book still on her knee. Little Jacinta flung her left hand out to her twin's cot and, as if he could see, Arty extended his right arm and their fingers touched, gently.

She smiled. They were really sweet, obliging children and so close to each other despite their physical and mental differences. Knowing about child development not only from her teaching but also from books and papers while in the profession, she thrilled to watch her own children's progress. At almost four years old, they were still delightfully childish and rompish, as her mother would say. In many ways, they thought the same way, liked many of the same things. Yet, despite her resolve to ensure that they had a mix of toys to share and opportunities to develop their individual imaginations, Arthur's art was starting to depict wheels, cars and mechanical things while Jacinta drew houses and babies and other people. Esther was fascinated by these gender-typical developments and was beginning to believe her mother's oft-quoted theory of 'Nature over Nurture'. *Mama has a head on her shoulders, that is certain.*

Downstairs again, she put the kettle on to make a cup of tea. She and Frank had been talking after dinner and she realised his interpretation was more rigid than hers; was more that children should not be allowed to develop naturally in their own time but that their development, at least in some areas, could be engineered.

She took in a mug of coffee and he smiled his thanks.

'Esther, now the children are in bed, let's talk some more about this Nurture theory.'

'Must we, Frank? It's been a long day.'

He took his coffee and she sat down. He had obviously been thinking while she was upstairs so she sipped her drink and listened. To be fair, in his own way, Frank had recognised the changes in his elder son but his response differed from hers. He thought to split up the children – in one way at least. He ordained – Esther's sarcasm was openly expressed on her face – that now Ralph was seven, he should be promoted to a room of his own; until an extra room could be made for Ralph, he thought the two boys could share.

Esther was quick to disagree; she put her coffee down on the table. 'Oh no, Frank, let's not rush into things. Ralph and Kathy are sharing quite happily, and I think they're young enough to do so – their gender development is only just beginning. What's more, they're almost the same age in many ways, like sharing their homework times and helping each other. And they don't disturb each other's belongings like Jacinta would if she shared with Kathy. Kathy's a tidy child, Jacinta anything but! And poor Ralph! We cannot make a seven-year-old schoolboy share with a preschooler who needs lifting out every night. No, it wouldn't do at all. Do believe me.'

'Esther, I think of this in a father's way and I'll decide what's best for my son. This is not just school stuff, it's the growing up of a young man. I think I know more of that than you do with your book learning and teaching of girls.'

'Frank, let us talk sensibly about this…'

'I have made my point, Esther. Your teaching was all with girls. This is not a time for theories, but a time for facts. I have stated my wishes and I am his father. Now I suggest you consider well my wishes and how it can all be effected. You can think about it while I go out with Josh to the club.'

Suddenly a wave of incredible anger swept over Esther. She stood upright so suddenly that Mog scuttled out of his basket nearby. 'Francis Flack! We have the family we both wanted. It's one I can raise to a standard we both expect, with my educational know-how! Yet here you are now denying my skills, gainsaying my abilities, my intelligence and my authority. I know where it comes from, this inherent chauvinism of yours. It raises its ugly head…and, if I'm confusing my metaphors, I couldn't care less! So I'm only fit to teach girls, girls the lesser breed are they suddenly? How dare you, Frank!'

He tugged his coat from the hook in the hall and pulled open the door. 'I'm not staying here with you shouting like to waken them all – and Mrs Blum and all the neighbours! I'll be with my brother at the Hahndorf Football Club.'

'That's it, take your male opinions and run from the truth! You're twisting my judgements. I've nurtured Ralph throughout this interminable war while you spend your days in the workshop or drive around to customers. The business has been your life, the children have been, and always will be, mine!'

Then he was gone. A motor started outside.

She yanked the door open. 'So you had it all planned, both of you! Going to that haven or hell hole – whichever – drinking beers one after the other!' A slam of the door and she plonked down among the cushions.

Ralph's voice came from upstairs. A tentative appeal, 'Mama, can I have a drink?'

Oh darn it, they'll all have heard.

41

Putting a smile on her face, she settled him again, sat between his and Kathy's beds, talking nonsense to them until they went off to sleep. She sat back in the old wicker chair there, allowing her anger to smoulder unseen and mostly unheard as she continued in whispers.

'I was convinced I could persuade Mama and Papa of our mutual respect and likeness, how Frank had measured all other likely candidates against me until realising I was the one he wanted and why – my "cleverness, my education and my ambition for teaching", that's what he wrote. Mama wasn't fully persuaded then. She had been concerned that Frank's ideas of female independence were different from mine. She thought it possible he might have absorbed more of his father's rigidity and might want me to confine myself to running a house, caring and cooking for him – all that. And how could I have doubted my motherliness? Or whatever it's called. I do love my children. They are themselves but they are mine too! I will help them become what they want to be in life. And it's not by separating them from each other. I don't know why or when Frank changed his thinking. When our children's welfare had been a concern he had usually accepted my point of view. Now, I sense his own history is catching up with him. He's starting to take a leaf from Papa Herbert's book on favouring sons over daughters. Ah well, think clearly, Esther.'

Arthur called out; she moved to the other room. She tucked the little boy into bed, dimmed the lamp and went softly downstairs.

She made a mug of chocolate and sat in the inglenook; Mog settled onto her slippered feet. Apple wood was burning in the stove with its own particular lovely fragrance permeating the sheltered little annex and soothing her fractured temper.

On another tack, she wondered if there was a problem between

Miriam and Josh, that Josh called so frequently to partner Frank to the football club. Miriam had said some time ago they were trying for a child; Josh of course talked of having a son.

There was a sudden thud as wind caused some smoke to blow down the chimney. She moved, disturbing Mog, who looked at her in disgust before springing onto Frank's usual chair. Rain was hammering on the windowpane, noisily enough for her to wonder if it would break the pane. It was a nasty night of weather. She didn't like the idea of Frank being out in this rain and wind; the wind was building up and thudding above the roof on the metal drum of the chimney. She hoped they were all right driving that dratted old truck of Josh's.

She picked up the paper and idly turned the pages. That British PM and his prophecies were repeated in one report. Her skin prickled in fear at the word 'prophecy'. God forbid there would be another war in twenty-five years. If it happened, her Ralphy could be taken to be a soldier, as would little Arty. Oh no! She was to be thirty-eight in September; if that next war happened as prophesied, she would then be over sixty. Mama… well, Mama is only now just sixty-three.

She shivered, and bent down to cuddle warm, furry, purring Mog. 'Dear old Mog, tell me to exercise my common sense. The twins are not quite four years old and so they'll still be in primary school in five years' time. Another five years after that, when I'm nearing fifty, Ralph should have his own bedroom and his artistic and sculpting talents should be refining themselves if they're to be part of his life. That's what Frank wants, of course: a son to take on the business. Oh, he can be so pig-headed, and so blasted male at times! But how artistic is artistic? Kathy has the gift of drawing – a few lines and there's a recognisable subject. And the expressions on her subjects' faces. Evie thinks she has a burgeoning talent but Kathy at the moment wants to be a doctor like her big cousin Susannah and Doctor Elena. Hmm, things change. You know, Mog, they're all different and they'll all have their chance but he's *not* going to force Ralph to share a room with a toddler. Nor will Kathy.'

A gust of wind thudded the lemon gum against the window frame again. Esther yawned but there was no point going up to bed; Frank would only wake her when he arrived home. Hopefully he would have had enough beer to mellow. At least he would stay dry, the silly man, even in Joshua's peculiar little vehicle.

Then the telephone rang. It was Miriam, Joshua's wife, crying. 'Oh, Esther, a farmer just telephoned to say Josh ran his truck into a drainage ditch by one of his fields. I've already phoned Papa Flach and he's whizzing off to see what happened and he'll call at your house on his way back. Papa said not to worry, you'll be his first call.' She put the phone down before Esther could answer.

Not that Esther would have known what to say. She had just exhausted herself criticising Frank's attitudes. *Oh, dear God! Let them be safe. They can always buy a new car or truck, whatever it is, but there's only one Frank – and Josh of course.*

'Hey, Mog! Was that an engine? Josh? Or the wind…'

With a violent gust, the front door banged open. It was Herbert looking exhausted and very muddy and supporting a wobbly Frank.

'He is unhurt, Esther, so is Joshua. However, I am their father so they have both suffered – that I hope – from my tongue lashing all the way home. I am now to take Josh to his Miriam and I trust she will let him know about his stupidity.'

He almost threw Frank onto a chair, then flexed his arms and stretched his neck. He turned at the door. 'In the days of horses and carts, a man could get drunk and not worry, for the horse would lead him home. But now, these mechanical transports have no brains and when their drivers are likewise, that is when trouble overtakes. The farmer is very decent, him. He will tow the truck to my house tomorrow.'

He gave a funny little wave. 'Goodnight, Esther,' and pulled the door hard, to close against the wind.

Esther turned to Frank. His head was in his hands, his elbows on his knees, and he was moaning. He looked so muddy, wet and pathetic. She moved towards him then was suddenly seized with an impulse to laugh, an impulse she quickly stifled. It was sheer relief but he wouldn't see it that way; he would take it as a slight at his behaviour. So, saving his dignity, she rinsed out her cup, bade him goodnight and took herself off to bed, Mog escaping with her.

'Moggy, he told me only this morning that the war is over – that was before he started his own. So now, with his self-inflicted wounds, he can interpret my actions as he wishes. In Mama's words, he can put that in his pipe and smoke it! Now you, puss cat, can go down those stairs, find your favourite step. Go!'

Next morning, Frank was subdued. Nor did Ralph mention their shouting of the evening before. Thankfully, Esther invited schoolish topics for chat when busying herself with the children. The wind had dropped, the rain holding off, but they dressed in their waterproof macintoshes – a gift brought from England by Uncle William – and set off with Mrs Blum, who'd take them to school. She wanted the shops, she said.

Frank went up to his workshop, saying only a brief thanks as she put his breakfast in front of him, and then he spoke to the little twins.

Later, as Esther was setting the two little ones to some drawing and colouring in, Willem came for their coffee and told Esther how Mister had the drafting table up. 'I'm to tell you, Missus Esther, that he's doing the drawing for two new rooms to add to the side of the house, one up and one down, and when done he wants you to give your opinion.'

'You know, Mog, when Frank finishes that…goodness me, what with all the legalese and paperwork, I think Ralph will be ready to leave primary school!'

42

Very little was said by Frank about the football club interlude but from his rather downcast appearance over the next few days, Esther surmised that Papa Herbert hadn't held back in his chastisements. She almost felt sorry for the two brothers, but decided it was best not to comment; best to allow it just to blow over – one of her papa's frequent adages.

Mama Kate had rung, commenting on Josh's new love for beer halls and bars. She confessed to Esther that she knew he and Miriam were having words; she had comforted Miriam one day but not really found out the cause for her tears. She said she was at a loss to know how to help.

Then Esther had an idea. 'Do you feel that Miriam might like to be more involved in the township, in the community, Kate? You know, to be busier? I seem to remember Frank telling me she worked in the office of a newspaper in Lobethal, Tweedvale or whatever it is now. I know she used one of those typewriters, or is it that she's called a typewriter, I can never get that right.'

'Goodness, Esther, whatever she was then, she's married now and Josh still has the idea that he must provide for her, that she should be content caring for him and her home.'

'I know, Mama Kate, but if I may, Miriam and Josh live with you and Papa Herbert and Evelyn in your house. She has no house of her own to clean, wash, organise…'

'Esther, please tell me you don't think we make her welcome!'

'No, no, Mama Kate. You know me better than that. But time may be hanging and she may feel she has too much free time, she may feel aimless. With Josh busy all day and at the workshop…'

'Oh, I see, Esther…hmm. I suppose, come to think of it, I manage much on my own now… I'll think on it.'

Esther and Mrs Blum were busy at the joinery too, making marmalade from the lemon, orange and mandarin fruit. Esther was always reminded of her mother when she was involved with the citrus, though here in Hahndorf she had no cumquats. She knew of her mother's success with drying them and some she cooked in sugar syrup to preserve them. She had told Esther how they were very popular on the market stall. She was discussing this with Mrs Blum when Dr Elena came to the door, knocked and called, 'Yoohoo!' She had a standing invitation to walk in if they were busy indoors.

'Esther, I'd like to introduce you to my new intern.'

Esther nodded and beckoned her to come in, then dried her hands. She turned from the trough. 'Susannah!'

Mrs Blum gave her a gentle shove. 'I can manage from here, mum.'

'Oh, do come in and oh, Susannah! You are Elena's trainee? Oh, how wonderful! I imagine Mama Kate is pleased!'

Smiles all round.

'She is. I wanted to come to see you because I owe you so much, Aunty Esther. If it was not for you marrying my Uncle Frank, I don't know that I would have persevered with the study. Oma told me you only married him because he wanted you to tutor me…'

'Oh no, Susannah, that's not quite so. Tutoring you was an added interest your uncle knew I could not refuse, that's all!' *Goodness me, surely that's not what's being said.*

They all laughed and Elena said they had time to stay so Arthur was sent running up to his dadda's workshop to let him know. Jacinta helped Mumma take a cake from the pantry and put out some tea plates.

Frank arrived within minutes and kicked off his boots at the door. 'Mrs Blum's bringing in coffee, she said.' He was smiling widely and gave Susannah a vigorous hug. 'So you're now a qualified doctor.'

'Oh no, Uncle Frank, quite a way to go yet. I've opted for this year of practical experience. I'll be here with Doctor Elena for some months and then next year I return to university part time for the second semester. On other days and nights I have some hospital studies to undertake; that will be for at least the following year. Then I'll have options how to specialise or go into general practice like Doctor Elena. But it's all beginning! I'm living with Oma and Opa. But oh, do stop the squeeze. I like to breathe, you know!'

She turned to little Jacinta, who was watching this new lady doctor with wide open eyes. 'Hello. Are you the little one who wants to be a doctor?'

'No, thank you, Aunty Susannah. That's Kathy. I'm only three years and nearly four. She's gone to school. I want to be a teacher like Mumma and Oma Kate. I can read.'

Even Esther was surprised at this. 'Oh, my lovely girl! But Susannah's your cousin, Jassy.'

'She's growed up, Mumma.'

Elena smiled. She would always have a soft spot for this one, her flame-haired little baby lamb. She took Jacinta onto her knee and explained about cousins and aunties.

Coffee was brewed, mugs filled and cake brought from the pantry. Frank was grinning at Susannah, obviously thrilled at her news.

Elena was obviously happy with the children but apologised for disturbing their jam-making, 'But I knew you'd like to see Susannah and I thought it was a time of day when I can lock up and pop over.'

'Oh, Elena, you know you're always welcome…but you had to lock up?'

'Yes. Betty my nurse has a day off today but also I've lost my secretary – she's gone to another job in Adelaide. When we return, Susannah and I must look to see if there's someone in the paper's classified section writing for a position.'

'Oh yes, of course, that would make it difficult for you. Oh!' Esther had an inspiration. 'Susannah, may I suggest you talk it over with Elena and then perhaps…Miriam?'

Susannah looked askance at her Auntie Esther. 'Oh. Well yes, she was…and is…if Josh…'

Elena laughed. 'Well, that would be lovely if it could be agreed. I know Miriam and like her. She did work in an office, didn't she? It would be making appointments and things like that?'

Susannah thought it an excellent idea. 'I've had a few chats with Aunty Miriam. She likes to be busier than living with Oma and Opa allows.' She sat, eating the cake. 'You know, if Uncle Josh would allow it, that's the question, but I do know he wants them to save up for a house of their own and it's taking too long. Perhaps Dr Elena and I can talk and then if she would like, I'll talk to Oma and Auntie Miriam. You know, Auntie Esther, you really do have some clever ideas!'

A little hand clasped her arm: Jacinta. 'Aunty 'Lena's drinking her coffee so she wants her knee. I like having a growed-up cousin. Will you be my friend?'

Susannah smiled and hunkered down. 'Little one, I'll always be your friend if you're mine.'

Jacinta looked surprised. 'But you's all growed up. When I am, I can be a teacher, can't I? Mumma was one too.'

Frank grinned. 'I think your mumma is so pleased and surprised, little Jassy, she's lost for words. You see, your mumma is one of the very best teachers in this whole state. She showed you how to read, didn't she?'

Susannah got down Jacinta's level again. 'And, little cousin Jassy, she taught me how to do mathematics and exams so I can be a doctor with Doctor Elena. She knows all about little children and big ones, isn't that right, Uncle Frank?'

Frank looked across her to Esther. 'You're quite right, my clever niece. I'm most happy to have such a clever woman as my children's mother – they're having a wonderful start in life.'

Esther raised her brows at her husband, who smiled before heading back to the workshop. *It seems I may have won this battle, if not the war!*

43

The hotel's beer cart, pulled by two splendid Clydesdale horses, stopped outside the joinery showroom.

Esther stood up from the table in surprise. 'Frank, put your coffee away and tell me what this is, being delivered on such a dismal, overcast August day.'

'This' turned out to be an upright piano – well-worn and a little battered, but still a piano.

Frank went to open the main door for the two cellarmen, aprons and all, who eased it through and asked where it was to go. Esther was wordless.

Frank directed it to a position next to the big dresser. 'It needs tuning up, my Esther, but the man in the hotel says Allans in Rundle Street will send up someone to make it shipshape. That's what he said.'

She found her voice as Jassy and Arty ran out to see the horses and, laughing, were chased by the two cellarmen. 'Oh, Frank, how wonderful! Oh, it's a Wertheim – they have a lovely tone I believe. Anna Strang at the church has a Wertheim – she says they're made in Melbourne or Bendigo was it...no, Bendigo Street in Richmond. But – the man in what hotel?'

'The Union, Ess! They're doing some work there and smartening it up a bit. This was to go down into the cellar and I made them an offer. Do you like it?'

She smiled at his earnest expression. 'Oh, my Francis, I love it, love it! Now I can play with the children and teach...'

He bent over, laughing. 'I knew that word would come into it somewhere. Always the teacher! As long as you enjoy playing it yourself, my dear girl. It's for you. It's your birthday tomorrow, my Esther, the first of September. I could think of nothing you'd like more.'

She ran over and gave him a long, loving kiss. 'I am so lucky, Frank. Thank you.'

'I am the lucky one, Liebchen. I have you.'

It was time for him to get to the workshop; he needed to talk to Willem about the new balcony rails of the hotel and to Michael for some ideas to decorate the posts.

Esther ran her fingers through the keys – a flat C but…goodness, she was out of practice. Mama had suggested she try to buy another piano, saying, 'Keep the music in your life, Esther' – her metaphor for happiness. *Mama, now I can and I will – I'm truly blessed and know it.*

'What was that piece …ahah!' The melody, or a few bars of it, literally jumped into her head, one of Mama's special favourites…Chopin, naturally! What was it called? Concerto Number 2, as Mama always called it; she loved to sit and play it. A lovely trilling piece yet restful in its way. She dawdled a few notes from memory. *Can't remember enough…*

'Mumma, I like that one,' whispered Jacinta. 'Can I work it, please?' She quickly pulled up a little stool and started to press the keys. Despite a few wrong ones, tuned or not, they had a gloriously mellow tone.

Watching the children discover the surprises of the keyboard, she suddenly had a flash of insight. This was such a caring, thoughtful gesture from Frank – not at all the usual business asset and carefully considered expenditure of their general budgeting. Frank had known of her love of playing of course but he had never until now been able to afford to buy a piano. But this? And now? It was much more than a sorry gesture for when they rolled the truck, he and Josh. No. This was a genuine gift of love from him, and it demonstrated so much about the inherent goodness and perceptiveness of the man.

Oh, Frank, has it taken me all these years together to understand you and appreciate you? All these years I've wondered how to define love. No book reading, or studies, could tell me. Yet it was here all the time! Truth to tell, it's the sum of many parts: pleasures in sharing, giving and feeling – all those – wrapped in a bundle that needs no unravelling.

There was a knock on the huge showroom window.

'Oh, Mama Kate! Do come in. Look at this: Frank's huge surprise! It's for my birthday. But how can I help you?'

'I just want you to know what a brilliantly clever idea it was of yours to involve Miriam in the surgery office. Josh was a little put out at first but then I gather Frank talked him round to more modern ideas…'

'Frank? Did he? Oh, I am glad.'

'…and of course Josh approves of Dr Elena being suitable. Both my boys had some old-fashioned ideas but thankfully the elder one learned from a wise wife!' She held out her arms for a big hug from Jacinta then turned to Esther and gave her one too. 'Thank you, Esther. It's only her first day today but Miriam was as bright as a button this morning. She has skills she was worried about losing and as a result felt without value. Esther, I know you worried about similar things once before, did you not? Clever you. Now I must go. Herbert has asked me to chase up some errands for him so I'll leave you with your lovely surprise piano. Do invite us for your first sing-song, won't you?'

Jacinta ran to the gate to farewell Oma.

Esther turned to run her fingers along the keys. She closed the piano's lid. 'I remember little Anna Dodd asking me once if pianos can answer when we talk to them. Well, my dear surprise, Mr Wertheim, I know you'll have a beautiful tone so I'll try to get you your best voice as soon as I can. I'll telephone Allans and ask them to send their tuner as soon as they can.'

She called to Jacinta to come in from the roadway outside.

'Regardless of Mama's dislike of her telephone, I'll ring her this evening and tell her about this lovely piano. She will be thrilled! And her listeners can listen all they like. However, there's every likelihood Mama will telephone me tomorrow for my birthday.'

She picked up little Jacinta and whizzed her around the showroom on her hip. 'My goodness, little one, you are solid aren't you!'

Jassy giggled, slipped down and ran off back to her dolls and drawings.

Mog slipped in during the distraction.

'You furry, sneaky horror of Mogdom! Patter back to your own quarters. Do you realise it's at least a fortnight ago Mama said she'd write. Last time Rosalie was showing some brilliance in something and to my shame I forget what. However, Mama was to write me the details and she hasn't. I know it's a busy time for her, but I said I would write and haven't written either. Not good enough, Esther! I'll ring her this evening and her neighbours can twitch their ears. I haven't spoken with her for ages…well, since just after Ralphy's birthday – that's a couple of months ago. Oh, goodness me. I must see if she's managed to shed that cold…and tell her that finally her daughter has grown up!'

From indoors, Mrs Blum was calling the littlies for their lunch. Mog was gently booted ahead of her mistress.

Esther smiled, humming a few bars of the Chopin Number 2. 'Come on, Mog, pitter patter please! The melody's coming back to me and it'll stay in my head, I know. Mama has always loved her piano, and so enjoyed playing, and very often from her favourite Chopin. Frank calls me the teacher, but I was taught every lesson I know, no matter what, by my funny, quixotic yet so sensible and clever mama.'

Then the telephone rang.

44

It was a cold day, but the sky was clear. Frost was forecast for later and, with such a clear sky, Esther could well understand she might need an extra blanket on the bed that night. Over towards the north-west, the sun's light was edging some fluffy cumulus clouds, like the halo-clouds she had spun stories around when she was small, believing they were the province of angels. In the distance, a line of trees marked the course of the river.

She felt Rosalie's warm hand grip hers. 'Are you all right, Aunt Esther, or would you like to stay here for a while on your own?' She leaned over and tucked away a stray hair peeking out from the edge of Esther's cloche felt hat.

Esther noticed how the long shadow cast by the single tall pencil pine tree scythed between her shoes. She turned to see its length, 'beyond to behind', as Mama used to say when describing such a phenomenon. To Esther, it brought to mind the long hand of the grandmother clock in Cumquats' dining room.

She refocused. 'I'm fine, dear girl. I'll walk back through the vineyard later.' She smiled to see the elegant fifteen-and-a-half-year-old skip off along the furrow, her short, short skirt displaying her long tanned legs, her ballet dancing legs. *She'll be famous one day.*

Her own suede shoes were stained with the wet from the grass and she shook first one, then the other, as she stepped onto the gravel walkway. Moving towards the seat to the left of the pencil pine, she looked down at the dates of birth on the headstone at its base. Papa's name first, Mama's below. Today would have been Mama's seventieth birthday, 16 June 1926. Nearly seven years since she died, about eleven since Papa…

Sitting on the neatly carved wooden seat, Esther pondered on what her parents might have thought of the growing youngsters of the family.

'Remember Susannah, Papa – you liked her and Mama claimed she started it all! She's already becoming known for her medical research into the causes of what are called strokes, like Papa had. She also advises on prevention, treats sufferers, lectures in Sydney. Also, your four Flack grandchildren, my brood, living in Hahndorf? Then there are the Symonds ones – six of them, based here at Cumquats, including the two sets of twins.

'My own twins could not be more different from each other, and not yet eleven. Jacinta's bound to be a future pacifist and politician. She's busy at home studying for the big exam held at the end of the year so she can go into the high school. Arthur Junior, who cares less for tests of any kind, is a clever young artist and intends to apply for the School of Arts as soon as he can leave other lessons behind. I think he's too young for such decisions and yet he's already exhibited a couple of works, sponsored by his aunt Evelyn – you remember Kate's daughter? Evie adopted her mother's name back in the war years and signs her work as Tweedie.

'Oh Papa, Mama, I wish you could know them now, as they've grown. Ralph at fourteen is Frank's pride and joy. Frank tries to hide it but he can't. The boy has inherited his gift for carving, too.' She smiled. 'He's a decent young person in anyone's eyes, and also artistic. He's learning sculpting and carving with good teachers and that has really been all he ever wanted to do, so he can help his father in the business. You know, he's almost completed the beautifully carved backs of six dining chairs. Michael will make the actual seats and legs, he's very good at that. Ralph has promised to carve the backs of a set for Katherine when she marries.

'And that's what Kathy wants to do, Mama – marry. You know, Mama, I wish you could hear this – I like to think you can – Kathy has her life mapped out and oh, Mama, does it sound familiar? Kathy wants to marry, but only after becoming a teacher – like me, she says – and then, Mama and Papa, she avers, "I'll have lots of children then I can teach them all that you have taught us, Mumma." Really heart-warming. Kathy has a lovely nature and a keen perception. I feel she'll one day be a wonderful teacher.'

The gravel crunched. 'Are you awright, old girl?' It was George, striding along towards her; concerned for her. 'Rosalie said she left you here a while ago and the evening's closing in to be a cold one. Thought you might need a coat.' He handed it to her and its woolly warmth, even now, still smelled of Mama and her horse, old Gemini.

She felt tears come to her eyes as she pulled one of the lapels over to her nose and breathed deeply. Time has passed but…

'Hey, c'mon, old girl. Sorry. Didn't want to make you cry, just took it off the hook at the door as I came out. Spur of the moment thing. Who'd guess that old horse would have a heart attack and roll onto her. Look, she didn't wear this coat that day… Erica's got the kettle on the hob and said to tell you there's a tot of whisky to add to it. That'll warm you up! She hopes to join us later.'

Dear George, in so many ways like Papa; same gruff nature but without Papa's sophistication. She moved towards him and they walked home, warmly wrapped arms around each other. She told him how Frank would be ringing later, though under the new system he now had to book the call. She laughed with George as he described declining to go to watch William's twins at their football match that afternoon. They were both football mad and so alike still, George found it hard to tell them apart when they were chasing a ball and covered in mud.

'Gets embarrassing, cheering one when it's the other on the ball. Done it too often. William hopes they'll develop some physical differences later, as my boys did. My two are eighteen but these two aren't eight yet. Plenty of time. Mind you, he still hopes one of his will follow him into law! Got his plans, typical Will. Could even be his Alicia – she's a sharp little miss and she so young. She has very adult opinions, that one, quite a surprise for one yet to start school!'

Aaron met them at the door. Taller than his father but otherwise a copybook Symonds, he took Esther's coat, tossed it over the hook then did the same with his father's. 'Pa, let's have your boots or Aunt Erica will have me hung and quartered. The girls have just polished the floor, so she tells me.'

Esther had to smile. 'Has Erica gone to the surgery, Aaron?'

'Yup, Aunt Esther. Well, to Anna's place actually. Got a baby on the way. Do you remember Anna, Dodds that was? It's her first one. They've been married a while so this is quite an occasion. They live in town but her husband's a parliamentary secretary and looking to go into politics fully. Sounds good, but he often has to go away. Actually, Aunt, politics is people, isn't it? There's an administration and business side to my horticultural degree – leaves my options open for when I'm qualified. Mind you, ages to go yet, three years. To know the land, know the product, and get to know the people, local politics may be a useful sideline. I think it's fascinating talking to people and by helping Uncle Will, like I do sometimes, I meet quite a few. But – oh, sorry – I was told to tell you there was a hot drink ready when you want it.'

There was a loud 'Hellooo' from along the hall. 'Is that you, Az? I want a hand.'

Alex was repairing one of the ceiling lights in the piano room, once called the big dining room, so they walked down. 'Hello, Aunt Esther. You can tell me if it suits the room. Grandmama always wanted one like this and I found it recently in a little Adelaide shop.'

'It' was a miniature chandelier and as the ceiling plaster had a rose etched on its surface, the new fitting matched perfectly. The room was so familiar to Esther: tall, open windows, the long dining table at the end, the large and rather shabby cushions on the sofas and, nearest to her, Mama's piano.

Still my favourite room. What was it Mama said? 'Let's sit down in here where it's cool and quiet and we won't be disturbed'. *It was when I broke the news about wanting to marry Frank. Seems so long ago. Before the world war, even. Oops, he's waiting for me to answer...*

'Alex, it's a good choice. It's really attractive and complements the etchings on the ceiling so well.'

Alex climbed down the ladder and gave her a shoulder hug. He was shorter than Aaron by a couple of inches and had, as he had earlier informed her, inherited his mother's father's nose! Not a steam engineer as once was planned, he had become involved with electricity and was indeed studying electrical engineering under an apprentice master. Esther hid a smile – she had once found these twins so alike she couldn't tell who was whom. *Now they are growing into their own personas. Lovely boys.*

She scanned the room. The same couple of horsey paintings on the wall. Mama's piano polished and the candelabra brasses sparkling. Sheet music at the ready…she gasped. So recognisable, it was Chopin, Concerto Number 2…well-thumbed and with pencil notations in Mama's writing.

Alex heard the gasp; he looked over. 'I know it's a bit shabby, Aunt Esther. It's just that it's one of Grandmama's favourites. Silly of us I s'pose but we prop it up there open when no one's playing. It just makes us feel like she's still here. She was playing it you see, that morning, the morning when the sun was shining and she said to Aunt Erica how the breezes were too sweet to miss and she took the old horse for a ride.'

That morning. The one when Frank gave her the piano. That morning when this piece of music, the concerto, had sprung into her mind. It had not been unbidden, just unlocked. Mama was the key. She remembered how she tried a few bars on the old piano from memory. For Jacinta. Then the telephone had rung. That call.

She felt she was spinning. Those bars, the notes in glowing relief swept through her brain. She grabbed Alex's arm, exhaling, trying to calm herself. 'Alex, that music, that piece…'

Ever caring, he curled his arm protectively around her shoulders.

The very room seemed expectant; the breeze overloud, all embracing; the very air redolent with the perfumed sweetness of wet grapevines beyond the window. Up above, the little chandelier swayed gently, its chain trilling, quavering sweetly to a familiar rhythm. Esther glanced at the sheet music on the piano; it slid downwards and over the bracket, drifted horizontally towards her…and she reached over to secure it in her grasp.

Eyes closed, she raised it to her face and breathed its well-fingered surface. Alex's expression demonstrated his concern. Between her fingers, the old paper felt warm, supple, its music ready for her to pursue. She opened her eyes, scanning the well-loved mapping of notes, staves and bar lines.

Alex dropped his arm and she smiled; a sad smile prompting Aaron to step forward, eyebrows raised in enquiry to his brother. Esther shook her head slowly and hugged the sheet music even more tightly. The boys moved as if to support her but she lifted the finger of one hand to stay their movements.

They waited, uncertain, as she closed her eyes and dropped her chin. Her whispering was barely heard, her breath rippling the edge of the precious paper. 'Oh, Mama. I remember how we sat in this room and I told you of my plans, my decision. As time went on – and you knew – moments of doubt insinuated themselves into my happiness. I quashed them each time. You told me to keep the music in my life…well, it is, Mama, and I shall. I think I have always known, and now realise that you know I made the right decision. It may have taken a few years but now at last, I am content, Mama, thankful and at peace. I feel my battles are truly over.'

Then the telephone rang.

Acknowledgements

Works consulted

Bolton, Margaret, *Prisoners of War*, Pocket People 2, Ginninderra Press, 2015

Cuffley, Peter, *Chandeliers and Billy Tea: A Catalogue of Australian Life 1880–1940*, Five Mile Press, 1984

Fox, Anni Luur, *Hahndorf: A Journey through a Village and its History*, Fox Publishing, 2002

Gibbs, R.M., *A History of South Australia from Colonial Times to the Present*, 1992

Goldsworthy, Kerryn, *Adelaide*, New South Publishing, 2011

Ross, John (ed.), *Chronicle of the 20th Century*, Chronicle Communications and Penguin Books Australia

Speck, Catherine, 'Nora Heysen, Art and War for a German-Australian family', in Monteath, Peter (ed.), *Germans: Travellers. Settlers and their Descendants in South Australia*, Wakcficld Press

Online sites consulted

Hahndorf – Hahndorf Maritime Museum

Hahndorf History – Flinders Ranges Research

Pneunonic Influenza Lists 1919; Trove Abstract

Field Marshal Bernard Montgomery – www.histnuleamingsite.co.uk/world war

The Story of Metters' Wood Stoves, Pittwater, NSW

Wilhelm Conrad Roentgen – Biography – Nobel prize

Australian Glass Manufacturers

Thanks

Sincere thanks to my writing colleague Mr Trevor Schaefer for allowing me to read and absorb material from his Honours thesis (1982) entitled The Treatment of Germans in South Australia 1914–1924 (Department of History, University of Adelaide).

My thanks also for the freedom to visit the home of the Heysen family, The Cedars; the German Migration Museum based in the former Hahndorf Academy; St Paul's and St Michael's Churches in Hahndorf; the Lobethal Archives and Historical Museum; the National Motor Museum at Birdwood; and, not least, the State Library of South Australia.

Special thanks are owed to my publishers, Stephen and Brenda Matthews of Ginninderra Press, for their unfailing professional guidance; to my friends and colleagues of the Tea Tree Gully Library Writers Group and of NEW Inc. for their collective and continuous encouragement; the Tea Tree Gully Library for their continuing support of local writers; to my family for their tolerance; and, last but certainly not least, to Fred for his meticulous proofreading, his patience and his (hopefully deserved) confidence in me.